D1491362

Books by Gary Meehan
True Fire
True Dark

Coming soon
True Power

GARY MEEHAN

Quercus

New York • London

Quercus

New York • London

© 2014 by Gary Meehan
First published in the United States by Quercus in 2015

Any member of educational institutions wishing to photocopy part or
all of the work for classroom use or anthology should send inquiries to
permissions@quercus.com.

ISBN 978-1-62365-615-7

Library of Congress Control Number: 2015940798

Distributed in the United States and Canada by
Hachette Book Group
237 Park Avenue
New York, NY 10017

Manufactured in the United States

10 9 8 7 6 5 4 3 2 1

www.quercus.com

For Tom

One

Agitation pulled at Megan. What was the banker doing back there in his hidden offices? Was he lost in paperwork, searching for Lynette's authorization letter? Did he have his feet up, sipping a cool drink while his customers stewed in the stifling heat? Or was he watching with a nervous thrill as witches surrounded the building?

Clerks glided past, paying them no attention, serene in the presence of money. Eleanor caught Megan's fidgeting and stretched out a calming hand. "Relax," she said. "Sisters are meant to be used to hard seats and slow dehydration."

"We should get out of here while we still can," said Megan. They should have planned this better: worked out an escape route; brought more weapons; worn something more practical than the bulky robes of a Sister of the Faith, whose constant itching explained the sisters' legendary sourness.

"It'll be fine. Banks don't like giving up money."

"Even if it's not theirs?"

"Especially if it's not theirs."

To distract herself, Megan pulled out a carving of the Saviors she'd bought from a street vendor. It was nothing more than a hacked-up chunk of work with some varnish slapped on it, not worth even one of the three pence she'd been conned out of.

"What've you got there?" said Eleanor, leaning over.

Megan showed her. "It's for—" she lowered her voice out of habit "—Cate." She ran her thumb over the wood and winced as a splinter pierced her skin. "Might have to file it down first. Plenty of time for that, huh?"

"You will get it to her," said Eleanor. "I promise."

If you let me. The countess was the only one who knew where Megan's daughter was, who knew if she was even still alive. Sometimes Megan stared into the dead of night and feared Eleanor had done something terrible to thwart the witches, a fear Eleanor's continued reassurances as to Cate's safety couldn't quite quash.

The banker reappeared. He was all gray skin and spindly limbs, as if drawn by a child with a morbid streak. "I'm afraid we can't find the authorization for this transfer," he said, holding a scroll out to Eleanor.

"Maybe it went to our *New* Statham branch. People do get confused."

"We've just come from there," said Eleanor. "Well, I say 'just' . . ." They'd got caught up in the army that was marching south to Eastport. The journey to Statham, which should have taken two days, had taken four. "They told us to try here." She proffered the scroll back to the banker. "Lynette's signed this. And there's her seal. Look."

"Yes . . ." The banker accepted the scroll and squinted at the lump of wax that had once sealed it. "What is that meant to be exactly?"

"Lynette's sigil," said Eleanor. "Gerbil rampant." She shrugged. "All the good ones were taken."

The banker's mouth narrowed to a slit. "For a sum this large, we do need authorization from the client's branch."

"In Eastport?"

"Yes, well . . ."

A sum this large? The banker seemed paranoid over the few shillings Lynette, who had served Eleanor's family before the first war against the witches and had helped them in Eastport, had promised them for living expenses. Megan got up and stretched her atrophied muscles, all the while trying to peek at the scroll dangling from the banker's fingers.

"You haven't heard anything from Eastport?" said Eleanor.

"The last bird arrived weeks ago," said the banker. "The witches seem reluctant to help us replenish our stocks."

"What about couriers? Traders? Refugees? Is anyone making it out of the city?"

The banker shook his head. He held out the scroll. Eleanor made to take it; Megan got there first. She had just enough time to register the amount being transferred—twenty thousand sovereigns—before Eleanor snatched it off her.

Megan mouthed a "What the hell?" at Eleanor. The countess shot her a warning look.

"Are you sure there's nothing you can do?"

The banker shook his head with the solemnity of an undertaker. "Is there anything else I can help you with?"

Megan thought the "else" a tad specious. "That'll be all, thanks," she said, grabbing Eleanor and bundling her toward the exit.

Megan pulled Eleanor through the broiling streets, jostling past soldiers encamped in Statham for redemption or recreation before they marched on Eastport, pushing aside vendors who shoved trinkets in their faces, elbowing the face attached to the hand that sneaked in from behind and tried to get inside her robes.

She found a quiet alcove and dragged the countess into it. "*Twenty thousand* sovereigns?"

"What can I say?" said Eleanor. "Lynette married well. Invested better."

"You know that's not what I meant. What the hell are you planning on buying with that kind of money?"

"Your safety."

A sprinkling of dust fell on Megan's shoulders. She looked up and found herself being jerked out of the way just as a chunk of brick plummeted down and punched the ground where she'd been standing.

"What the . . . ?" Megan reached inside her sleeve for a knife, looked around for assailants, someone to assail.

"Relax," said Eleanor. "It's just a crumbling building." Ancient statutes forbade the demolition of any buildings standing when the Saviors had walked, and if the occasional pilgrim was crushed by falling brickwork, this was obviously God's will. "Let's get out of here."

She led Megan back out on to the streets. "Have you got anything left," she asked Megan, "or did you spend it all on tat?"

"It is *not* tat."

"Sorry, I didn't mean it like . . . I just don't know what we're going to do now."

Megan's stomach growled at the realization she didn't know where her next meal was coming from. "Maybe we can join the sisters for real."

"You ready to give up men, money and misbehavior?"

"Two of the three at least," said Megan.

Eleanor suddenly stiffened. "It was good meeting you, Sister Moira," she said, her tone officious.

"What?"

Eleanor bent in to kiss Megan's cheek. "Down by the fountain," she murmured. "*Don't* look. There's a priest watching us. Pretend we've just met and walk back the way we came."

Megan's muscles tightened. *One of them?* "I'll bear your wise words in mind, Sister Edla," she said, imitating Eleanor's stiff tones.

She slipped her hands into the sleeves of her robes, seeking reassurance in the knives she had stashed there. Forcing her steps into a regular pattern, she moved off, her neck so tense the muscles were starting to cramp.

She reached a market stall piled high with jars and pots and vials filled with all manner of colored liquids. In their reflective surfaces, a miniature version of Eleanor shimmered over to the dry fountain where the priest stood. He looked unthreatening: a middle-aged man with a pot belly and a bald pate reddening in the sun. So why was Megan's pulse racing?

Eleanor made the sign of the circle over her heart and then, imperceptible unless you were looking for it, tapped her breast twice. The priest hesitated, head twitching as he checked for observers, then returned the sign of the star-broken circle. Megan almost had her knives out of their scabbards before she realized the stallholder was looking at her strangely.

"Can I help you, sister?"

Megan slid her weapons back home and gave the stallholder what she hoped was a reassuring smile. "Just, you know . . ."

"Looking to stash a nice little something up your sleeve?"

"You're accusing a Sister of the Faith of stealing?"

The stallholder was unmoved by Megan's faked indignation. "More unilaterally accepting unsolicited donations."

The vendors in Statham certainly had a larger vocabulary than their Eastport counterparts. "I was only browsing."

"Yeah. Had a priest here the other day. He was 'only browsing.' You know how much perfume he . . . ?"

Priest. Megan remembered why she was here. She scanned the myriad reflections. No sign of Eleanor. She spun around. The countess and the priest were both gone. She hurried down to the fountain, trying to spot Eleanor in the crowd. Had the priest dragged her off? He couldn't have overpowered her, surely? But maybe there were other witches in the city.

There. Eleanor was leading the priest somewhere. Megan hurried after them. The priest looked back. Megan quickly sidestepped, ducking behind a soldier, whom she realized too late was relieving himself against the wall.

She backed away from the noxious stream trickling in her direction. "Sorry, sister," muttered the soldier, his voice slurred from drink. "You wouldn't believe the line for the outhouses. Guess everyone's trying to forget what's, you know . . ." Fear clouded his eyes. Not of Megan, but of what was to come, what was waiting for him at the end of the long march south.

The priest's attention was back on Eleanor as the two of them squeezed through the crowds. Megan made after them. Eleanor could have told her what she intended before she'd shooed her away, but that would have only given Megan time to object. If the priest was a witch, there was only one thing they could do. Her stomach knotted at the thought.

They reached a crypt, a circular building of weatherworn limestone surrounded by a low wall generations of asses had polished into a serviceable bench. A few people sat there: lovers sharing a private moment in a public space; soldiers calming their nerves with a shared bottle; bewildered pilgrims who had come to Statham for a bit of quiet contemplation only to find an army on top of them. Eleanor headed for a side door. The priest scurried into the crypt after her, his sandals catching on uneven flagstones. She ushered him into the building, then caught Megan's eye. Megan counted to ten. She checked her knives and followed them inside.

* * *

The sounds of the city faded as Megan crept down a spiral staircase, her shadow slinking around the curved walls as if trying to peer ahead. The air became as dead as the building's occupants. Further below came the slap of leather against stone and Eleanor's aimless chatter, probably intended to cover Megan's pursuit.

She reached the bottom. Footsteps in the dust led to a door of rotting wood. It was ajar, more torchlight flickering through the narrow gap, tasting the stonework.

Megan stepped behind it and slipped out a knife.

". . . you were with?" the priest was saying. "Was it her?"

"Just some sister from Percadia."

"She doesn't look Percadian."

"What's your interest in her?" asked Eleanor.

"You haven't heard the good news?"

"My branch of the order encourages silent contemplation," said Eleanor. "Quite boring really."

"Joanne's prophecy has come to pass."

"Oh . . ."

The priest started to recite. Megan was taken back to that night in the Forbidden Collection in the Eastport temple, when she had learned the terrible truth about her baby, why her sister had manipulated her into getting pregnant.

Fear not, O True
God will watch over you

When the world has gone
Four score times around the sun
My sisters will be born again
To clean the world of its stain
And in their sixteenth year
A Savior each will bear
A daughter and a son
Jolecia and Ahebban
Born to a dead father
The True they will gather
To save them from the scourge
The false will be purged
No more the liar, the priest
Only His eternal peace

It was nonsense, of course, the ravings of a madwoman lamenting the crushing of her religion by the priests. But the witches believed it, believed it to the point of excluding everything else, and had returned to Werlavia forty years after their defeat. But this time they had come with an army and guns supplied by the Diannon Emperor, which the Faithful could only fight with blades and hope.

"You've found the sisters?" asked Eleanor.

"One Mother is in Eastport with the True," said the priest. "She was blessed with the birth of a Savior."

Megan silently cursed. She'd been hoping the baby had been stillborn or, better, that the delivery had claimed mother and child. A horrible thing to wish, but after all Gwyneth had been responsible for, including the murder of their grandfather, it would have been just punishment. And the death would have invalidated Joanne's prophecy, saved Megan and her daughter from the witches.

"And what of the second Mother?" asked Eleanor. "You think the girl I was talking to was her?"

"She . . . she continues to be blinded by the priests' lies. Maybe you can help teach her the truth . . ." The priest paused. "My lady."

"What?" Apprehension filled Eleanor's voice.

"Is that not the correct term of address for the Countess of Ainsworth?"

"Oh hell."

"Your father fought against us, but you can redeem that sin. Accept—"

Adrenalin surged through Megan. She took a step back and kicked out. The door flew inwards, eliciting a crack and a yelp as it smacked into someone on the other side. Only when she was confronted by the priest gawking at her did Megan realize the yelp had been female and that Eleanor was staggering around the tomb with her hands cupped over her bleeding nose.

"Was the dramatic entrance really necessary?"

"I didn't know you were there."

"That's why you don't kick the—"

The priest launched himself toward the exit, slamming an elbow into Megan as he passed.

Caught off guard, she spun and fell, palms stinging as the rough stone scraped the skin off them.

Eleanor waved blindly, flicking drops of blood into the air. "Get after him!"

Megan pushed herself to her feet and charged up the stairs as fast as the cumbersome sister's robes would allow her—for obvious reasons, they weren't designed for chasing after men. The initial burst of adrenalin soon gave way to the sapping effects of the climb. Her body still hadn't recovered from childbirth and rebelled against the sudden exercise. Acid burned in her thighs. She needed to rest, possibly throw up, but if the priest got away and told Gwyneth and the other witches about her . . .

If it had been anyone else she was chasing Megan wouldn't have stood a chance, but priests, even those who had betrayed their vows, rarely did anything more strenuous than lift a flagon of ale. His wheezing form hove into view. Megan grabbed at his ankle. He kicked out, catching her on the jaw. Her vision juddered. The priest pulled his leg from her grasp and scrambled up the few remaining steps. Sunlight flooded into the staircase as he barged the door open.

Megan collected herself and chased after him, but by the time she got outside he had disappeared into the crowd. Footsteps clattered behind her. She bent over, hands on her thighs, panting as she waited for Eleanor to catch up.

"I lost . . . I lost him."

Eleanor handed Megan the knife she had dropped and dabbed her injured nose. "Well, we wouldn't want to leave the plan only *half* screwed up, would we?"

"You could have told me there was a plan."

"There wasn't time," said Eleanor. "I assumed you'd guess what was going on and not, you know, kick a door in my face."

There was a commotion: shattering pottery, cries of protest, snatched apologies. Megan and Eleanor glanced at each other and set off in pursuit. They found a vendor sifting through the remains of an upturned stall while onlookers offered commiserations but no actual help.

"A priest did this?" said Megan.

The vendor contemplated the fragment of what had once been a vase, its jagged edges raw as a fresh wound. "Bastard." He tossed it over his shoulder.

"Where'd he go?"

The vendor jabbed a finger down the street, at a ramshackle warehouse thrown up by the kinds of builders who didn't intend to stay in town after its completion. Megan and Eleanor hurried to it. Inside it was empty but for heaps of garbage someone had swept into the corners for others to dispose of. The sun punched through holes in the high ceiling, forming hazy columns of light in which dust danced.

"He must have found a back way out," said Eleanor, her voice echoing in the vast space.

Megan squinted. The walls seemed intact—there were no telltale slivers of light that betrayed the existence of another exit. "He's still here," she said.

"Where?"

Megan looked again. This time she saw them: steps hammered into the wall. Her eyes followed them up to an office tucked into the top corner of the warehouse. Did something just move up there, or were her eyes adjusting to the gloom? Whichever, she pointed up to it. Eleanor nodded and flicked out a knife.

The steps groaned as they crept up. Megan tried not to look down lest she see joints straining or the ground receding to the point where its solidity tipped from reassuring to threatening. One step was missing, the only evidence of its existence splinters of wood and bent nails sticking out of the wall. Megan stretched over the gap and wondered if it would really have been that hard to install a guard rail.

They reached a small landing at the top. Megan took a moment to steady herself. A flimsy door constructed from broken-up crates blocked their path. Scuffling came from the other side.

"You can kick this one in," whispered Eleanor.

Megan put her shoulder to it instead. She burst into a box-like room barely ten feet in each direction, with holes cut into the walls to look out on to the warehouse floor below. It was empty apart from a desk, upon which scraps of paper and parchment fluttered in the gust of her entry.

Megan frowned. "There's no one—"

The door flew back shut, smacking into Eleanor just as she was crossing the threshold. A priest had been hidden behind it. He advanced on Megan.

Two

Megan whipped her knife into a defensive position. The priest held up his palms. "Hey!" he cried. "It's me!"

"What the . . . ?" Megan sighed in relief as she realized the priest was Damon. "Why didn't you say something? Do you know what you did to me?"

"How do you think *I* feel?" said Damon. "I thought someone was coming to kill me."

Eleanor barged through the door, rubbing her nose. "What the hell are you doing here?" she said to Damon. "Where have you been? And what's with the stupid beard?"

Damon stroked his blond goatee, the only hair on his head now that he had shaved his scalp to complete his priestly disguise. "You don't like it?"

"You look like your evil twin."

"As someone with an actual evil twin, I'm not sure I appreciate the comparison," said Megan.

Damon held out a porcelain vial to Eleanor. "I got you a present," he said. "It's a perfume jar."

"A what?"

"You put perfume in it."

"Why would I want something to put perfume in?"

"You can't just let it run free," said Damon. "It'll evaporate."

Eleanor looked unimpressed. "What is it with you two? There's a war about to start and you're both off buying trinkets?"

"I wouldn't say buying—"

"We're after a priest," said Megan. "You see one?"

"You might want to narrow that down a bit," said Damon. "There couldn't be more priests here if someone announced a free bar."

"This one was fleeing."

"Not as uncommon as you might think . . ."

"Did you?"

"I did see one run into the Drowned Man."

Eleanor spun on her heel. "What are we waiting for?" She headed down to the main warehouse floor.

"I thought we were getting reacquainted," Damon called down after her, "swapping stories, that kind of thing." He shrugged and turned to Megan. "She still . . . ?"

"Uh-huh."

"And how are you doing?"

How *was* Megan doing, running around a foreign city while her daughter was being brought up by a strange family and Gwyneth plotted to destroy the world? If she thought about it too much, she might not be able to prevent herself from dropping to the floor and weeping forever.

"Same as ever," she said. "Come on."

"You don't want to wait here for a few minutes more?"

"How much do you owe?"

"That's not the relevant question," said Damon.

"What is the relevant question then?"

"'How badly does he want it back?'"

"Don't worry. I'll protect you."

Megan made her way down the steps, hugging the wall for support. Damon trotted behind her. "I got you a present," he said.

"Is it a perfume vial?"

"Perhaps . . ."

The Drowned Man was packed, full of soldiers splashing around in spilled beer and baying for enough booze to keep them drunk for the whole march south. The air was fetid with the stench of sweat, leather and vomit. Priests monopolized the tables, but none was the one they were looking for.

Damon tapped Megan on the shoulder. "Let's go to the bar," he shouted in her ear.

"You think this is the time to be drinking?" said Megan, though she had to admit she could do with one.

"If you're going to hide in a crowd, hide where it's thickest."

They pushed their way through the bodies. The soldiers, seeing their robes, reluctantly made way for them. Damon offered them blessings in return; a boyhood spent in a seminary training to be a priest had taught him the forms.

Down at the far end of the bar, a cowled figure in priests' robes was hunched over a tankard, trying to make himself look as small as possible. "Get Eleanor," said Megan.

She squeezed down to the priest, smearing God knew what on her robes in the process. His eyes widened in alarm as he realized who it was. Megan poked a knife into his ribs and pointed to the exit. The priest looked around. The wall of bodies prevented any dash for freedom. Megan pressed her knife in harder. The point dented a spongy mass of flesh. The priest nodded hesitantly and pushed away from the bar.

They shuffled their way through the crowd, Megan's hand trembling as she kept her knife against the priest's lower back. Drinkers flashed annoyed glances at them as they eased their way through. The swamp-like atmosphere was curdling her stomach and making her head throb. Any moment now, she expected someone's gaze to fall on them, a hue to be raised, arms to grab her and wrench the blade from her grip.

They reached the door. Here, if anywhere, was where the priest would make a break for it. Megan grabbed his shoulder and pushed close into him.

"Don't do anything stupid," she said.

"Pardon?" said the priest, craning his neck around.

Megan stood on tiptoes so she could speak into his ear. "I said, don't do anything stupid."

"Don't do anything . . . ?"

"Stupid!"

The yell was heard not only by the priest but by the hundred or so troops crammed into the inn. Conversations dropped, cups paused before lips, eyes swiveled in their direction.

Megan licked dry lips. "Er . . ."

Damon sliced through the crowd. "Anyone lost a sovereign?" he said. "I handed one in at the bar."

The inn's population appeared to have been carrying with them a large chunk of their campaign salary in gold, judging by the stampede to the rear of the building. Megan and Damon bundled the priest outside, where they found Eleanor waiting. Together they marched the man around to an alley by the side of the pub, which overcrowding had pressed into service as a latrine.

Megan slammed the priest—no, the *witch*—against the wall and held the point of her knife against his neck. "How did you know we were in Statham?"

"I didn't."

"You're looking for us though. Me and Eleanor?"

"We're all looking for you, Mother." He looked at her, imploring. "It's not too late. Accept the True. Lead us to the Savior."

Megan's blade pierced his skin. A droplet of blood welled up and trickled down his neck. "There's no chance in hell I'll—"

"No matter what you do to me, you cannot deny your child his destiny," said the witch. "The Saviors will bring peace to Werlavia. The aristocracy is dead. The priests' lies have been exposed. There is only the True."

The stench of ammonia in the alley was making Megan's eyes water. At least, that was what she told herself. She would never let the witches have her daughter, turn her into a tyrant who gloried in the deaths of those she deemed her enemies, and all in the name of God. Cate wouldn't become a second Gwyneth.

"Let's do this and get out of here," said Eleanor.

The witch looked her directly in the eye. Megan's knife quivered against his throat. She knew what she had to do to protect herself, to protect Cate. It wouldn't be the first time she'd killed. But in cold blood?

The witch took a gentle hold of Megan's hand and edged it away. "She can't do it," he said to Eleanor. "She knows in her heart it would be an offense against God."

Eleanor whipped out her own blade. "I'll do it then," she said. "He's used to me offending Him."

Before Megan could react, the witch gripped and twisted her wrist. Searing pain shot up her arm. She cried out, dropped the knife. The witch shoved her away and lunged for the weapon. Eleanor was on him before he could reach it, her blade ramming between the man's ribs. The witch let out a pathetic gasp and crumpled to the floor. Blood bloomed across his chest. He shivered, then fell still.

A voice echoed down the alley: a man's, trying to effect command. "What's going on here?"

A soldier strode toward them, an officer in brand-new armor edged in gold. He looked about thirty, with the deep tan of a farmer and a jawline sculpted with a razor. Eleanor slipped her knife into her robes. She looked at Megan and Damon. They didn't need the army asking questions. If it slipped out who Megan was, who her daughter was . . .

Damon crouched over the witch. "One minute he was complaining about the pies, the next . . ." He pressed down on his chest, as if trying to resuscitate him. He only succeeded in squeezing out fresh blood.

The officer spotted the knife the witch had snatched off Megan and picked it up, flicking it to shake the urine off. "You know anything about this?"

"It's a knife," said Damon. "It stabs, cuts, picks the dirt out of your fingernails. What're they teaching you in the army these days?"

"There's no blood on it."

"You passed basic observation, I see."

Eleanor swished over to the solider, sighed and ran her fingers through her hair. The dye was growing out: her roots had regained their natural copper, though the ends were still singed black. "We found him like this," she said, polishing the soldier's armor with the sleeve of her robe. "A fight, I guess. The strain of going to war. People have too much to drink. Tempers fray . . ."

The soldier plucked her hand off his chest but held it for a little longer than he should have, stroking her elegant fingers with his thumb. Eleanor stared up into his eyes, a smile twitching on her lips.

"He's not the first," said the soldier. "I'd better go find a coroner. And a wheelbarrow."

"Don't you have men to do that—" Eleanor tilted her head to take in the single pip on his shoulder "—lieutenant?"

"I suppose I could get one of the corporals to do it . . ."

"Excellent," said Eleanor. She slipped her arm through the lieutenant's and nudged him toward the entrance of the alley. "That gives us time to get to know each other. Buy a sister a drink?"

"I guess." The lieutenant turned to Megan and Damon. "You two wait here."

"Why?" said Damon. He jerked a thumb at the dead witch. "Worried he's going to run off?"

"There'll be someone along shortly."

Eleanor led the lieutenant up the alley. As soon as they were out of view Megan and Damon exchanged glances and hurried the other way. Megan didn't look back at the corpse. They'd had no choice, she told herself. He'd attacked them; he would have told Gwyneth where they were. Still, guilt gnawed at her. Another life ended, and she'd been responsible.

They found themselves down at the riverside. Out on the Rustway—so called for the sequence of disintegrating defensive chains that lurked beneath its surface—a flotilla of war galleys edged out to the open sea. Sailors leaned over the bulwarks and waved at the crowd that had formed along the water's edge to see them off. Megan offered up a silent prayer that they would defeat the witches, free her from this hunt, allow her to reclaim her daughter. It was a prayer for herself more than for them. She hoped God understood.

"What now?" asked Damon.

Megan fanned herself with her hood. The encounter with the witch had left her hot and sweaty and the suffocating robes weren't helping—the sisters obviously thought chastity's first defense was body odor. "We wait for Eleanor to get that soldier so drunk he doesn't remember a thing, then meet back up with her," she said. "I guess. You know what she's like about sharing information."

"You got somewhere to stay?"

"Not unless we can put the landlady off a bit longer. Have you got any money left or did you lose it all?"

"I think technically I lost more than all of it." He shrugged. "I owe an acolyte ten shillings. There was this game with a bat and ball. You know, back in my day, an acolyte would've let a priest win."

"We're broke then?" said Megan.

"Lynette not come through?"

"Bank's complaining about the paperwork."

"What's the plan then?" asked Damon. "Beg in the streets? Mug a paralytic private? Scavenge our way back north?"

Megan leaned on a set of railings that were slowly being eaten by rust and gazed out on to the river. The departing war galleys now looked no bigger than children's toys. The ground troops would be moving off soon, leaving Megan and the others to scavenge in an empty city with nothing more than a few pilgrims for company. And witches. She doubted the one she killed had been the only one in Statham, and the army's absence would only embolden them.

"We need food and shelter . . ." she said.

"Doesn't everyone?"

". . . to be where the witches least expect us . . ."

"No argument there."

". . . and protection if they do find us."

Damon looked wary. "Are you saying . . . ?"

Megan nodded. "Only one thing for it. We'll have to march with the army."

Three

Damon looked at the gulls gliding above their heads and wondered what they made of the army grinding its way south: a gigantic beast stripping the land bare and churning once-verdant land into mud; a massive cut slashed down the continent. This was the easy part too, when the only casualties were caused by brawls and beer. Once they met the witches . . . He shuddered. Thank God the priest's robes would keep him from the front lines.

He spotted Eleanor among the sea of weary marchers and made his way over to her, each step accompanied by a squelch as the mud tried to claim his sandals as tribute for stepping on it. The summer rains had started as soon as they had left Statham, and thousands of feet and hoofs had made the ground more liquid than solid.

"Greetings, sister," he said, making the sign of the circle. "Any sins to confess?"

"No."

"You can tell me anything, even about the things you get up to late at night when you think no one's watching. They're not necessarily ruled out by the Book of Faith. Believe me, I've checked."

Eleanor rolled her eyes. Damon spotted Megan fifty yards ahead of them, her shoulders hunched as she trudged along. "I'm surprised you agreed to this," he said. "You wouldn't have your own reasons for coming down here, would you?"

Eleanor grimaced as she pulled her foot clear of the mud. "What kind of reasons?"

"Lynette."

"I'd like to make sure she's all right, yes."

"Megan told me about the money," said Damon. "That's an awful lot of shoes for a girl. Or is it boots you're looking to buy?"

"I don't know what you're talking about," said Eleanor.

"*Army* boots."

"Yes, I got what you meant by boots. I don't know why you think I'd need them."

"You don't want to avenge Daddy's loss?" asked Damon. Eleanor's father had fought with the last king, Edwyn the Fifth, in the first war against the witches. Their defeat had led to the overthrow of the aristocracy by the priests, who had proceeded to crush the witches, armed only with righteousness, the power of faith and a five-to-one numerical advantage. They had been keen to downplay the last when Damon had been in the seminary.

"Now *you* don't know what you're talking about."

They continued to trudge along, accompanied by the background rumble of a thousand muttered complaints. A cart stuck in the mud blocked their way. Damon scraped his soles clean on one of its slats, even though he knew his sandals would be dirty again before he had taken two more steps. Sometimes it was enough to be clean, or relatively clean, for a few seconds.

"You seen that lieutenant you were simpering over?" he asked, trying to sound casual.

"I was not simpering," said Eleanor. "I had to stop the guy reporting us, that's all."

"Why didn't we hit him like we normally do?"

"He's on our side."

"Never stopped us before."

Damon found himself on a dry spot, a square foot of grass in the eternal swamp. He stopped, reveling in a brief moment of firm footing. Soldiers flowed around him, their progress slow and inexorable as lava. He should let them pass, march on by until he was alone in the wilderness. There were plenty of parts of the Realm untouched by war where he could hide until all this was over.

A few steps ahead, Eleanor turned around, waiting for him to catch up, and Damon remembered why he had joined this sorry band of men. If he fled, that was it, he'd lose his chance with her. If he was to win her, he'd have to stick around and commit brave deeds. The only trouble was, brave deeds often left you dead, and dead guys never got the girl.

The army descended the slopes of the Speed Valley and reached the border with Ainsworth at Clibbur Point, where the river looped back on itself so much it was in danger of cutting off the land. A party of Sandstriders was waiting for them, silk robes fluttering in the hot air from their fire, faint expressions of amusement on their bronzed faces. They were from the desert lands of the Andaluvian peninsula south of the Endalayan Mountains and had broken away from the Realm's rule centuries ago.

"Why are they here?" asked Megan.

"I heard the priests are negotiating an alliance with the Sandstriders," said Eleanor. "Well, I say negotiating. More dictating."

"They still expecting the Sandstriders to come back to the Faith?"

"This is the priests we're talking about," said Damon. "They're probably expecting conversion, reparation and a groveling letter of apology to Edwyn the Second—" he cast a sly glance at Eleanor "—and his heirs. All for the glorious chance of dying with us."

Soldiers started to set up camp, supervised by priests whose advice made up in certitude what it lacked in expertise. Megan left them to it and drifted down to the River Speed, where a contingent was debating the best way to cross now the witches had burned all the bridges. The Sandstriders' vessels, plus a few rafts and rowing boats abandoned by refugees fleeing Ainsworth, bobbed around on the water, but they weren't enough to transport an army. Not one without a very patient enemy anyway.

On the opposite bank trees swayed in the evening breeze. Home, or what was left of it, was that way. Megan yearned to reclaim it, to take Cate to Thicketford, but she didn't know how. She was reliant on others to do everything for her and it was driving her crazy. She needed the army to defeat the witches, Eleanor's people to keep her daughter safe and anonymous; even her food was provided at the whim of strangers. Megan understood the most of what was going on, but could do the least about it.

She looked downriver, westward, toward Eastport. The sun dappled the surface of the water a deep golden before sinking beyond the horizon. More memories of home came to her: lying on the banks of the Heledor watching the day surrender to night. Was Gwyneth remembering the same place as she prowled around her captured city? Did she have any desire to go back there, to undo what she had done?

Ripples disturbed the sheen of the Speed. Megan squinted. Was that . . . ? She shielded her eyes with her hand. A boat was approaching, its oars gently splashing in the water. It could only have come from Eastport.

Heart racing, Megan picked her way through reeds and bushes to where the vessel had landed. Hollering from the camp indicated she wasn't the only one who had spotted the unexpected visitor. A squad of soldiers, their uniforms in various states of disarray, assembled at the top of the bank, axes and maces ready to offer the kind of greeting that precluded snacks and sherry.

An armored man clambered off the boat. Aged, battle-hardened eyes that suggested grief and cruelty in equal parts. Megan had just enough time to recognize Tobrytan, the witch captain who had led the assault on Eastport, before someone was dragging her into the crowd and yanking her hood up.

"We didn't come all this way just so you could stand dumb in front of the first witch we ran across," whispered Damon. "Especially not *that* witch."

He tried to pull her further back to the camp, but Megan held her ground. She peered through the thicket of bodies. The soldiers held a quick conference among themselves and pushed forward one of their number to confront Tobrytan.

"What do you want?" he said, unable to suppress the quaver in his voice.

"To talk to the Supreme Priest," said Tobrytan.

The soldiers broke out into nervous laughter. "You serious?"

"They're always serious," Damon whispered into Megan's ear. "It's one of their more endearing qualities. That and their love of crochet."

The soldiers had another conference, which largely consisted of them shrugging at each other. Eventually they beckoned to Tobrytan and started up the bank. Two of Tobrytan's crew leaped from their boat. There was a clatter of drawn weapons. Tobrytan gave the soldiers a knowing look. They relented and let the rowers join their captain.

Megan and Damon followed as the witches were marched to the heart of the camp, hanging back just enough not to attract attention. A crowd formed a wide circle around Tobrytan and his crew, muttering curses and insults, though nothing so loud as to give away its source. Several bows peeked out from the tightly knit bodies, their aim so wavering the men on the opposite side of the circle were more at risk than the witches.

A herald sounded. The crowd parted to make way for Grandfather Derian, Supreme Priest and Secretary of the Realm. He was old, eighty at least, and every step seemed to require deep reserves of willpower. The official history claimed he had commanded the priests' siege of Trafford's Haven, but Megan knew enough of official histories to remain skeptical of them, and enough of what had happened at Trafford's Haven to know it was nothing to be proud of.

A servant scurried up and unfolded a chair. Grandfather Derian lowered himself into it with all the grace of a pregnant sow and curled arthritic fingers around the head of his ornate walking stick. He studied the witches through watery eyes, head resting on a multitude of chins.

Tobrytan stared back, unimpressed. "Where is Megan of Thicketford?"

Megan couldn't suppress a gasp at the sound of her name. The crowd was too caught up with events at the center of the circle to notice. It didn't stop her tugging her hood down as far as it would go.

"Who?" said Grandfather Derian. "Where?"

"She's under the care of the Countess of Ainsworth," said Tobrytan. Grandfather Derian twitched. "A name you do recognize, I see. I'm surprised you let her live."

Grandfather Derian leaned forward. There was something unnatural about his teeth, the way they caught the light with an iridescent sheen: they were pearls, filed down to form dentures. "Endalay is of no consequence," he said.

Megan caught a harrumph that could have only come from Eleanor, hidden somewhere in the crowd.

"What do you want with this Megan?"

"This is what we offer you in return." Tobrytan reached under his breastplate and pulled out a scroll, which he threw to the ground at the Supreme Priest's feet.

"What's that?" said Grandfather Derian.

"Names," said Tobrytan. "Give us the M—Give us the girl and they live."

"Hostages?" said Grandfather Derian. "Is that the best you can manage?"

"One of your own is included. The High Priest of Eastport."

"We're not interested in threats," said Grandfather Derian. "And as for this girl, who cares? You've seen the army we've assembled here. You know you can't defeat it, no matter what weapons you sold your souls for."

"You will never defeat us," said Tobrytan. "Do you want to know why?"

He motioned to his escorts. There was a flash of steel. Knives appeared in the hands of the witches. They raised the blades to their necks, and, with no hesitation or sign of fear, slashed their own throats.

Blood spurted in wild sprays as they crumpled to the ground. Tobrytan made the sign of the star-broken circle and bathed in the macabre shower, a triumphant expression on his face. Megan covered her face with her hand, muffling her scream of shock, wanting to turn away but transfixed.

"Find me two men in your army prepared to do *that*," he demanded. The Supreme Priest grimaced. "There must be two brave souls among the thousands you forced here." To a man, the crowd took a step back, unwilling to become a casualty in the rhetorical warfare. "You can't, can you?" continued Tobrytan. "Your men know they're fighting for your lies, whereas the True—" he spread his arms to indicate his fallen comrades "—know they're fighting for God."

"You confuse madness with belief," said Grandfather Derian. "A parody of the Faith for the real thing."

"We follow the True Faith, the one you tried to suppress. You condemned us as witches and demon-worshippers, but your lies found you out."

Tobrytan marched around the edge of the circle, addressing the crowd. "Do not let the priests come between you and God. The Saviors have returned to show you the way. Bring Megan of Thicketford to us, and you will find your reward."

The Supreme Priest signaled to his guards. They rushed forward and seized Tobrytan. He made no effort to struggle. Showed no alarm, no fear. He was utterly prepared for his fate.

"Slink back to Eastport," Grandfather Derian said to him. "Tell your men, your leaders, the witch mother you worship, that we are coming to teach you the real meaning of the Saviors' teachings, and that they will accept them or suffer the same fate their ancestors did at Trafford's Haven." Tobrytan flushed at the dead city's name. "Do you understand?"

Tobrytan fixed the Supreme Priest with an unwavering gaze. "I will deliver your message."

The soldiers dragged him around in a half-circle and threw him to the ground. Tobrytan picked himself up and stalked back toward the river, the crowd parting to form a wide corridor. For a moment, his head turned toward Megan. She stiffened, terrified he'd recognized her, but he continued on to his boat.

Soldiers dragged the bodies of the dead witches away. The army began to disperse. A sister dashed forward and retrieved the scroll Tobrytan had thrown on the ground. Megan recognized her movements: Eleanor. She took a couple of deep breaths to steady herself, then caught up with her.

"They know—" she looked around for eavesdroppers "—that girl's here."

"No, they don't," said Eleanor. "They're trying to flush her out, put her name out there. Tonight a thousand men will write home and mention a Megan the witches are hunting. Look on the bright side. Those kinds of numbers, chances are *someone's* going to spell your—her name right."

"I don't think that's what she cares about," Megan said through gritted teeth.

"No," said Eleanor, stopping under the glow of a lantern in a quiet part of camp. "She does have more pressing worries." She unrolled the scroll. Her hands started to tremble.

"What is it?" said Megan, stepping up to her.

Eleanor handled the scroll over. Megan scanned the names scratched into the parchment. A few she recognized: senior priests, prominent merchants who had dined at the palace when she had been a serving girl there. In the middle of the list was Lynette's name.

"I have to get her out of Eastport," said Eleanor.

"They're bluffing," said Megan. "Why kill her? What would be the point?"

"Since when have the witches needed a point to kill someone?"

Duckboards shuddering underfoot warned them of a visitor. "Well, that was the same old blend of pomp and psychopathy," said Damon. "You'd think they'd mix it up a bit, wouldn't you? Throw in a dance routine."

"How can you joke about something like that?" said Megan.

"Because if I think in any depth about what just happened, I'll go catatonic with despair."

Eleanor took the scroll from Megan and twisted it in her hands. "I can't leave Lynette to die," she said. "Not like I did Silas."

Like we *did*, Megan mentally corrected. "There's nothing we can do," she said. "We have to hope the witches are bluffing."

Canvas cracked as the wind caught the flap of a nearby tent. Eleanor crumpled up the parchment and flung it into the mud. Megan felt for her. She knew only too well the pain of someone you loved being in danger and your being able to do absolutely nothing about it.

Four

Megan detected something wrong as soon as she woke, even before her eyes adjusted to the dim light and took in the empty space next to her. The subconscious indicators of Eleanor's presence—her scent, her breathing, her radiant superiority complex—were missing.

She shot up. Around her, Sisters of the Faith—here to mend the wounded and tend to the dying—snored and mumbled in their sleep. Megan tiptoed through the narrow corridors between their bodies and slipped out of the tent. The camp was quiet. Stars twinkled coldly in the night sky.

She took a step forward. A man cleared his throat behind her, making her jump. "Sister Edla said you were to stay in the tent."

Megan turned around. It was the officer from Statham, the one who was meant to have forgotten about them. "Perhaps Sister Edla would like to give me her orders in person."

"She said to give you this."

The officer brandished a scrap of paper. Megan accepted it. "Thank you, captain."

"Lieutenant."

"What's the difference?"

"Five shillings a week."

Megan shuffled along so she could get some light. "Dear Allie," she read. "I know you're missing me so I did this sketch of my—" Her eyes widened.

"Other side."

Megan flipped the paper over with not a little relief. "M. Had to do this. Do *not* follow. Aldred will look after you. Back soon. E."

"I'm Aldred, by the way," said the lieutenant.

Megan tore the paper in frustration. Eleanor had gone to Eastport on some stupid mission to rescue Lynette. She was going to get herself killed, and Megan would lose not only her sole friend but the only person who knew where Cate was. She swore vehemently enough to make Aldred blush. That was what Eleanor wanted: if Megan couldn't find Cate, then neither could the witches.

No, she wasn't going to let that happen. "I'm going after her."

"Sister Edla said—"

"Do you have *any* opinions of your own?"

"Not once a woman's told me what to think." Aldred took a gentle but firm grip on Megan's arm. "I have to ask you to return to your tent, Sister Moira."

Megan didn't need a commotion. She let herself be guided back inside. And immediately started cutting a back door in the canvas.

The warships loomed above them like slumbering leviathans. Damon sat stock still, hardly daring to exhale as they drifted toward them. He stared up at the decks, dreading that every shimmer across his retina was a witch looking out on to the Speed and noticing the small boat bobbing toward him.

"Of all the stupid things we've ever done," he muttered.

"At least Megan's not here," said Eleanor. "She'd have us attacking the ships." She waved a hand in warning. "We're moving too far right. Take us left a bit."

"Port," said Damon.

"Huh?"

"It's port on a boat, not left."

"Does it really freaking matter?"

"Well, if you're not going to enter into the spirit of—"

Too late. There was a thud and a wet scrape as the boat hit the right-most warship. Damon cringed. Eleanor swore under her breath. They craned their necks, examining the portholes in the hulks for telltale lights. Damon felt like a flea fearing it had disturbed the dog.

There was no reaction. The collision must have been written off as a piece of flotsam. Eleanor leaned over and pressed her hands against the slimy hull of the warship. Damon copied her. Together they pushed themselves away.

The current picked them up and exaggerated their motion, sending them into a slow spin as they traversed the narrow channel between the two ships. Damon moved the oars to correct their yaw. Eleanor waved him away with a chop of her hand. A man was leaning over the bulwark. Eleanor grabbed a bow from their stash and strung an arrow. Yew creaked as she drew back and aimed.

Something splatted into the water. The guy up top was throwing up. Too much wine, Damon guessed, one last blowout before battle commenced. More chunks pitter-pattered into the river. There was a low moan, then the man stumbled from view.

They cleared the ships. Eleanor let her bow go slack, a release of tension Damon could empathize with. He wrapped his hands around the oars and looked to her. She nodded. Gently he pushed them toward the south bank. Further down the Speed, Damon could make out the shapes of another quartet of warships skulking on the water.

Eastport's riverside should have been a riot of light and revelry and, possibly, rioting, even at this time of night. Instead it looked as it was in mourning. A dim glow above the rooftops of the outer city at least hinted at some life there; the center was almost a void. Damon thought of the rumors he'd heard, that the witches had sealed Eastport's inner city and slaughtered everyone who wouldn't become True. He swallowed. Rumor might be right.

The prison loomed above them, its walls sheer and impenetrable. "You sure Lynette's here?" he asked Eleanor.

"Where else would she be?"

"*Not* here?" said Damon. "We could have tried the less-liable-to-get-us-killed places first."

"You didn't have to come, you know."

Oh, but Damon did. She'd asked him and not the half-witted officer who'd supplied them with weapons. It meant Eleanor still relied on him, still turned to him when she was most in need. Perhaps one day that need would grow.

"We need to find the sewage outlet," said Eleanor, scanning the wall. "We'll be able to crawl through it and into the prison. There'll be gates, but after centuries of piss flowing through them they'll be rusted to hell."

"Seems a remarkably coherent plan," said Damon. "For us, anyway. How long've you been thinking about this? Not a spur-of-the-moment thing, I'm guessing."

"Someone as rich as Lynette was always going to be a target. I feared it might come to this."

"And you'd have to make a withdrawal?"

"This is not about her money," said Eleanor.

"We're going to rescue some poor people as well?"

"Just keep looking for an outlet," said Eleanor. "It'll be the worst-smelling thing around. Well—" she tugged at the leather uniform she was wearing, from which the insignia of the Faith had been removed "—second worst."

"It's not my fault. You said get something practical. You didn't say it had to smell of roses and lavender."

They cut through the river, past the water gate, securely chained and unused for decades to the best of Damon's knowledge, and down to the western end. Damon racked his brain, trying to recall the times he'd stared at the prison from the river or the far end of the jetties. He swore he'd seen sewage outlets, their undersides stained with effluent. Maybe someone else had already attempted a rescue this way and the witches had blocked them off.

"There," said Eleanor, pointing at a spot a few feet above the waterline.

"You sure?" said Damon.

"It's a hole. How sure do you need me to be?"

"Words I never dreamed you'd utter."

Damon brought the boat to a stop. Eleanor threaded a rope through an iron ring that had been hammered into the mortar between the stonework. When she tightened the rope, the ring wiggled loose a bit, like a tooth starting to decay, but it held.

Eleanor stood up so she could peer into the opening, rocking the boat. Damon gripped the sides to stabilize it. "That what we're looking for?" he asked. The outlet was a rough square, about three feet in each direction. Large enough to crawl through, but no larger.

The countess wrinkled her nose. "Uh-huh." She tied her hair back, then jerked a thumb at Damon. "You first."

"Why me?"

"If we're going to get stuck in there, I want fair notice."

Damon sighed and got to his feet, swaying with the motion. He pulled himself over to the outlet and hauled himself up. His legs flailed in the air, like those of a mouse caught in the jaws of a snake, before he slithered inside.

The tunnel was rapidly losing any cozy qualities it might have had. The narrow walls seemed to be squeezing inwards, threatening to crush Damon. Every time he saw a brick jutting from the ceiling or the floor, he feared it heralded a squeezing of the available space. So far, the obstacles proved to be nothing more than the product of bad masonry. He breathed a sigh of relief whenever he crawled past one, occasionally crying out as he misjudged the clearance.

They reached the first gate. As Eleanor had predicted, the bottom of the bars were crumbling with corrosion. Damon propped his torch up against the wall, away from the stream of God knew what that trickled down the center of the tunnel, and stretched a hand backward.

"Hammer."

Eleanor slapped a war hammer from the bag of supplies Aldred had supplied into his palm. Iron met stone with a deep chime as his arm was immediately dragged to the ground. Damon dragged the hammer forward and considered his options. There was no room to swing it, so he rammed the head at the most rusted part of the gate. A clang reverberated around the cramped tunnel. He hoped the thick walls would muffle the sounds to the prison's inhabitants.

He continued to attack the gate. His arm started to ache. The hammer was designed to be wielded with brute force, and he was designed for neither brute nor force. "Are you all right up there?" asked Eleanor. "Want me to go see if I can find a small child to give you a lift?"

"Maybe if we swapped positions and you condescended at the gate, we'd get through faster?"

Damon gave one last heave. The gate came free with a clatter. He shoved it out of the way and resumed crawling.

The incline became steeper, the climb harder on his aching arms and thighs. He wasn't helping himself by trying not to breathe in. He filled his lungs with dank air. His eyes watered. On second thoughts, he preferred asphyxiation.

An opening appeared over his head. A vertical tunnel leading to one of the higher floors of the prison. He held the torch up. Ancient iron rungs were hammered into the walls for maintenance access. Not enough light to see how far up they went or how secure they'd be. Damon continued on his current path.

His right arm scuffed the wall. He must have veered off course. He pushed himself to the left. The wall that side blocked any movement. *Uh-oh.*

"We have a problem," he said. "I'm a bit stuck."

"How's that a 'we' problem?"

"Hang on, I might be able to . . ."

Damon wriggled forward. The walls clamped on to him. "A bit stuck" turned into "oh my God I'm going to be here forever." The flames of his torch licked the air in front of him. His face was getting very warm. He blew frantically. The air only encouraged the flames.

He twisted so he occupied the diagonal of the passage and squeezed his arm forward, grimacing as rough stone flayed the skin on the back of his hand. He grabbed the torch and threw it further down the tunnel.

There was a splash. The flames spluttered and died.

"Why has it gone dark?"

"That's right, focus on what affects you." Damon felt around with his free arm. "It gets wider again."

"I'm very pleased for you. Can you get a move on? Something's trying to crawl up my trouser leg."

Clenching his teeth, Damon wriggled through the gap. Halfway through, he was able to free his other arm and drag himself along. Although the tunnel he emerged into was no larger than before, it felt as roomy as a mansion.

There was a clunk behind him as Eleanor threw the sack of supplies ahead of her, then frantic grunting.

"I can't move!" she cried.

"Imagine that."

Eleanor squeezed in the gap beside Damon. At last they could stand upright. There was a sequence of planks above their heads with an egg-shaped hole cut into them, through which moonlight shone. They'd found the production end of the sewer system.

Damon tested the planks. They weren't secured very well. "Hammer?" asked Eleanor.

"Hammer."

He smashed through the planks and clambered up through the toilet into the garderobe beyond. He collapsed on the flagstones, glorying in relaxation, the space and a smell that was merely mildly unpleasant.

"Now I know what a turd goes through," he moaned. "Saviors, I have never so needed a bath."

"You don't know how true that isn't," said Eleanor, grunting as she heaved herself up. She let out a long

"Hmm." Damon could tell by her tone she was frowning. "I was expecting it to be more . . ."

"'After them!'-y?"

". . . especially after all the noise you made."

"Oh, I'm sorry. Maybe next time you can get your boyfriend to supply us with a padded hammer."

Damon noticed Eleanor didn't bother to deny the "boyfriend" part. He hoped it was because the accusation was too fanciful.

Eleanor looked around and spotted a surcoat dangling from a hook. She tore it into strips and wiped herself down. Damon followed her example. A pitcher stood on the windowsill. They washed themselves, gasping at the iciness of the water.

"Any idea where to look?" said Eleanor.

"You're the old convict," said Damon. "You don't know?"

"I was in here for a few hours. We didn't get around to the guided tour."

"I thought you'd been planning this."

"Only hypothetically," said Eleanor. "I don't have maps or anything."

"So we're back to the old dynamic strategy of employing a fast-reacting approach to events as they unfurl?"

"You object?"

"No," said Damon. "It feels strangely reassuring to know we're winging it."

They snuck out into the corridor. It was quiet, the only sound the scuffling of their soles as they scurried from shadow to shadow. There were no guards patrolling and all of the cells they peeked into were empty. This surprised Damon. He thought crimes against the witches expanded so as to fill the available prison space.

"I don't like this," he whispered.

"You were the one complaining about the danger."

"Lack of obvious danger makes me worried there's lots of nonobvious danger waiting for us around the next corner."

"How do you manage to lead a life being so paranoid?" said Eleanor.

"By being this paranoid."

"Saviors, you sound like my father."

They crept along until they found a deserted guards' station.

An icy breeze blew in from the river, sneaking into the gaps of Damon's uniform and making him shiver. He pulled his jerkin tighter, but that only served to dislodge the stench festering there.

"Maybe there's some record of where everyone is," said Eleanor.

"Including handy instructions on how to break them out and a shilling for the stagecoach out of here?"

Eleanor lit a candle; whether to aid in her search or better glare at him, Damon didn't know. The greasy glow—cheap tallow only for the ranks—revealed a mold-spattered room dominated by a splintered oak table that looked as if it had been used for butchering the more unsavory types of meat, a company of tankards filled to varying degrees with souring wine and a blackboard covered in names arranged in a grid. A ring of keys hung next to it.

"See," said Eleanor with a triumphant grin.

"Don't see a shilling."

Eleanor began searching the grid while Damon reached for one of the cups. "Is this really the time to be drinking?" she asked.

"I'd say it was the perfect time to be drinking," said Damon. He had a sip of the wine. "Not turned to vinegar yet. Whoever had the party hasn't been gone long."

"You sound disappointed you missed it."

"No, but . . . I don't like this."

"Well, it's got to have gone off a *bit*," said Eleanor, distracted.

"How many jailers do you know who are literate—" he waved at the board "—never mind this organized?"

"The witches might be evil murdering bastards, but they're well-educated evil murdering bastards."

"It's almost as if someone wants us to find them."

"You think this is a trap?" Eleanor tapped on the board, leaving a small black circle in the chalk. "She's in cell block number nine." She lifted the keys from their hook and blew out the candle. "Let's do this and get out of here," she said.

"It'd be rude to keep the trap waiting."

They headed back into the corridor. "Which way's number nine?" asked Damon.

"Um . . ."

"Shall we find number eight and take it from there?"

They crept along, trying to minimize the sound of their footsteps despite no evidence anyone was around to hear them. Damon tripped on a loose flagstone and shot an arm out to stabilize himself. The wall was clammy, like a cadaver dragged out of the water.

"There might be a reason the witches have no guards here," he said.

"It had crossed my mind."

"Are you prepared for that?"

"At least I'll know what happened to her," said Eleanor.

Wails made them shrink against the wall, human voices that had lost the will or the ability to form words. They shuffled down until they reached a junction. Eleanor unstrapped her bow and notched an arrow.

"Go check," she whispered to Damon.

"Why me?" he whispered back. "You're the one with the weapons."

"I'll cover you. Or shoot you in the back. The jury's still out."

Damon stretched past Eleanor and peered around the corner. She encouraged him on by poking her arrow in his buttock. He gasped and scurried forward.

A line of cells stretched out before him. Moonlight shone through barred windows and cast silvery shapes on the floor. No one challenged him or, more importantly, tried to decapitate him.

He recovered his bravado. "Anyone order the economy jailbreak?" he shouted down the corridor. A multitude of replies came back. None of them expressed the level of gratitude he'd been expecting. Or, on reflection, any.

Eleanor bustled around the corner. "Lynette?" she said, checking each cell in turn. "Is there a Lynette here?" She stopped and beckoned to Damon. "Keys!"

"You have them."

"I do not—oh."

She pressed her bow and arrow into Damon's hands and fished in her pockets. It took her half a dozen tries—once trying to ram a key in a gap in the timbers that formed the door—before she found the one that fitted. She flew inside.

Damon hung around at the entrance, fiddling with the unfamiliar weapon. Cells made him nervous—he'd spent his adult life trying to avoid them—and this was worse than most: a cramped cave with slime-streaked walls and the stench of decaying flesh. A dead woman was stretched out on a stone block that served as a bed, her dark skin shrinking into her skull.

Another woman huddled in a corner, dressed in the rags of what was once a fine gown. Her head was buried in her arms and she was muttering scraps of prayers. She didn't react to Eleanor's calls. The countess had to crouch beside the woman and lift her head up.

"Lynette, it's me. Eleanor."

The woman blinked, tears swimming in her eyes. Beneath the grime, beauty was only just beginning to lose the battle with age. "My lady?"

"I think we can drop the formalities in the circumstances." Eleanor got up and held out a hand. "We're getting out of here."

"There's no way out." Lynette pushed herself to her feet. Her legs gave way. Eleanor caught her.

"We have keys."

"No good," said Lynette. "The witches barred all the doors."

"Why would they . . . ?"

Fear seized Damon. He dashed to the window. A warship was maneuvering out on the river, bringing its broadside parallel with the prison.

"I think I've figured out how they're planning to execute their prisoners," he said. "They're going to use them as target practice. And for 'them,' read 'us'."

Five

Megan snuck away in the small hours, when the air was sharp in the lungs and the camp was quiet but for twenty thousand collective snores. Tied up among the smattering of craft down by the bank she found a small rowboat that looked more or less seaworthy. She threw in a sack of supplies—food, water, a spare uniform, a few extra knives—she'd scavenged from the sleeping army, and cast off. The strong currents of the Speed caught the vessel. She only just managed to jump on board before the boat was snatched away.

Megan didn't have to row much; instead she just used the oars to correct her course and keep her safely in the center of the Speed. The world slipped by in silhouette, as if it was a figment of her imagination. She wriggled out of the sister's robes. It felt good to get them off. Not only because they were heavy and ungainly and smelled like rotten vegetables, but because they carried with them a promise of sanctity she could never fulfill.

The uniform she changed into felt more her, even if it was tight across the chest and she had to saw a couple of inches off the legs.

Not foolhardy enough to tackle Eastport in the glare of the sun—and hoping Eleanor wasn't either—she spent the day hidden in the reeds by the remains of the Washbrook bridge, dozing and suppressing the part of her that screamed this was a really stupid idea. It was the longest she'd spent on her own since the night the witches had destroyed Thicketford. Was that why she was doing this, because she was scared of being alone?

Night fell once more. Megan pushed off again, slipping silently down the Speed. She had hoped to catch up with Eleanor before they reached Eastport, but there was no sign of another vessel. Maybe she'd taken a horse. She could have reached the city a day ahead of Megan, which meant she'd be either dead or on her way out. Or having Cate's whereabouts tortured from her. Megan grabbed the oars and increased her pace.

She reached the fringes of the outer city. Warships lurked on the horizon. Megan made herself keep going despite the instinct to turn and flee. She pulled the oars up and let herself drift. A splash might catch the moonlight and then the attention of a watching witch.

The shoreline darkened. For a moment Megan panicked, thinking she'd overshot and was now heading for the open sea. But no, she'd drawn level with the inner city, though she wasn't sure if the dingy shadows she was seeing were buildings or merely the memory of them. Still, the blackness suited her purpose. She steered for the shore.

A jetty rushed toward her. Megan did her best to counteract her momentum, but she still thudded into the posts with an ominous crack. She cringed, fearful the noise and vibration had alerted lurking witches. Nothing scuttled out. She threw out a rope and secured her vessel.

Keeping low, as if losing a few inches of height would keep her hidden, Megan scurried into the city. Devoid of life, Eastport was a forbidding labyrinth. It was only when she spotted the palace looming down a side street that she got her bearings. One of Lynette's possible prisons, the others being Lynette's house and the city prison itself. Her throat tightened at the thought of the last.

Where would Eleanor have gone? Maybe she should find a vantage point and wait for the inevitable pandemonium—the sound would certainly carry in this silence. No, she had to be doing something. She couldn't just hang around, risking being too late to come to Eleanor's rescue. She should try the palace. It'd be easier to break into than the prison, and it was closer to Lynette's house.

Decision made, Megan padded through the empty streets. A curfew, she tried to persuade herself, but didn't a curfew need enforcers? The mere threat of the witches might be enough to keep people indoors. She risked a peek in a couple of windows. No one peeked back.

She reached the back of the palace. It looked deserted. No, wait, was that a glow in one of the windows, or just her eyes playing tricks? She blinked, let her eyes adjust. Definitely a light, and it was moving. Someone was in there.

Megan hurried along the perimeter, looking for a way in. One door failed to yield; the next proved just as obdurate. She tried the windows. One hinted it might be open to persuasion. She wedged a knife in between frame and sill and pushed. The window rose with a squeal. Megan froze. Had anyone heard? No sign of anyone. She pushed her fingers into the half-inch gap she had created and lifted the window the rest of the way.

A couch cushioned her drop. She paused, resisting the urge to curl up and sleep, listening for signs of activity or, more specifically, frantic pursuit. There was a tiny scratching. Something scurried across the tiles.

Megan tiptoed down the corridor. Something slammed in the distance. She headed toward it, then ducked back into the shadows as she caught sight of two witches. Once she had regained control of her heartbeat, she risked a peek. They were dragging a figure along. A priest.

She slipped in behind them, hopping between hiding places, hoping the stomp of the witches' boots and the moaning of the priest would cover her approach. The surroundings began to look familiar. Double doors opened. Megan could see all the way into the great hall, down an aisle of soldiers, past the forbidding forms of Tobrytan and a dark-skinned woman—Diannon?—in leather armor, and all the way to the throne. Once it had been the seat of the Endalays and after them the High Priests of Eastport. Now Gwyneth occupied it, light from the chandelier high above her head dappling the pure white furs she snuggled in. There was something else. Gwyneth was holding something—cradling something. Megan's mind went to the fetid hut, when she had held her daughter for the only time before Eleanor had taken her away.

The doors slammed shut. Megan blinked away tears and crept out from her hiding place. Alcoves faced each other in the corridor. Access to the galleries that overlooked the great hall. Morbid curiosity drove Megan up, made her forget about Eleanor and Lynette.

The gallery was dark and smelled of wood varnish, sour wine and stale sweat. Megan crawled along, watching the action flicker down below through the gaps in the rails. The soldiers she had followed heaved the priest along and threw him to the floor in front of the throne.

Tobrytan was muttering something to two of his men. "They have their orders?" said Gwyneth.

"Yes, Mother."

"Go, then," Gwyneth said to the two witches. "And may the Saviors protect you."

The witches looked to Tobrytan, who nodded. They departed.

Through all this, the priest remained unmoving on the floor, a terrified worshipper prostrating himself at the feet of a pagan goddess. Megan inched closer to the edge. It was Father Galan, High Priest of Eastport. The last time she'd seen him he'd tried to hang her, or rather her unborn child.

Gwyneth rose and circled him, rocking her baby as she did so. "I'm sorry, father. Would you like a seat?"

"We don't have time for this, Mother," said Tobrytan. "We have to get to the ship."

"Of course, captain." Gwyneth turned to the Diannon woman. "Afreyda, if you would . . . ?"

"If I would what?" said the woman. Her words were slow and over-articulated. Stathian wasn't her first language.

"If you would separate Father Galan's head from his body, I'd be *most* grateful." She looked to the soldiers. "Did someone bring the spike?" There was a murmur. "Honestly, do I have to do everything myself?"

The Diannon woman, Afreyda, hadn't moved. "What are you waiting for?" Gwyneth demanded.

"I did not agree to be your executioner."

"You agreed to do anything I commanded."

"Anything the True commanded," said Tobrytan.

"They're the same thing," snapped Gwyneth. She stepped up to Afreyda. "Do it. *Now.*"

Afreyda held her ground, staring down Gwyneth, her hand clenching at the sword sheathed at her waist. Gwyneth glared back. Megan was reminded of childish contests, when she and her sister had competed to see who could make the other laugh first. Invariably, they'd crack at the same time, a consequence of being twins, they'd always claimed. Now the stakes were so much higher.

Tobrytan placed a hand on Afreyda's shoulder and edged her aside. "I'll do it," he said.

He drew his sword. Candlelight flashed across its blade, making it look as if it was on fire. Two soldiers grabbed Father Galan and heaved him to his knees. The priest made the sign of the circle and started reciting the funeral prayer.

As Tobrytan took up position, Gwyneth swayed. She looked at the baby cradled in her arms. "This is what'll happen to your enemies, sweetheart. They'll die at your feet. Every single one of them, until all who remain are True."

Revulsion coursed through Megan. *I pledge to defend His people.* She thought back to deaths she'd witnessed: Wade hacked down in the wheat fields; her grandfather shot outside his own home; Silas butchered above her head. *I pledge to uphold the Faith and destroy its enemies.* Could she do nothing while another person was murdered? *I pledge obedience to God and His priests.* If she didn't believe that, she might as well declare herself a witch and have done with it.

But what could she do? She looked to the heavens for inspiration. The light of the chandelier dazzled her for a moment. She looked away, noticed the chain holding it up, followed its path. It terminated up in the tower that topped the great hall. How to get up there? A dark archway at the end of the gallery. Megan scurried over to it, keeping low. Stone stairs wound upward. She scrambled up them.

She found herself on a narrow walkway ringed by clerestory windows and marble busts of Eleanor's ancestors, who looked as unimpressed with Megan's actions as the countess herself would be.

Down below, Father Galan was still praying. "Are you going to recite the whole damn Book of Faith?" said Gwyneth.

The chandelier chain was wrapped around a roller. A lever locked it into place. Megan lunged at it, heaved with everything she had. The chandelier plummeted with a metallic clatter. There was a holler of alarm, then an almighty crash. Crystals and candles smashed into the floor and at least one witch, if the scream was anything to go by.

The great hall went black. "Run, Father Galan! Run!" Megan shouted. The slap of footsteps told her the

High Priest had at least tried to take advantage of the distraction.

Megan had her own escape to consider now. She lifted one of the busts—with difficulty—and propelled it through a windowpane. She threw herself after it, wincing as a jagged tooth ripped through the leather of her pants and scraped her shin.

The tower was higher than she'd reckoned. It was at least ten feet down to the roof of the palace. The commotion continued inside. They'd be coming for her. No time to be scared. She squatted, twisted, grabbed the windowsill, dangled for a moment, then let herself drop.

Despite rolling with the fall, it still felt as if someone had taken a hammer to her legs. Megan lay on the roof, seeing both real and imaginary stars. A shape appeared up on the tower. The Diannon woman, Afreyda. Saviors, she'd got there quick. Megan pushed to her feet and set off across the roof.

Tremors underfoot told Megan her pursuer had found her way down. She picked up her pace, then lost her footing as the world underneath turned to ice. No, not ice, she realized as she squeaked and slid: the glass ceiling over the atrium, cracked by the impact of her fall. It shifted beneath her weight.

She scrambled for the stone solidity of the roof proper. Afreyda was nearly upon her. Closer to her own age, Megan could see now. Tight-fitting leather armor protected an athletic body. Jet-black hair hung in a long ponytail braided with gold filigree. Tattoos coiled around the edges of her face, the ink almost indiscernible. Megan had seen the design before, on the bodies of the witches. The Diannon Empire was supplying troops as well as guns, it would seem.

Afreyda stepped on to the glass. Megan pulled two heavy daggers from her belt and looked her straight in the eye. Afreyda cocked her head as if to say, Really?

Megan flipped the knives around and slammed their hilts into the atrium ceiling.

An anguished creak became a shriek. The glass, already weakened by Megan's fall, shattered in a sequence of waves. Afreyda leaped for safety as shards fell around her, catching the moonlight like crystal rain. She grabbed the edge of the ceiling and hung there, fingers straining as she fought the pull of the atrium floor far below. Megan gave her an apologetic shrug and hurried on.

A drainpipe offered Megan a way to the ground. She shimmied down it and dashed into the nearest alley. There had been no sign of Lynette or Eleanor at the palace. One option down, two to go. She hoped the prison would be less infested with witches.

The alley opened out on to the main thoroughfare leading down to the docks. Megan skidded to a halt. A witch was marching down the street, toward the river.

Damn, they were still looking for her. What should she do? Wait until he had passed and hope he didn't check this alley? Megan heard clomping—too close behind her. No choice. She dashed across the street and disappeared down a passageway opposite.

Megan wasn't as disappeared as she'd hoped. The witches cried out, hurtled after her. A pile of crates was heaped against the wall. Before she had time to think what she was doing, Megan raced up them as if they were giant steps and dropped into the yard beyond.

There was scuffling on the other side of the wall. She froze, held her breath. The ground shifted beneath her feet. The sacks of refuse she was standing on were rearranging themselves, adjusting to her weight. She was going to fall.

A boom filled the air just as her ass hit the ground. A gun had been fired. Had the priests' army arrived already? Were the witches firing on them? There was a crack of a second shot, then a third, then a continuous roar in which it was impossible to discern the individual shots.

The gunfire ceased. There was a low moan, as if Eastport was crying in agony, then a huge splash. Something big had hit the river. It sounded like the entire city.

The noise settled into an eerie silence. Megan reached for the top of the wall and heaved herself up. She was about to drop down when she spotted another witch coming down the alley, moonlight glinting off his lacquered armor. Crouching low, she eased a knife from her belt. She swallowed, realizing what she had planned, how easy it was becoming . . .

The witch drew level with her. Megan launched herself off the wall. She thudded into him, dragging him to the ground. Before he could react, she jerked his head backward and rammed her blade into his throat. Blood spurted on to her skin, almost comfortingly hot.

The witch's armor dinged against the cobblestones as his body shuddered its last. Megan eased off him, damning herself for her lack of remorse. She wanted to blame Gwyneth for forcing her into this, but she knew she didn't have to be here. She could be far away, her hands clean.

She checked up and down the alley. It looked clear, but who could tell in the darkness? She resumed her journey, mindful there was still another witch ahead of her. He could be hiding in the shadows, waiting to pounce on her like she had his compatriot. If he slit her throat, could she blame him?

The tinkling of running water warned her she was approaching Gaderian Square. She flattened herself against the wall and peeked around the corner. It was deserted, the cascading fountain performing for an absent audience. She crept into the square and looked to the skyline to reorient herself. She gasped when she saw the thick gray column reaching for the heavens, realizing where it was coming from. The prison. The witches would have no reason to fire on an empty building. Their other prisoners must be there. Eleanor must be there.

She hastened across the square. A voice made her halt. "You will not escape me a second time."

It was Afreyda. She raised her sword in a two-handed grip. The blade was short and slightly curved, polished so brightly her eyes reflected in the steel, and sharp enough to slice through marble. Megan brought her blood-smeared knife into an offensive position.

"Mine is bigger," said Afreyda.

Megan pulled out another knife and crossed her arms in front of her face.

"Mine is still bigger."

"I thought only men felt the need to compensate?"

The sword twirled and slashed the air in front of Megan. A show-off move. Megan jumped back, trying to remember the training Eleanor had instilled in her. Unfortunately most of it involved stabbing the other person before they realized they were in a fight. It might be better to make a run for it, find Eleanor. But looking at Afreyda, Megan could see there was no way she could outrun her.

Afreyda thrust. Metal shrieked as Megan beat her sword away with one of her knives. She lunged forward, swiping as hard as she could at the girl's legs. Leather rent. A thin red line on the edge of her blade told Megan she'd got more than clothing. Her opponent scowled, more in annoyance than pain.

The sword came down twice as hard as before, taking off a chunk of Megan's hair and the tip of her ear as she jerked out of the way. Blood trickled down her face, followed by stinging pain.

Another slash, a weak one, easily evaded. Too late Megan realized it was a feint. The girl spun and kicked her flush in the face.

Megan staggered back, head spinning, blood gushing from her nose. The flat of Afreyda's blade smacked each of Megan's wrists in turn, beating the knives from her grasp. Megan made a grab for the girl's arm, trying to push the sword away. A boot to the knee sent Megan crashing to the ground.

Afreyda's sword came to rest on Megan's neck. The blade stung as it nibbled her skin. Megan braced herself. At least the sharpness of the sword ensured her death would be quick.

Six

Damon shot from cell to cell, fumbling with keys, trying to find the right one for each lock while the building shook and his hands shook ever harder. Prisoners—Eastport's great and good—urged him on, one second pleading, the next barking contemptuous orders. *I could take care of myself, you know,* he thought of telling them, *get the hell out of here while there's still a here to get out of.* He couldn't though. She would know; judge him; find him no better than she suspected.

He looked through the bars of the cell he was trying to open. The occupant had his back to him, gawking at the witches' ship out on the Speed. A flash filled the room, followed by an almighty boom the smallest fraction of a second later. Dust and masonry blasted into his face. He staggered back, coughing and spluttering.

"Damon!"

"All right! All right!"

Damon stumbled to the door, operating by touch rather than sight. He jammed a key at random into the lock—had he used this one before? who could tell?—and twisted. God smiled on him. The lock yielded. He shouldered the door open and wafted the clouds away. Half the cell's wall was gone. Its occupant was sprawled on the floor. Blood oozed from a gash in his head. Chunks of stone were piled on his body as if someone had already started building his memorial cairn.

Eleanor coughed behind him. "Is he . . . ?" she asked. Damon shook his head. "We need to get out of here."

"Really?" said Damon, stumbling back into the corridor to join her. "I thought I'd hang around a bit, supervise the restructuring work."

"You're bleeding."

"Huh?"

Eleanor reached for his face. Damon thought she was going to slap him. Instead she brushed his cheek. She showed him her fingers. They were smeared with his blood.

"Oh, that," he said. "It's nothing. Just scratches."

Was she concerned about him? It was worth the pain if she was. Eleanor spoiled the moment by wrinkling her mouth and wiping her hand on her leather pants.

The prisoners they'd rescued—about a dozen after they'd filtered out the dead—were congregated in a huddle. Skeletal and covered in dust, they looked like specters come to haunt them. Eleanor beckoned to them and pointed up the corridor the way they'd come.

"This way."

A deafening boom shook the prison, knocking them off their feet. An ominous crack ripped above their heads. Chunks of ceiling became floor covering.

"That way!" Eleanor shouted, now pointing in the opposite direction.

"Getting the hang of the fast-reacting approach, I see."

They pushed to the front of the escaping pack as they dashed through the prison—it felt important someone with experience of running away in a blind panic led them, even though flight seemed in vain. It was like trying to outrun an earthquake. How long were the witches' ships going to bombard them? Until the building was nothing but rubble and corpses?

They reached a staircase. Eleanor urged everyone down it, waving them on like a teacher in a gym lesson. Damon tried not to look directly at them, but he couldn't help it, couldn't help seeing exhaustion fighting with desperation in their faces, naked fear exposing their vulnerability.

There was one last straggler, an old man who wasn't so much running as falling forward. He clutched his chest and toppled over, his face smacking into the floor. Eleanor scurried over to him, rolled him on his back. Blood spread from his smashed nose, coloring his gray face. She placed two fingers on his neck, searching for a pulse. A shake of the head confirmed its absence.

Eleanor started back for the staircase. The corridor shuddered as the witches hit them again. She lost her footing and went flying. Damon rushed to her. She waved him off as he tried to help her up, then relented and grabbed on to his arm.

They followed the others down the stairs and into the courtyard, dashing for the main gates. The air got a little fresher, the noise a lot louder.

"Been here before," said Eleanor, breathless. "It's not going to work." There was a squeal of aggravated iron as those in front grabbed the gates and began to pull them open. "Just goes to show every situation's different."

Damon turned to her. "You're telling me we went through all that shit—and I mean that in its most literal sense—and the freaking door was unlocked?"

"I don't remember *you* suggesting we try the front way."

One by one they slipped through the gap in the gates and into the deserted streets. Unspoken consensus drove them away from the river, into the alleys and ginnels that spiraled out from the prison. The surrounding buildings deadened the sound of gunfire, bringing some relief to Damon's shattered nerves.

Then it fell silent altogether. "The guns have stopped," said Eleanor.

"Does this mean the witches have gone?" said Damon.

"Or sent troops in after us."

"Can't you give me a few moments of optimism?"

Eleanor ran her free hand through her hair, sending up a cloud of dust that made it look like her head was on fire. "It's at times like this you have to ask yourself what's realistically going to happen in a situation like this."

Someone cleared their throat. "What?" said Eleanor and Damon together. The crowd pointed fingers down the street. A black-armored witch was swinging an ax. In one smooth motion, Eleanor notched an arrow to her bow. A whisper of air brushed Damon's face as she fired. The witch toppled to the ground. Someone offered up a brief round of applause.

"Impressive," said Damon. He leaned into Eleanor. "You'd already spotted him, hadn't you?" he whispered. "And you dried your hand with the dust in your hair."

Eleanor gave him a cheeky pout. Damon so wanted to kiss her. "If you think all you need to do is stand waving a big weapon, you deserve all that's coming to you."

She trotted over to the dead witch and began to relieve him of his weapons, which Damon passed around the rest of their party. "Question is, how many of his friends did he bring with him?"

"The witches don't really do friends," said Damon, "more comurderous fanatics."

Eleanor's head snapped up at the sound of approaching footsteps. She snatched up her bow and started as she recognized Father Galan, his face hollowed out and phantom-like in the moonlight. The tonsure had grown out a little, giving his pate the appearance of shrub land. Dirt and less salubrious substances stained his priestly robes.

"Don't shoot!" he cried, holding up his hands.

"Like you didn't hang us?" said Eleanor.

"What?" Father Galan bent forward. "Oh, it's you. So who was that at the palace?"

"Who was what where?"

Damon knew instinctively. "Megan," he said. "She came after us."

The sword lifted from Megan's neck. She knew she should try to roll away before the blade sliced down, but the kick had left her uncoordinated, and even if she could command her muscles, she had no energy left to power them.

The blow didn't come. Metal clattered on to stone. Footsteps approached. Someone rolled her over. Megan opened her eyes. Damon swam into focus.

"My head hurts," she said.

"And you thought you'd cure it by decapitation?"

He helped her to her feet. She put a hand to her ear, wincing as she touched sliced cartilage. It came away sticky. "How's it look?"

"Well, you've lost a little weight."

"That bad?"

"The top quarter-inch or so of your ear," said Damon. "Quite endearing. Apart from the blood of course."

Eleanor was covering Afreyda with her bow. Behind her was arranged a motley crew, brandishing weapons with all the conviction of a new father faced with his first diaper change.

"Are you going to explain what you're doing here?" Eleanor said to Megan.

"After you do."

There was a tense pause. "We'll talk about this later." Eleanor jerked her bow at Afreyda. "Do you want me to . . . ?"

"I don't know." Megan approached the Diannon girl. "Why are you fighting for the witches?"

Afreyda clenched her fists. Her eyes flicked down to her fallen sword. "Don't," said Megan. "You won't be faster than Eleanor. Tell me why you were fighting."

"The True said they would spare my mother if I served them."

"Your mother?" said Damon. "Was she from the Diannon Empire as well? Forty-ish. Long hair. Dark-skinned like you?"

"Yes."

"And there're no others from the empire in the city?"

"No," said Afreyda. The Diannon Empire stretched across a continent a treacherous ocean away. Ships from the Realm rarely went there, unless they were part of an insurance scam, though the odd merchant did make the opposite journey.

"Then your mother's dead."

Afreyda's face dropped. Her head shook compulsively. "No! She cannot be! You must be wrong. You have to be wrong. She promised!" Megan didn't need to ask who "she" was.

"Who was that woman in your cell?" Eleanor asked Lynette.

Lynette looked a little catatonic. "What, my lady?"

"The woman in your cell. What was her name? Where did she come from?"

"I . . . er . . . Mafreyda. I think. She had some kind of illness."

"What kind of illness?"

"I think we can safely say it was nontrivial," said Damon. Megan glared at him. "What? We're meant to be nice to behead-y lady now?"

Afreyda looked around the small crowd. Her face crumpled, her expression a mixture of bewilderment and grief. Tears filled her eyes, desperation clouding her features. Megan knew the feeling, the pain that crushed your heart, the onrush of fear as you realized you were on your own in the world. She forgot the fight.

There was another lost girl in front of her, another girl betrayed and abandoned. She couldn't stop herself from wrapping her arms around Afreyda and holding her as she sobbed her heart out.

Skin peeled away from leather with a wet rasp as Eleanor gently pried Megan away from Afreyda. "We should be going," said the countess, pressing a rag against Megan's wounded ear, from which blood still dribbled. "We don't know who's out here."

"No one," said Father Galan. "The witches have fled."

Afreyda nodded. "It is true. Our ships were to be the last."

"Where're they going?" asked Megan.

"I do not know."

"It has to be somewhere."

"Not necessarily," said Damon. "The whole point of fleeing is you're running *from* somewhere rather than *to* somewhere."

Megan ignored him. It was second nature by now. "Would they be going to the Diannon Empire?"

"No," said Afreyda, a haunted look in her eye, "not there. Not if . . ."

"I heard Dustor," said Father Galan, "but who knows?"

Was that it? Had the witches taken their revenge for Trafford's Haven and scarpered? Like a victim who'd endured a bully's attacks, Megan wanted to believe the appearance of her big brothers had scared off her tormentor, but she feared things weren't that easy, could never be that easy.

Eleanor turned to Lynette. "Your place is close. Is it habitable?"

Lynette stared back at her, uncomprehending. Tears had made tracks in the dust caking her face. "What, my lady?"

"Can we use your place?"

"My place is close."

"I'll take that as a yes," said Eleanor. She took Lynette by the arm and started to lead her across the square.

Megan beckoned to Afreyda.

"We're bringing her with us?" said Father Galan.

"When you're doing the rescuing, you can decide who gets rescued."

Lynette's house was mostly intact. Some looting occurred for form's sake, but most of the heavier silver remained. They washed and changed into fresh clothes, then went in search of food. Down in the cellars, Eleanor found flour, dried meat and shriveled apples; the High Priest's professional acumen turned up a barrel of fine wine. Eleanor and Megan settled Lynette and Afreyda in the warmth of the kitchen while the others went off to get drunk and argue over who got relegated to the servants' quarters.

Lynette paced the kitchen, wringing her hands. Eleanor took her by the shoulders and parked her on a bench. She splashed wine into a goblet and got Lynette to drink some. A little color returned to Lynette's cheeks.

"Megan's been hurt," Eleanor said. "Why don't you see to her?"

Lynette looked up at the countess, a dazed expression on her face. "Huh?"

"Megan . . ." said Eleanor, pointing.

"I'm all right, really."

Lynette turned her gaze to Megan and did a double take. "What happened?"

"Er . . ." Megan glanced across to Afreyda, who was huddled in a corner of the kitchen, not registering what was going on. "Haircutting experiment went wrong."

"You girls and your fashions." Lynette's stupor lifted. She bustled over to the cupboards and began rummaging around in them. "I've got some ointment for that."

Megan leaned over to Eleanor. "Are you sure this is a good idea?" she whispered.

"Give her something to do. Take her mind off what's happened."

Lynette returned with a jar of gloop that combined the consistency of diarrhea with the odor of cat vomit. Megan bit back any objection and let Lynette smear it across her cut ear. Eleanor set about making bread. Megan, the granddaughter of a miller and baker, despaired at the countess's kneading style, which resembled a toddler having an argument with modeling clay.

"One day it'll be nice if you called on me not half dead," Lynette said to Megan.

"I'm just a poor country girl. I don't understand etiquette."

Lynette contemplated Afreyda. "You've been cut too." She pushed the jar of ointment across the table toward her. "Put some of that on it."

"I am fine."

"It'll get infected," said Lynette.

Afreyda nodded and picked up the jar. She dabbed a little ointment on to her thigh. Most of it smeared on her leather pants.

"You might want to take them off, dear," said Lynette. Afreyda's eyes widened a little. "Oh, don't worry, we're all girls here."

"A Diannon princess doesn't expose herself to lowlife scum," said a voice from the door. It was the High Priest, waving a cup upside down to indicate its emptiness.

"A princess?" said Megan. "Really?" She grinned at Eleanor. "She outranks you." Eleanor smiled sourly and punched her dough.

"A former princess, anyway," said the High Priest. "The Diannon Emperor stripped your family of their titles, isn't that correct?" Afreyda scowled, neither confirming nor denying his assertion.

"Former princess versus titular countess. How does that work out?" Megan asked.

"I wouldn't be too impressed," said the priest. "Princesses are ten a penny over there, I believe. Or ten a thousand gold pieces."

"You paid to be a princess?"

"Arriviste," muttered Eleanor.

"It is the custom," said Afreyda.

"Hope you got your money back."

Father Galan eased his bulk on to a bench. "I believe you were undressing," he said to Afreyda, a leer pushing his jowls apart.

"Give us the room," said Megan.

"And what put you in charge? The same thing as your sister?"

Megan slammed a knife on the table, feeling satisfaction as Father Galan jerked back. "Same thing that put you in charge all those years."

"God put me in charge," said Father Galan.

"Want to go confirm that with Him?"

Lynette patted Father Galan on the shoulder and gave him a placating smile. "Why don't we go see if we can find some more wine, father? I'm sure the Faithful are thirsty."

Father Galan allowed himself to be led away. Eleanor pointed at the dough. "I'll let that rise a while," she said, before scurrying after Lynette. Megan didn't know whether she was making herself scarce or eager to be where the booze was.

Megan patted the other girl's thigh. "Get these off then."

Afreyda kicked off her boots and squirmed out of her tight pants. Megan soaked a clean cloth in the water steaming in a copper pot hanging by the fire and checked the wound. The lightweight armor had done its job. Had Afreyda been unprotected, Megan's slash would have severed arteries; as it was, the cut didn't even need stitching.

Afreyda reached for the cloth. "No," said Megan. "Let me."

Unsure, Afreyda sat down and gripped the side of the bench. Kneeling in front of her, Megan parted the girl's legs a little to give her better access to the injury. Afreyda's thighs were well-muscled curves, iron wrapped in black silk. The edge of an undergarment peeked from under her jerkin, the frilly lace an odd contrast to the battledress.

"Why are you doing this?" said Afreyda. "Helping me?"

"Because I remember asking the same question not so long ago," said Megan, cleaning the wound with gentle rolling motions and brushing away flakes of dried blood.

"I tried to kill you."

"*Everyone's* tried to kill me," said Megan. "These days I'm taking it as a sign of affection."

As she patted the cut dry, a memory came to her. "I've seen you before, haven't I? Here in Eastport, a few days before the witches invaded."

"The True do not like being called that."

"Can't say I care," said Megan. "There was a man with you, I think."

"My father."

"What . . . what happened to him?"

"The True killed him."

"Why?"

"I do not know," said Afreyda. "She told me if I fought for her, she would release me and my mother."

"I'm sorry."

"Why?"

"I don't know," said Megan, an ointment-smeared finger paused in midair. "I feel this overwhelming urge to apologize to everyone I meet."

She smeared the ointment over the cut. There were more tattoos on Afreyda's thighs. She traced one with her fingertip. Afreyda shuddered.

"Did the witches do this to you?"

"What? No. They are to honor my ancestors."

"Ancestors?"

"Is that not the right word?" said Afreyda. "Your parents and their parents and their parents. When they pass on, they intercede on your behalf with the gods."

"No, you were right. It's just that the witches have these tattoos too."

"My people have had them for thousands of years." Afreyda's head drooped. "And I will need another two."

"I'm sorry," said Megan. "Again."

Afreyda nodded thoughtfully. She picked up her pants and wiggled her finger through the hole. "These need repairing."

"I don't sew."

Afreyda pulled a stiletto out of her boot—a girl after Megan's heart—and started to punch needle holes in her pants. Megan set about making the dough less like building material and more like foodstuff. It felt almost cozy for a moment, a reminder of days past with Gwyneth, until a draft on her neck heralded Eleanor's reappearance. Megan gritted her teeth. Time for the inevitable confrontation.

She followed the countess down to the cellar. It was freezing and almost pitch black. Only a few shafts of faint light pierced the darkness through windows set high in the ceiling. Something constantly plinked, ticking off the seconds: a leaky pipe or a bottle that hadn't been secured properly.

"You should have brought a candle," said Megan. "You wouldn't want to serve up an inferior vintage."

"I don't think anyone cares."

Megan took a deep breath. The cold air made her cough.

"You all right?" said Eleanor, slapping her back.

"Why did you come here?" demanded Megan, pulling away. "Why did you leave me?"

"You were safe with Aldred. Megan, you're the most important thing in the world to me, but not at the exclusion of everyone else."

"What if you'd got yourself killed? What would've happened to Cate? How would I have found her?"

"You think I didn't make arrangements?" said Eleanor. "I'm not some silly little girl who blunders in without a clue about what she's doing."

"Silly? I came to rescue you."

"You might want to think of how *that* turned out. Talking of which, was it such a good idea to bring her here? You thinking with your head?"

"Gwyneth killed her parents," said Megan. "Afreyda's no witch."

"And when she finds out who you are? You trust her not to sell you out?"

"She must've already guessed." Darkening blond streaks weren't going to hide Megan's similarity to her sister. "Especially after you used my real name."

"I did no—Oh, I did, didn't I? Lynette needed something to do, something to take her mind off . . . off whatever the witches did to her."

"I know. I understand." Megan shivered in the frigidity. "What do we do now?"

Eleanor wrapped her arms around her. "I quite like the idea of being where the witches aren't."

"Why did they go?"

"Joanne's prophecy drives them," said Eleanor, "but it also binds them. They don't think they can win without her. Without both Saviors."

"So it's too early to go for Cate?"

"You know it is."

Megan huddled deeper into Eleanor's embrace, wishing she hadn't allowed herself that brief moment of hope. The witches were still out there. Still searching for her, still hunting her daughter.

"One problem remains."

"I'm hoping Damon'll eventually wash."

"No . . ."

"Are you trying to point?" said Eleanor. "This isn't the best environment for visual clues."

"Father Galan."

"Ah." A pause. "You want me to deal with him?"

"No," said Megan. "I will."

Seven

Snores rumbled through the sleeping house. Megan crept into Father Galan's room—he'd commandeered one for his sole use—and dumped the remnants of his wine over his head. He spluttered awake, jowls flapping like a beached seal.

Megan held up a knife so moonlight rippled off its blade and traced a beam down the priest's prison-bleached skin. Father Galan quieted his objections and pushed himself up and away from the bed, as far from Megan as the topography would allow.

"Before we start," she said, "I want you to know it was me who stopped the witches killing you in the palace."

"I guessed." Father Galan wiped his face with a blanket. He surveyed the stained bedclothes for a moment as if considering sucking the wine out of them. "This is about the child, isn't it? Is it alive?"

"She's safe, a long way from here, and she's going to remain that way. If you have a problem with that, tell me now and I'll kill you quickly."

"I have no reason to harm her. Unless she becomes a threat to the Realm."

"She's a baby. How can she be a threat?"

"In that case, what do you have to fear from me?" said Father Galan. "Besides, I believe I'm in your debt." He pointed to the ewer by his bedside. "Pour me some water, would you?"

"You've got to be—"

"Joking? Yes. And testing you." He gestured to the knife in Megan's hand. "You like it, don't you?"

"Like what?"

"The power that comes with violence."

"I do what I have to."

"Oh, of course," said Father Galan. "One can always find justification: it's me or him; I was provoked; he needed to be taught a lesson. You're enforcing your will with a weapon, which is all well and good until someone finds a better weapon."

"Are you saying I should lay down my knife and pray the world sees the error of its ways, because even I can quote a few lines from the Book of Faith—"

"Which was written a long time ago in a world very different from ours. Not everything it says is applicable today or means what you think it does. One must look to the wider lessons given to us by the Saviors, not focus on the few specifics that justify the position we want to hold."

"I don't care about theological arguments," said Megan. "I care about my daughter. The priests—what do they know about me? About Cate? Do they know the truth about the witches?"

"You aren't going to get all literalist on me, are you?"

"She's no demon spawn. She isn't one of the Saviors either. Killing her won't gain them anything."

"I wouldn't know what my colleagues have planned," said Father Galan. "The witches have had me locked up since they invaded Eastport."

"You must be able to guess where their thoughts are leading."

Father Galan looked grim. "None of them would want to be *seen* killing a baby . . ."

"But if they could do it unseen . . . ?"

"What crimes would any of us commit if no one ever saw them?" Father Galan took Megan's hands in his. "You want my advice, my child? Get as far away from Eastport as you can. And keep getting away."

The vanguard of the priests' army arrived at dawn. The gates were opened and the population allowed to return to the inner city, but guards were posted everywhere.

Too many awkward questions might be asked if they
tried to slip away now; best to wait until life returned to
normal. If it ever did.

The prisoners returned to their own homes, leaving just Megan and her party at Lynette's. Despite her
misgivings, she found it good to rest in one place for
a while, to remember feet weren't meant to ache. She
wondered what Cate was doing. Too young for anything interesting, just cuddles while dozing in the
afternoon sun. Megan imagined her daughter's tiny
heart beating against her own, her breaths gently
blowing against her skin. How much growing up was
she going to miss? By the time Megan saw her again,
Cate might be walking, talking, or a grown woman
who couldn't understand why her mother had sent her
away.

Megan spent most of her time out in the interior
courtyard, which Lynette and nature had turned into
a now-neglected garden. Ivy covered the brickwork like
raggedy clothes, and a few rose bushes still displayed
flowers, though petals had already started to flutter
to the ground. Stone benches gave her somewhere to
stretch out, her only companions statues sculpted by
an artist who could most generously be described as
"experimenting." The solitude was good after the hustle
and bustle of the army, when she'd had to be forever on
her guard.

Damon wandered outside, carrying cheese and bread steaming from the oven. He proffered them to Megan. She reached out then halted. "Did Eleanor bake this?"

"One of Lynette's old servants came back," said Damon, budging her up and sitting down beside her.

Megan broke off a piece of bread. The warm texture reminded her of home. "Any news on the witches?" *Or Gwyneth?*

"The glorious victors are too busy arranging the party to worry about the enemy they never defeated," said Damon. "There's a big party at the palace for the great and the good. And the priests." He sliced himself some cheese. "Lynette's going. We're not invited. Bit rude, considering you're the only casualty of battle." Megan's fingers went to her ear, whose ragged edge was greasy with the ointment Lynette continued to apply. "Well, you and that soldier Eleanor shot."

"And the one whose throat I cut," said Megan.

"You kept that quiet, you little slasher, you."

"It was either me or him."

"Don't think anyone's going to mourn two dead witches," said Damon. "Well, maybe two other witches."

Two other witches. A memory came to Megan, of the men Gwyneth and Tobrytan had dispatched before attempting to behead Father Galan. What had been their orders?

She jumped up. "Where's Afreyda?"

"Up in her room," said Damon, "praying. Do you know the Diannons worship their dead ancestors? All of them, even the sketchy uncle who was always a little too keen to babysit. No wonder we haven't seen her for days. She's probably only up to her great-great-great-grandparents."

Megan hurried back into the house and up the winding staircases to the room Afreyda had claimed as her own. It was a dusty space up in the attic, which Megan doubted had been used for years. A miscellany of candles flickered on the periphery, casting dancing shadows on the sloping walls.

"It's one of those religions, is it?" said Damon, looking around. "Let me guess—founded by someone with large investments in the tallow industry?"

Afreyda knelt in the middle of the room. Her eyes snapped open. "Get out, heathen."

"Heathen?" said Damon. "Me? I'm not the one who's deified my Uncle Bob."

Afreyda looked confused. "I do not have an Uncle Bob."

"*Everyone* has an Uncle Bob."

"I don't either," said Megan.

"We all know *you're* special."

Megan shot him a dirty look. She crouched in front of Afreyda. "We're sorry for disturbing you—"

"We?" said Afreyda.

"Damon'll be sorry later when he wakes up in a pool of his own blood. But we need to ask you—what happened to the other two soldiers at the palace?"

"What other two soldiers?"

"Tobrytan ordered two soldiers to . . . I don't know . . . something."

"That's what I like about you," said Damon. "Your preciseness."

Afreyda shook her head. "I don't remember what he ordered. I was too busy chasing after you."

"What's your problem, Megan? It's two witches—"

"Two witches who are still in Eastport."

Damon gawked. The gown Eleanor was wearing wasn't so much a dress as a framing device for her cleavage. If there wasn't already a war happening, men would raise arms for a chance to win her.

"You're going to this party at the palace?" he asked.

Lynette, who was bustling around Eleanor with pins in mouth, adjusting the garment for the countess's fuller figure, mumbled something. Eleanor translated. "I'm her plus-one."

"You couldn't get a plus-four, no?"

"What do you want?"

I can barely remember, thought Damon as his eyes traced the figure-hugging silk. "I was wondering if Lynette had a balm. My face is a bit itchy."

"You shaved, I see."

"Like it?" said Damon, stroking the unfamiliar smoothness of his chin.

"It makes you look like a twelve-year-old."

"Not a look you go for?"

"They put you in prison for that kind of thing," said Eleanor. She shooed him toward the exit. "There'll be some balm and lotions down in the kitchen."

Damon was reluctant to leave so soon. "Megan thinks there are witches in Eastport."

Lynette jerked, jabbing Eleanor with a pin. The countess flinched, made to say something but cut herself off. She crouched down and took Lynette's hand.

"Two of 'em," continued Damon.

"I heard," said Eleanor. "Maybe they can set up home and bring up lots of little witches." She plucked the pins from Lynette's mouth. "Why don't you get us a drink?"

"Of course, my lady." Lynette scurried out.

"You're not worried?" said Damon.

"Of course I'm worried," said Eleanor, dropping the pins into a sewing basket. "I'm always worried. But there were always going to be witches left in the city."

"And if they think to check here? You don't think we should at least stay in one of Lynette's hundred other houses?"

"You think the witches didn't have a complete list of her property? They can find us here; they can find us anywhere."

"And at least here people call you 'my lady.'"

Damon drifted around the room. Eleanor looked just as good from the back. "Do you think this a good idea?" he asked.

"Am I showing too much?" said Eleanor, tugging the sapphire material—the same color as her eyes—so it covered a fraction more of her creamy skin.

"No, *no!*" said Damon, shaking his head furiously. "I meant the last scion of the House of Endalay showing up at her family's former seat of power."

"We're just meeting a few people, that's all."

"People? That's very democratically minded of you."

"Important people."

"Oh, *that* kind of democracy."

Eleanor lifted a blond wig from its stand and put it on, adjusting it while checking her reflection in a plate of polished silver. "The Supreme Priest is dying. The doctors say he's unlikely to see out the year."

"One less Saviors' Day present to buy."

"Some . . . people think it might be best if we had a change of leadership."

"You'd need one, with a dead Supreme Priest," said Damon. "Not sure I want to live under a necrocracy. Sounds a bit creepy."

"System rather than personnel."

Dismay flooded Damon as he realized what Eleanor meant. "Saviors, you're planning . . . ? You know what the priests'll do to you if they find out? They'll kill you. And your accomplices. Especially your accomplices."

"That's where Lynette comes in."

"You're going to bribe your way to the throne?"

"More of an investment really," said Eleanor. "Once I'm in control of the treasury . . ."

"Treasury? Have you heard yourself? The priests aren't going to restore the monarchy, especially not to someone who . . . What is your claim exactly?"

"I'm the only one stupid enough and alive enough to make one." She flicked her hand. "Some great-great- . . . great-grandfather or other."

"You told Megan about this?"

"She's the one I'm doing this for," said Eleanor. "The priests want to do the minimum possible. They're not interested in actually defeating the witches. We should be going after them, fighting them on our terms, not theirs. The priests think the witches are like the Sandstriders or the Snow Cities: raiders who can be chased away with a show of force. We have to find them and destroy them. Every last one."

Damon thought of flippantly asking who she meant, the priests or the witches, but given Eleanor's history it could be both. This wouldn't end well. This *couldn't* end well. The priests would never give up power. Eleanor would end up rotting in some dungeon until a paid-off jailer knifed her in her sleep. Or, worse, she would actually be crowned queen and he would have lost her forever.

Eleanor waved at the door. "Do something useful and organize a carriage."

"What for? It's only half a mile to the palace."

Eleanor lifted her dress to show off her shoes. The last time Damon had seen such devices applied to a person's anatomy they had led to a confession. "You expect me to walk in these?" she asked. There was a hint of a smile on her lips. An attempt at ingratiation?

"It's people like you who are the reason the city's polluted with manure and you can't move in Gaderian Square." Damon made to leave.

Eleanor called him back. "This stays between us, right."

"You don't want me to tell Megan?"

"Saviors, no."

The presence of a large army that wasn't going anywhere made it a simple matter for Damon to hire a horse and cart from a bored quartermaster for five shillings. He helped the women on board—Lynette in a demure sable gown; Eleanor heartbreaking in her tight-fitting silk, the blond wig retained in lip-service to disguise—and nudged the horse into the street. It refused to move.

"You got a horse that won't start?" said Eleanor, tossing a damaged helmet out of the cart.

Damon prodded the horse's flank with a whip. He was loath to provoke something five times his size. "It just needs warming up."

Eleanor leaned around and plucked the whip from his hand, brushing against him as she did so. Her sweet perfume triggered raw desire. His imagination ran through a hundred scenarios his decade in a seminary had taught him were wrong.

There was a crack and the cart bucked into life. Eleanor handed the whip back to him. "You need to put your wrist into it," she said.

"Believe me, I will."

They got to within a street of the main square, where the palace was situated, and then hit traffic. Everyone was arguing with everyone else, claiming ever-more-impressive war records to assert priority. Damon slipped a feedbag over the horse's nose and settled in. They could be here for a while.

An officer made his way through the morass of carts and carriages and horses, getting them moving again with the usual military combination of shouting and brandished steel. As the jam cleared and he moved closer to their position, Damon recognized him: Aldred. Judging by the way Eleanor was checking herself, she'd recognized him too. Damon's stomach sank a little.

"We'll get you through in a minute," Aldred said to him. His brow furrowed. "Don't I know you?"

Damon's usual responses in these situation were "No," "I was miles away" and "You can't prove it." Eleanor got in before he could say anything.

"I have a bone to pick with you, lieutenant."

Aldred peered around Damon into the back of the cart. His eyes widened. Damon detected a certain slackening of the jaw. "Sister Edla? That's quite a . . ."

"We thought it might encourage donations to the order," said Eleanor, adjusting herself. "Now, about Sister Moira . . ."

"I couldn't follow her into a tent full of sisters, could I? How is she?"

"In one piece. Mostly."

"Good, good." Aldred craned his neck to see behind them. "Oi! You let your horse shit there again, you eat it!"

"The horse?" said Damon.

"The manure."

"Are you coming to the party?" Eleanor asked Aldred.

"They only let important people into those kind of things, not junior officers who'd trail cack everywhere. I'll be on duty all evening. If you find me when you leave, I'll make sure your driver has a clear way out."

"I'm not her driver," said Damon. "I'm just, um, driving." He turned to Eleanor. "Tell him."

"He's a temp. The agency sent him. Seriously considering not tipping."

"I could spare one of my men if you need a replacement," said Aldred. "Or I could even, if you don't think it too presumptuous, drive you home myself."

"We're kind of stuck with him now," said Eleanor.

A servant bustled forward and puffed out his chest, a proxy for pomposity. "What's the delay here?" he demanded. "My master—" Aldred snapped out a fist and laid him out cold.

"Shouldn't you have waited to see what he wanted first?" asked Eleanor.

"It'll be the usual," said Aldred. "Once someone gets a carriage they think the world revolves around them."

"Speaking of which . . ." said Damon, jiggling the reins.

"I'll go see what I can do." Aldred gave them—well, Eleanor—a bow and wandered back up the road, shouting and exhorting.

Lynette peered at the servant Aldred had decked, who was still sprawled out on the dirt-spattered cobblestones. "Should we move him?"

"What do you think's going to happen to him at the speed we're going?" said Damon. "He's going to get nudged to death?"

"He might be hurt."

"Of course he's hurt. Some thug punched him in the face."

"The lieutenant is not a thug," said Eleanor. "The military do things a little more . . . percussively, that's all."

"Still," said Lynette, "I think we should . . ." The carriage blocking their way moved on. "A gap's opened. Quick!"

Damon cracked his whip. Aldred had to dive out of the way as the cart lurched forward and headed into the main square.

Being cooped up in the house, even one as big as Lynette's, was getting to Megan. With Eleanor and the others gone to the palace, every noise in the silence had her jumping and reaching for her knife. How quickly sanctuary could turn into a prison. She'd explained her fears to Eleanor, but the countess had waved them away, ascribing them to paranoia.

She persuaded Afreyda to go out with her into the city, where she could at least suffer the regular paranoia over muggers, pickpockets and conmen. Eastport was regaining its vitality, especially now there were thousands of soldiers to fleece. The two girls shared a pie and a flagon of ale at a table outside a cafe, for which they were charged double what they would have been before the invasion. Megan didn't begrudge it. It was a tiny bit of compensation for the damage she'd brought upon them.

Afreyda was quiet. Megan could guess why. "Do you want to talk about it?" she asked.

"Talk about what?" said Afreyda.

"About your parents. How you feel about . . . about . . ."

"Sad."

"How sad?"

Afreyda shrugged. A dog padded up to their table, all ribs and fleas.

Megan dropped it a hunk of pie. The dog sniffed it, whimpered and scurried off down the street.

Megan pushed the rest of her dinner aside. "Sorry, I'm not very good at this. I just want you to know that I know what you're going through."

"Have you ever lost the only people you love in the world?"

"Yes."

"And was your sister responsible?" said Afreyda, a hint of spite in her voice.

"Yes."

"Did you not . . . ?"

"Know my sister was a murderous psychopath who wanted to set herself up as a religious icon?" finished Megan. "She could be a bit moody at times . . ." She stared down into her cup, watching the occasional bubble race for the surface and pop out of existence. "I look back and think I should have suspected *something*, but who could ever have imagined that?"

There was a commotion. A pair of servants armed with cudgels barged their way through the streets, clearing the way for their master, a merchant draped in finery and enough jewels to pay for the rebuilding of the city. One of them slammed into Afreyda, sending her sprawling across the table and her drink splashing over the edges. Her eyes flashed. She jumped to her feet, hand going for her sword.

Megan pulled her back down. "It's not worth it." Master and servants continued on their way, oblivious to their offense.

"He spilled my drink."

"That's not enough reason for disembowelment." A few blocks over, it might be a different matter. "He's obviously going to that party at the palace. We don't want trouble with the priests." Megan pushed her cup across. "Here, have mine."

Afreyda grunted. "Palace. Priests. It is like the Emperor's court. We should raise the people while all the rulers are in one place and do away with all of them."

"Is that why you're here?" said Megan. "Did you revolt against this Emperor of yours?"

"He had oppressed the people too long."

"And he's still oppressing them, I'm guessing?"

Afreyda reached for Megan's cup. "He has the gunpowder."

"Like the witches," said Megan. "Like the . . ."

The pieces fell into place: the witches' evacuation; the two soldiers left behind; the party for the leaders of the Faithful; gunpowder. Megan shot out of her seat so fast she almost knocked the table over. Her thighs stung where they had hit the edge.

Afreyda brightened. "We *are* going to teach them a lesson?"

"It's not that," said Megan. She jabbed her hand in the direction of the inner city. "We have to . . ."

She couldn't contain the energy rushing through her. She broke into a run, hurdling over the detritus littering the street and shouldering her way through passersby. Eleanor was going to be in the palace. She had to get her—she had to get everyone—out of there.

Megan caught up with the merchant who had spilled Afreyda's ale. She cried to him to get out of the way. He ignored her. She slammed into him. The transferred momentum sent him sprawling against a makeshift stall. Withered fruit bounced everywhere. Megan tripped over it and tumbled into the packed mud.

There was a cry of indignation. Female. Afreyda was struggling with the merchant's servants. They had her by the arms. She jerked her elbow upward, catching one of them under the chin. Blood spurted from his bitten tongue. His companion smashed his club into her stomach. She doubled over and vomited her dinner all over the street.

Megan's head snapped between them and the street ahead. No time to waste—she could come back for Afreyda later. She picked herself up, ignored the pulped fruit dripping from her front and managed a couple of steps.

A thunderous explosion rocked the city. Screams filled the air. Clouds of dust and ash billowed into the sky. The witches had blown up the palace.

Eight

There must have been some events between driving toward the palace and being face down on the main square, but Damon couldn't remember them. Pain pulsed up and down his body; battered joints demanded attention like needy children. From all around him came the screams and hollering of people and animals and God knew what, piercing the ringing in his ears.

He pushed himself to his feet, dreading the spear of agony that would tell him something was broken. None came. That was something at least. He looked around. Dust smothered the air. He couldn't make out the houses on the side of the square or the palace at the far end. The figures ricocheting around in the gray were mere impressions on his retinas.

Eleanor? Where was Eleanor? He stumbled around with the coordination of a drunk. He tried to shout, but one breath of the filth in the air sent him into paroxysms of coughing. Someone barged past him, sending him spinning. He lost his footing and hit the marble again.

Strong arms hauled him to his feet. "Where's Sister Edla?" demanded Aldred, gripping Damon's collar so tight anyone would think he was responsible for whatever the hell just happened. "Where is she?"

Damon managed a croak. "She's . . ."

Aldred shook him. Damon spotted the cart, insubstantial as a sketch in the fog. It was on its side, one of its wheels still spinning. The horse was gone, fled in the panic. There went his deposit.

Aldred released him and rushed over to it. Damon staggered after him. Eleanor was bent over Lynette, trying to wake her. Blood dripped from a gash on Lynette's temple.

Eleanor looked up. Her wig was askew. Kohl tears were leaving black streaks in the dust that caked her face. "I can't . . . She won't . . ."

Aldred ripped off his gauntlet and pressed his fingers against Lynette's neck. "She's still alive," he said. "We need to get her out of here."

"You think?" said Damon.

"You, boy, help me."

"Who are you calling—?"

"Damon!"

"All right, all right."

Damon and Aldred slipped an arm each into Lynette's armpits and lifted. Her head lolled freely. Blood smeared across Damon's cheek as her wounded temple brushed him.

Eleanor picked up Lynette's feet and they set off. Damon hoped Eleanor knew where she was going, because he didn't have a clue. They could be going around in circles for all he knew, treading the same bit of the main square for eternity.

The air cleared as they moved away from the palace. Bodies sprawled over the ground. Some moved, some were still. Some bled, some trembled in shock. Some received attention, some suffered alone. They maneuvered around them, muttering apologies and condolences that would have been ignored even if heard.

Damon recognized the streets they had driven down a few minutes—was it minutes?—ago. The strain of carrying Lynette was becoming unbearable. Couldn't they take a rest now they had got away from the square? Any moment now he expected his arm to pop out of its socket. Why couldn't Aldred do this by himself? Wasn't that what the military was good for, carting things from place to place? Keeping the people safe certainly wasn't on their agenda.

There was no rest until they reached Lynette's home and laid her out on the kitchen table. Eleanor fretted around, hands shaking as she dabbed at Lynette with a wet cloth. Aldred took her by the shoulders and eased her on to a bench.

"Let me."

"Yeah," said Damon, massaging his throbbing shoulder. He swore his right side was now two inches longer than his left. "He's got experience with war wounds. Broken nails, dislocated eyelashes, all manner of horrors."

Eleanor looked at him blankly. "Get some wine," snapped Aldred.

That was one order Damon could live with.

Megan crashed into Lynette's kitchen, Afreyda hot on her heels. She found the owner of the house stretched out on the table, Eleanor with her head in her hands and a spilled cup at her feet and Damon slumped against the fireplace, knocking back wine as if in a one-man drinking contest. Elation at finding them alive gave way to dread.

"What's going on? What's Lynette doing there?"

"She isn't on the menu, if that's what you're worried about," said Damon.

Aldred appeared. He laid a sheet over Lynette. That would never keep her warm. They needed blankets, to get the fire going. The soldier covered Lynette's face. *Oh . . .*

"I've failed someone else," murmured Eleanor. Her face was paler than the corpse on the table. Dust caked her skin and clothes, save for streaks under her eyes that tears had washed clean.

"You haven't failed anyone," said Damon, his voice hollow.

"You were at the palace?" said Megan.

"The main square," said Damon. "Things went a bit . . ."

Megan stared at the shape under the sheet. A spot of scarlet bloomed on the linen. *Another victim for you, Gwyneth.* "The witches had a load of gunpowder hidden in the palace."

"Sneaky bastards," said Damon. "Quite clever really."

"They're cowards," snarled Aldred. "Hiding behind their guns and gunpowder. They should face us in a fair fight."

"A fair fight where you'd have a ten-to-one advantage? Everyone fights the battle that best suits them. Muscle-bound lunks bash people. Innocuous little girls slip knives between ribs. The witches blow people up."

"Do you know how many of my friends died in the palace?"

"No," said Damon. "Were they better people than those you didn't know?"

"Show some respect to the dead, boy."

Damon raised his goblet. "God, born of the eternal universe, ultimate arbiter of man, take these souls we deliver . . ." He downed his drink and looked upward. "You're probably familiar with the rest by now. You've heard it enough recently."

Aldred struck out, catching Damon across the mouth with the back of his hand. Damon slithered down the fireplace in stops and starts, as if he couldn't make up his mind whether to collapse or not. Aldred towered over him. He was twice Damon's size, a father chastising a rebellious child.

He made to deliver a follow-up blow. Megan kicked out, catching the lieutenant in the back of his knee. His leg buckled. He stumbled a few steps, then lurched around. His hand went for his sword. Megan flicked out a knife. Afreyda shot across the room, her own blade flashing.

"Stop it!" yelled Eleanor. Everyone froze. Glances flicked between weapons that were drawn or about to be. Damon fingered his burst lip. "She's dead, and your reaction is to squabble? Megan, Afreyda, put your weapons away. Lieutenant, when you've put up with Damon for months on end, *then* you have the right to hit him. Damon, shut the hell up."

They buried Lynette out in the courtyard—a spot of calm in the chaos of the city—lowering her body into the shallow grave while the moon tried to punch its way through the hazy atmosphere. Candlelight flickered high up in one of the attic rooms. Afreyda was honoring Lynette in her own way, asking her ancestors to protect the departed in the afterlife. Who was to say they wouldn't? Surely God wouldn't condemn them for asking?

Damon intoned the funeral prayer in the traditional way—his voice slurred from drink—while Megan held Eleanor's hand and tried to look anywhere but at the shroud lying in the dirt. Eleanor blamed herself, but Megan knew it was she who should have figured it out earlier. The witches wouldn't have left without leaving a nasty surprise, a macabre punch line. Why have all that gunpowder if you weren't going to use it? *Damn you, Gwyneth.*

They covered Lynette, taking turns with the shovel. Megan picked a rose and placed it on the mound. Damon produced a flagon of wine. They shared it in memory of Lynette. Eleanor and Damon needed to do more sharing than Megan.

There was a distant hammering. Damon massaged his forehead. "Has my hangover started early or is there someone at the door?"

"Aldred said he'd call," said Eleanor, "let us know what's going on." She made to get up. Her hand slipped, scraped against the stone bench she was sat on. She bumped back down with a wince. "Maybe you could . . . ?"

Megan nodded and headed for the door. Afreyda had beaten her to it and was staring through the peephole, her sword drawn. Megan gently placed her hands on her shoulders and moved her aside to peer out. Aldred was bouncing on his heels in the street.

Afreyda turned to Megan, their proximity meaning her breath was warm on Megan's cheek. "Do you want me to get rid of him?"

"It's all right," said Megan.

She unlocked the door and beckoned Aldred inside. He stared at Afreyda, confused. Megan ushered him down the corridor and made to follow. Afreyda set off back to her own room.

"You can join us, you know," Megan called out after her.

"I do not want to intrude on your funeral rites."

"You're not," said Megan. "It's mainly just drinking."

"A lot of your rites are mainly just drinking."

"You can't accuse the Faith of inconsistency."

They went out into the courtyard. Aldred made the sign of the circle by Lynette's grave. "They're still pulling bodies from the palace," he said. "I say 'palace.' There is no palace anymore, just rubble."

"Any survivors?" asked Eleanor.

"A few. The Supreme Priest is dead though. Most of the War Council."

"What about Father Galan?"

"Who?"

"It doesn't matter," said Eleanor. "Who's in charge?"

Aldred shrugged. "Who knows? A few of the captains are trying to organize the troops who haven't deserted. Everyone's making a break for it."

He took off his helmet and shook out the dust from his hair. Eleanor offered him a cup of wine. He emptied it in one and held the cup out for more.

"Saviors," he said, shaking his head. "Six weeks of officer training didn't prepare me for me this."

"Six years at the Imperial Officers' Academy wouldn't prepare you for this," said Afreyda. "We weren't used to the other side having gunpowder."

"You went to an officers' academy?" said Megan.

"It is the best school in the empire. Its graduates conquered a continent."

"I thought you were kind of against that?"

"I am," said Afreyda. She shrugged. "It does not take away the accomplishment."

Damon shook the last few drops out of the wine jug and frowned into its empty depths. "What do we do now?" he asked. "Wait for the witches to show up again and take them on?"

"We'd need a disciplined army to even think about that," said Aldred. "What we've got at the moment doesn't even qualify as a rabble."

"We run," said Megan.

"Right now?" asked Damon.

"Why? You need time to bid farewell to the wine cellar?"

"We'll make a decision in the morning," said Eleanor. "When everything's clearer. Including my head. Damon, go down to the cellar, get some more wine."

"Why me?"

"Because I really don't want to be on my own in a dark, enclosed space right now."

Damon stumbled off in the manner of someone not entirely on speaking terms with his legs. Megan drew a knife and started to sharpen it, scraping the whetstone down its edge in slow, deliberate strokes. Running again, but would they ever find somewhere safe? What was the alternative? Stay and fight? One girl against an army; what could she possibly do?

Eleanor rested her chin against her knees. "What's your story, lieutenant? What did you do before all this?"

"I've got a farm."

"Wife waiting for you back home?"

"She died."

"Oh," said Eleanor. "I'm sorry."

"It was a long time ago," said Aldred.

"Still," said Eleanor, "you must miss her."

"Not really. She only communicated by complaint. I had a peaceful couple of years and then all this happened. I bought a commission. Thought it'd be safer than enlisting."

"Bad move. Junior officers are always the first ones to die. Sent to lead the troops on the front line." Eleanor looked to the smoky sky. "Only this time there's no front line."

"You have experience of the military?" asked Aldred.

"My father was a general."

"He was a priest?"

"Saviors, no," said Eleanor. She twisted her mouth as she realized the implication of what she'd said. "What I meant to say was . . ."

Aldred looked to Eleanor and then to Megan. She stopped sharpening her knife midscrape. Unease prickled her skin.

"It's you," he said. "You're the ones . . . You're why the witches are here."

His hand, unconsciously or not, dropped to his sword hilt. Megan dropped the whetstone and brought her knife into a fighting position. Eleanor twisted off her seat and reached behind her back for her own weapon.

"Hey!" said Aldred. He twisted his neck around. Afreyda had her sword drawn and ready. "What the . . . ?"

Damon returned with the wine. He took in the scene with a studied nonchalance. "We've reached that stage of the evening, have we?"

There was a strained silence broken only by the tinkling of liquid filling Damon's cup and the distant wails of the city mourning its dead. Megan shifted her weight, wondering how a casual conversation had burst into an armed stand-off. Was it always going to be like this, never knowing who you couldn't trust, who you would have to fight?

Aldred slowly withdrew his hand from his sword and showed his palms. "I don't want any trouble."

Eleanor nodded. She sheathed her knife and motioned to Megan and Afreyda to do the same. After a moment, Megan slipped her knife back into her belt. No fight. This time.

"What do the witches want with—?"

Megan cut Aldred off with a jerk of her hand. He shut up, bemused. The wails were getting louder, coming their way. She exchanged worried glances with Eleanor. They hurried to the door. People were careering down the street, almost trampling on each other. Lamp- and moonlight caught snatches of their expressions: terror, desperation, panic.

Aldred squeezed past them and grabbed a passing soldier by the collar. "What is it?" he demanded.

"The fleet, sir," wheezed the soldier. "It's back."

"And?"

"Only one ship, sir. The witches destroyed the rest."

Nine

Megan wanted to flee right away. The witches would come to reclaim Eastport, destroy the army before it could reorganize itself. They'd be trapped inside the city, and after that how long before someone gave Megan away or the witches found her of their own accord? Eleanor talked her out of it: joining a stampede in the dark was a recipe for getting separated from not just each other but one's own limbs. They'd leave at first light, when the frenzy had died down and they'd rested.

Megan couldn't rest though. She prowled the house, flitting from window to window, trying to pick out news from the hubbub that continued to stream along the streets outside. Any minute she expected to hear news that the witches' ships had been sighted on the Speed or the distant boom of guns heralding an attack. Eventually weariness claimed her and she dropped off on a window seat, head resting against the cold glass.

She awoke with a start, ignorant of what had happened in the moments it took for consciousness to return. The morning sun was beginning to bleach out the stars. Megan stretched the stiffness from her neck and limbs and went in search of Eleanor.

The countess was in Lynette's study, rummaging through a pile of papers and parchments, her hair a tangled disarray.

"Where do we go now?" asked Megan.

"New Statham," muttered Eleanor, distracted by the document she was reading.

"Why there?"

"Three rings of very thick defensive walls."

"Edwyn the Third was *very* paranoid," added a third, slurred voice: Damon.

Megan couldn't see him. She peered behind a couch. He was flat on his back, outlined in empty bottles. He waved.

"Are you drunk?"

"If I'm not, I want my money back." He held up his arm. "Help us up, will you?"

Megan hauled him to his feet.

"We can't wait for you to sober up," said Eleanor.

"I'll be fine. Fresh air, a bit of water." He picked up a bottle, jiggled it to confirm the presence of liquid and swigged from it.

"Water?" said Megan.

"*Mostly* water," said Damon. He pointed to the sheaf of papers in Eleanor's hands. "Bringing something to read?"

The countess scowled and stuffed the papers into a pack. Damon gave her a knowing look. Neither was in a hurry to explain to Megan what was going on. Despite her instinct to put it down to another of their petty arguments, Megan couldn't shake the nagging feeling it was something she should be worrying about. As if she needed something else.

People streamed out of Eastport like the last breaths from a dying body. Officers pretended they were organizing the exodus, but collective wisdom was doing that, dragging the populace in a ragged column along the road that cut through the forest on the south bank of the Speed. Every so often, a rumor would ripple through the crowd and a thousand heads would crane around in fear, expecting the witches to be on top of them.

Damon plodded along with all the enthusiasm of a plague victim. Afreyda was stoic, as reserved as ever. Eleanor kept checking the soldiers; she hadn't said so, but Megan knew she was searching for Aldred. They hadn't seen him since he had left last night to try to round up what remained of his men.

They reached Washbrook, where they refreshed themselves on the chilly waters of the stream that babbled into
the Speed. The village was long since deserted. A few
people were milling around the remains of the bridge: a
woman carrying a baby, looking like she needed to sleep
for a fortnight; a girl of about ten or so; a boy a couple of
years younger; and an old man contemplating the splintered pillars sticking out of the water as if using them to
get over the river was some puzzle he had to solve.

Megan nudged the woman and pointed upriver. "The
army built a bridge at Clibbur Point."

"Huh?"

"You can cross there."

The woman called out to the children and the old
man—her family. They fell in with the rest of the rabble,
pushing down the path that wound between the Speed
and the forest, a current of people in a pale imitation of
the remorseless river. The road degraded from paved
stones to mud, the missing surface no doubt lining
some thief's backyard.

As they walked, Megan snuck glances at the baby
slung across the woman's chest, her heart becoming
heavier with each one. The possibility of seeing Cate
again felt more remote than ever.

The woman caught her staring. "What is it?"

"Nothing," said Megan. "I'm Me—" she checked herself "—Moira, by the way."

The woman looked wary. "Loretta."

"Do you want me to carry her for a while?"

"He's a boy."

"They're not uncommon," added Damon from behind them. He was keeping the older children entertained with wild tales Megan feared might actually be true.

"Do you want me to carry *him* for a while?"

Loretta considered for a moment, then handed the child over, sling and all. The release of her burden added an extra inch to her height. Megan stroked the boy's cheek with the back of her finger. The softness brought memories flooding back.

"He's beautiful," she said. "What's his name?"

"Edwyn."

"A little king. How old?"

"Six months," said Loretta. "I think. I've lost track of time, what with . . ."

"Is that what happened to his father? I've noticed he's not . . ."

"He was killed during the rebellion."

"Rebellion?" said Megan. Loretta stared at her as if she had just asked what water was. "Sorry, we're kind of, um, new around here. We . . ."

"We heard there was a nice craft fair," said Damon. "I was hoping to pick up some wickerwork, because who doesn't love furniture made out of grass?"

Megan shot him a look. "There was a rebellion?" she said to Loretta.

"When the ships sank in the Speed, Isen and some others took it as a sign from God to rise up against the witches." Loretta ran her fingers through her lank hair. "I hope you don't have to see the father of your children butchered in front of you."

Too late for that. Megan had a rare memory of Wade. She didn't know how culpable he was for getting her pregnant and how much he had been manipulated by Gwyneth but, like Loretta's husband, he had tried to do the right thing at the end, no matter how hopeless the odds.

"I'm sorry."

"At least they didn't make him fight for them," said Loretta. "At least he didn't forsake the Saviors for demons."

"You do know the witches don't worship demons, don't you?" said Megan.

Loretta looked at her blankly. "What are you talking about?"

"They worship the same god we do, follow the Saviors' teaching."

"Where did you hear *that*?"

"I—"

A boom echoed around the valley. As one, the crowd hit the ground. Birds whirled out of the woods amidst a torrent of squawks and cracking wings, fleeing for the sanctuary of the sky.

Edwyn started to cry, his little face reddening. Megan clutched him tight. "Shh, Cate, shh, it's going to be—"

"Give him to me!" shrieked Loretta. She snatched at her son. Megan made to resist, then realized what she was doing and let the woman reclaim her baby.

There was a flash from the opposite bank and the briefest impression of something tumbling through the air. The Speed erupted into a wall of spray, soaking them. People hollered, scrambled to their feet and scattered in all directions. One confused soul even threw himself into the river.

"Into the trees!" yelled Megan.

The crowd looked at her blankly until a boom upriver persuaded them of the wisdom of her order. They fled for the cover of the forest, trampling through long grass. Megan halted at the tree line, urging everyone on. Damon scampered past with the ease of a professional absconder. Eleanor and Afreyda brought up the rear, weapons drawn, as if there was anything a bow or a sword could do against guns.

There was a hush in the woods, as if they had stepped into a temple. People leaned against trees, faces pale as they caught their breath. Some sank into the undergrowth, sobbing silently. Megan knew how they felt.

"Maybe we should rest here," she said to Eleanor. "There's not—"

There was a screech. A man not twenty yards away from Megan was vaporized into a shower of blood and bone fragments, leaving nothing behind but a smoldering crater. Screams echoed through the trees. The crowd stampeded like animals scared by the huntsman's trumpet. Megan fought the tiredness in her legs and ran with them.

The forest gave way to inclined grassland. Clumps of civilians began to haul themselves up the long slopes, while guns continued to boom from various points on the river. A few hundred yards away, a squad of soldiers organized themselves into some semblance of formation. From the way Eleanor brightened, Megan assumed Aldred was one of them.

"We've come far enough, surely," said Damon, panting.

"I don't know," said Megan. She tried to reconcile her previous experience with the witches' guns with their present situation. They wouldn't be able to clear the trees, would they? They might have boats hidden, however, ready to transport the guns over the river, and even though guns were big and bulky and no doubt hard to move, she saw no reason to wait until the witches hove into view. "Let's keep moving."

"South?" said Damon. "You think anything good lies that way?"

"Home."

"Yes, well . . ."

Damon didn't have to say anything more. Megan knew she'd find no sanctuary there. That didn't stop a momentary fantasy she could run into the mill and bury herself in her grandfather's arms and he would make all the bad go away.

There was a low rumble. The ground trembled. Megan shielded her eyes and looked up the hill. All along the ridge, riders appeared, forming battle lines. Robes fluttered and snapped in the wind. They weren't witches. They were Sandstriders.

The ranked horsemen raised their arms as if in salute. Had they come to relieve them? Had the priests negotiated an alliance with their old foes from beyond the Endalayan Mountains?

There was a barked order, a deep hum, a whisper on the wind. A thousand arrows flew into the air. They blacked out the sky before arcing toward them.

Ten

Screams rang in Megan's ears. People dashed this way and that, panic robbing them of thought. Sandstriders one way, witches the other. Nowhere to go. No escape.

"The tree line," yelled Megan. It was the only hope. The forest canopy would protect them from the arrows and they'd be able to keep out of range of the guns.

The idea made its way along the lines. People scrambled back the way they'd come. The Sandstriders launched another volley. Arrows didn't so much thud into the ground as suddenly appear to be there. People flailed as they were hit. The lucky ones fell instantly; the unlucky ones were left to crawl through the grass, faces contorted in pain. An arrow sprouted in front of Megan. She leaped over it, unwilling to touch it even though its lethality was spent.

A strange wailing filled the air, like wolves possessed by demons. "What the hell is that?" said Eleanor.

"I think they're trying to scare us," said Megan.

"Shooting at us did that," said Damon.

The priests hadn't made an alliance with the Sandstriders—the witches had. It had all been planned from the start. Lure the Faithful to Eastport; destroy their leaders; then wait as the confused masses blundered into their trap, no more aware of their fate than a sheep driven to the slaughterhouse.

Aldred blundered through the forest, followed by a dozen or so soldiers. "You're all right?"

Eleanor nodded. "You need to prepare your men to fight."

"Against all them? There's thousands of them."

"You brought an army twenty thousand strong. They can't *all* have deserted."

"No, but—"

Everyone jumped for the cover of the nearest tree as a volley of arrows speared through the canopy. Several struck branches and spiraled out of control. One pinged off a breastplate and tumbled to the ground.

"Rally the men," said Eleanor. "Remember the fifth Pledge."

"Which one is that? I always get them mixed up."

"I pledge to defend His people."

Aldred pulled a horn from his belt. He filled his lungs and blew. A deep note sounded through the forest, bouncing off the trees, a question in search of an answer. For a moment, Megan thought there wasn't going to be one, then there was a distant reply, then another and another and hope surged within her.

The Sandstriders answered with their own war cry: the same eerie wail, twice as loud as before. There was a slow crunch of hoofs as they started to descend.

"Get out of here," Aldred said. "Find somewhere safe."

"Like we hadn't thought of that," said Damon.

"Stay within the trees," said Eleanor. "It'll cover you from their archers and cavalry."

"Like we hadn't thought of that," said Aldred. "Go on. We'll deal with these bastards."

Megan and the others stumbled away from the soldiers, deeper into the forest, kicking and slashing their way through the vegetation, grabbing whoever they could find. Some were prepared to follow anyone who looked as if they knew what they were doing; others resisted or had to be jolted out of their daze. From the thousands who had fled Eastport though, only a few dozen joined them.

Guttural cries and the chime of metal heralded the start of the fighting. A gun boomed, reminding them of the storm to the north. Soldiers stomped past, to whom Megan could only offer grim nods of encouragement. How many would still be alive in an hour's time?

It was hard to navigate in the dense forest. Megan, who had found herself at the front with Damon while Eleanor and Afreyda covered their rear, had been trying to steer a course away from the Sandstriders on the one side and the witches' guns on the other.

"Any idea where we're going?" asked Damon. "Or is this more a tactical retreat than a strategic one?"

"Clibbur Point," said Megan. "Cross the Speed there."

"That gets us away from one problem but kind of gives us another one. A witch-shaped one."

"No," said Megan. Her shortness of breath gave her time to put the pieces together. "The witches are shooting at us to drive us toward the Sandstriders. Why do that if the witches have their own troops on the other side of the river? They probably only have enough soldiers to man the guns."

"They could have a whole army over there in reserve."

"No, they couldn't, because that's the way we came. We would have noticed them."

"We didn't notice a couple of thousand Sandstriders out on a day trip from Andaluvia."

"Yeah, but we weren't look—"

A scream made Megan whirl around. A baby's wail. Instinct spurred her. She dashed through the forest, almost stumbling over a Sandstrider grappling with a woman. He raised his saber. Megan launched herself at him, thrusting her knife through silk and into an exposed armpit. The Sandstrider yelled in pain and dropped his sword as he made to grab the wound. Megan wrenched her knife free from his flesh, twisting the blade as she did so, and stuck it in him again.

He collapsed to the ground, a quivering wreck, blood quickly soaking his robes. No armor for those who traversed the baking desert wastes.

"Are you hurt?" said Megan. Loretta shook her head, clutching baby Edwyn close to her. "Is she . . . is he all right?"

"Uh-huh."

Loretta's eyes widened. Another Sandstrider was hurtling toward them, saber poised to strike. He fell and hit the ground, an arrow sticking out of his spine.

Eleanor ran over, wrenching the arrow out of her victim as she passed. "Where's the rest of your family?" she said.

"My . . . ?" Realization tautened Loretta's features. "Isen! Audrey!"

Damon looked alarmed. "Do we really want to draw attention to ourselves?"

"There are children out there!" said Megan. She took up the cry herself. "Isen! Audrey!"

"The Sandstriders won't kill kids," said Damon. "Enslave them, maybe."

Bushes rustled nearby. Isen and Audrey crawled out and scrambled to their mother. She pulled them close and muttered their names over and over.

"What about—?"

Loretta cut Megan off with a quick shake of the head, her eyes flicking down to the children clinging to her. No need to ask what had happened to the old man.

* * *

They reached Clibbur Point as the sun was heading for the horizon, throwing long shadows and adding a freshness to the air. The dense forest absorbed most of the sounds of the distant battle, though one or two of the most ferocious clashes still reached them. That and the thunder of guns. Those were inescapable.

Through the gaps in the branches, Megan could see the bridge the army had thrown up, all raw timber and irregular struts. The witches hadn't destroyed it. Was this a good thing or not? She stepped out into the scrubland beyond the forest. There was a flicker of movement on the peninsula opposite. She scrambled back to the safety of the trees just as a gun boomed and tore up the ground at the approach to the bridge.

"What do we do now?" said Afreyda.

Everyone seemed to be staring at Megan—all the lost souls they had gathered—looking for someone to give them hope, for someone to blame. "Any ideas?" she asked. The crowd was sullen, like schoolchildren avoiding the teacher's question. "Anyone?"

"We could send Damon across to annoy them to death," said Eleanor.

"They will kill him before he steps on the bridge," said Afreyda.

"We won't know until we try."

Damon smiled sourly at Eleanor. "How many are over there?" he asked Megan.

"Didn't see. Can't be many."

"Well, proceeding on the basis of blind hope . . ."

"I'll go look, shall I?" said Megan. No one offered to go in her place.

She selected one of the taller trees. She hauled herself up it and crawled out on to the highest branch she reckoned able to support her weight. Her heart skipped a beat as it bent underneath her. She clung on. It stabilized. She took a few breaths to calm herself and pushed the leaves aside.

Across the river she could see the remains of the camp: piles of trash, the occasional tent, palisades of sharpened tree trunks erected to protect against an attack that had never come. And there, hidden by one of the few patches of undergrowth that had survived, the smoke of a fired gun dissipating like breath on a winter's day.

She shuffled forward a little more, alarming a beetle that scurried away from her. A figure fussed about the gun—no, there was a second. Megan waited a minute, making sure no one else appeared. They didn't.

She shimmied down the tree and brushed scraps of bark from her hands. "There are only two of them. Someone needs to sneak over the water and take care of them before the others can cross." Silence followed this pronouncement. "Guess it's going to be me, huh?"

"We cannot use the bridge?" said Afreyda.

"It'd be a tiny bit obvious," said Megan.

Afreyda looked shamefaced. "I cannot swim."

Others piped up with declarations of a similar lack of skill, albeit with much less regret. No, Megan was being unfair. They were just ordinary people—women, children, the old—who were trying to cope with the destruction of their lives, the shattering of the hopes the arrival of the priests' army had raised. They were dazed, unsure what to do, eager to delegate to anyone who showed the slightest hint of willingness. Megan had been fighting for a year. These people would find the strength within themselves, if she could give them time.

In preparation for the swim, Megan kicked off her boots and pulled off her cloak and her outer jerkin. She thought about taking another layer, but she was already getting more looks than she felt comfortable with. Fortunately the crowd lost interest in her as soon as Eleanor copied her.

"You're coming with me?" Megan said.

"Of course."

"I would," said Damon. "I'm just not suicidal. Or homicidal. Or any 'cidal.'"

"That's all right too." Megan pointed upriver. "Go that way. We need you to cause a distraction."

"How?"

"I don't know," said Megan. "Taunt them."

"And once they start firing?"

"Taunt them some more." Megan pulled him and Afreyda close. She lowered her voice. "If we don't make it back, take everyone and keep going this side of the river. You might find somewhere to cross or get far enough away from the Sandstriders or we might have won the battle or . . ."

Afreyda squeezed Megan's shoulder. "We will protect them."

Megan gave her an appreciative nod. She set off with Eleanor through the forest. They followed the river as it looped past the tongue of Clibbur Point, heading north, then stopping before the path of the Speed swung back eastward. There was a clump of bushes by the water's edge. They crawled down to the shelter they offered. A fading finger of smoke gave away the witches' position. They probably couldn't see Megan and Eleanor with the steep banks and the detritus of the camp, but Megan didn't want to take the chance. She remained huddled behind the bush.

The river here was far narrower than at Eastport and the currents less formidable, but it wasn't going to be an easy swim. "Is this going to work?" she whispered to Eleanor.

"Can you imagine anyone hearing Damon and *not* wanting to shoot him?"

"Not that, I meant . . . never mind."

They waited. Megan shivered, half in anticipation of the cold water, half in anticipation of what she had to do.

No matter how many times she told herself this was war, that the witches had brought this upon themselves, that she had pledged thousands of times to destroy the enemies of the Faith, the fact she was planning to kill again troubled her. It was brutal, irrevocable, and not quite as forced upon her by Gwyneth as she pretended. They didn't have to go this way—they could find another— but expediency encouraged callousness.

Damon's voice broke on the river, clear but distant. "Hey! Witches! Why don't you come over—?"

The gun answered. "I've never seen anyone turn against him so fast," said Megan.

"Yes, you have," muttered Eleanor.

"Do you think he'll be all right?"

"We can but hope not."

Megan slipped into the Speed. The icy water enveloped her like a shroud. She fought the urge to crawl to the other side as fast as possible, instead adopting a graceful, if agonizingly slow, breaststroke. The guns were loud, deafening if you were stood next to one. You wouldn't hear an extra ripple on the river, would you? Not unless you had a second gun covering your blind spot . . .

Adrenalin surged in her veins at the thought. She lost her rhythm and flailed in the water. She was making things worse. She stopped, treading water. Eleanor drew up alongside and gave her a concerned look. Megan gave her a quick nod and resumed swimming.

Water sluicing off them, they pulled themselves on to dry land. Eleanor unstrapped her bow and ran her hand up and down the string, drying it as best she could. Megan oriented herself. If the witches were still aiming at Damon, they had circled almost completely behind them.

They struggled up the bank, slipping and sliding in the mud. It dried out as they reached the top, but the camped soldiers had left the ground a mess of troughs and ridges, like slapdash plasterwork. Megan and Eleanor scurried from cover to cover, zigzagging toward the witches.

They pulled up close to the gun emplacement and hid behind a tent whose ripped walls explained its abandonment. The two witch soldiers were fussing over the gun, stuffing it with gunpowder scooped out of a barrel like animal feed and an iron ball the size of a melon. Breastplates and helmets lay abandoned on the ground. Why suffer the discomfort when they faced no threat?

"Can you hit them from here?" Megan whispered to Eleanor.

"Shouldn't we give them another chance of blowing up Damon?"

"Can you?"

"One of them, no problem," said Eleanor. "The other'll be on top of us before I have a chance to notch another arrow."

"All right. I'll get closer. You shoot that one—" she indicated the taller of the soldiers "—I'll pop in and stab the other while he's busy wondering what the hell is going on."

Eleanor nodded. Megan dashed on tiptoes to the outcropping of bushes that led in a straggly line to the witches' position and crept along them. The cover wasn't perfect or complete. If one of the soldiers looked in her direction with anything more than a casual glance, they'd spot her. Why was she doing this again?

She was close enough now to smell the reek of sulfur, its hellish associations apt considering the circumstances. The gun itself was a sinister cylinder of cast iron mounted on wheels. The dirt was gouged where the soldiers had swiveled the gun to point at Damon's position.

Megan looked back to Eleanor. An arrowhead peeked out from the canvas. Megan eased herself between the branches. The soldier she'd designated as her target was still a good five yards away. Far enough to have recovered his senses by the time she got to him? She'd have to be quick.

There was a whoosh and a gargled cry. Megan leaped out of the bushes and charged at the soldier. It was only as she was slashing his neck that she realized he was already dropping to his knees. An arrow stuck out of his side. Eleanor had shot the wrong one.

The man she had spared made the most of his reprieve. He snatched up an ax and dashed toward Megan. She heaved his fallen comrade into his path. The ax flashed, buried itself deep into flesh. Megan cringed, then realized it wasn't hers.

She'd dropped her knife grabbing the solider. Her opponent stamped on it as he tried to wrench his ax from his dead colleague's arm. He was having trouble. The blade was stuck in the bone. Megan pulled one of the short daggers from her arm scabbard. The soldier lashed out, catching her flush in the face with the back of his hand. Megan staggered, her head spinning.

There was a crack and a pop. The ax came free, its blade thick with blood. Megan held her arms up, knife jutting out from the underside of her fist, as if they could protect her from the soldier's heavy weapon. Then an arrow hissed through the air and pierced his ribs.

He stumbled, face pale, eyes brimming with fear. He grasped at the shaft sucking the life out of him. He pulled, but his hand slipped off the arrow. Megan stepped forward and punched him in the throat with her knife hand. The fear left him.

Eleanor jogged over. "You couldn't . . ." gasped Megan, "you couldn't have shot the guy I told you to?"

"I did."

"The one *furthest* from the bushes."

"I suppose that would have made sense," said Eleanor. She shrugged. "Not my fault your pointing's sloppy."

Megan stepped past the smoking mouth of the gun and into the open ground beyond the emplacement's cover. She waved across to the other side of the river.

"It's safe!" she yelled.

"How do we know you're not trying to trick us?" Damon shouted back.

Megan turned her wave into something a little more offensive and went to rejoin Eleanor. The countess was studying the gun, poking it as if trying to determine whether it was still alive.

"Are they coming?"

"As soon as Damon stops wasting time."

"We could be a while," muttered Eleanor. "How d'you think this thing works?"

Megan pointed at a cord at the closed end of the gun that burrowed its way into the metal like a tapeworm. "Light that. Explosion. Stuff shoots out very fast."

"There's a metaphor in there somewhere." Eleanor walked around the gun. "I suppose it's too heavy to bring with us."

"Why would we?"

"Defense."

Megan remembered the fate of the *Fury*, one of the witches' ships. One of its guns had blown up, sinking the vessel. "We're more likely to kill ourselves than the enemy."

"I guess."

Megan wandered back out of the emplacement to see how the rest of their party was doing. Across the river, Damon was leading them out of the trees and on to the riverside path for the short journey to the bridge. He gave her a bow, though whether he was acknowledging her performance or his own was hard to say.

She caught movement in the corner of her eye. Downriver from Damon and the others, a quartet of Sandstriders were advancing down the road, sun glinting off drawn sabers. Megan made to shout a warning. She couldn't get the words out. She jabbed frantically. Damon made an exaggerated shrug.

"Behind you!"

Damon turned and swore loud enough to be heard back in Eastport. The others looked to see the cause of his distress. They started screaming.

"Get out of there!" yelled Megan.

The command was superfluous. There was a stampede for the bridge. Megan scrambled back to Eleanor.

"We have to . . ."

The countess had guessed Megan's plan and was trying to shove the gun back around. Megan joined her, pushing as hard as she could. Slowly the gun swung in the dirt, retracing the grooves it had left in the ground, jolting as it settled into the deeper ones of its previous position.

"Bit more," said Megan, gasping as she tried to recover her breath.

"What?"

"We need to take out the bridge."

They heaved again. The gun was reluctant to move from its home, jerking back as soon as Megan thought they'd got it clear. It took a back-breaking heave to free it and rotate it the necessary few degrees.

Eleanor grabbed steel and flint, which the witches had left in a tin by the barrel of gunpowder. "Go tell me when they're clear."

Megan nodded and scurried clear of the bushes. Everyone was streaming over the bridge, Afreyda bringing up the rear. The lead Sandstrider broke free and charged her. His sword swung. Hers replied. A clang echoed around the valley. Metal flashed as it spun to the ground. The Sandstrider's weapon had broken Afreyda's. Megan yelped in dismay.

"Get clear!" yelled Eleanor.

Megan spun around. "No! I didn't mean—"

Eleanor crashed out of the bushes and dragged Megan away. They hit the ground. Across the river, Afreyda thrust the remains of her sword into the Sandstrider's face. He staggered away, hands turning red as he pressed them to his wounds.

Afreyda dashed for the bridge. The other Sandstriders gave pursuit. Planks clattered as feet hit
them. The gun thundered with the roar of an angered
god.

The bridge disintegrated.

Eleven

Megan rushed down the bank, shouting Afreyda's name. The bridge had been reduced to scraps and splinters, like a toy stamped on by a bully. A body spun in the Speed as the current carried it away. The robes blistering in the water told her it was a Sandstrider.

There was a desperate squeal. Megan looked down to see two sets of dusty fingers clinging to the remnants of the bridge's span. She peered over the edge. Afreyda was hanging on, her feet dangling a few inches above the river.

"Will you help me up *this* time?"

Megan knelt and grabbed one of Afreyda's arms. "Can I have a hand here?" she shouted. "Damon!"

He dashed over and grabbed Afreyda's other arm. "On the count of three," she said. "One, two—"

An arrow thudded into the bridge between them. Megan's arms were almost ripped out of their sockets as Damon released Afreyda and scurried backward.

Afreyda dangled in midair, her eyes wide with fear. She gritted her teeth, swung her free arm up, got a grip on the bridge's edge.

On the other side, a Sandstrider was fumbling for another arrow. "Get back here!" Megan screamed at Damon.

He hesitated, then crawled back. Together they started to haul Afreyda up. The Sandstrider drew back his bowstring. He looked dazed, inebriated by the explosion, but the three of them together made an awfully big target. Megan and Damon wrenched hard. Afreyda shot over the edge. They collapsed into a heap just as an arrow whistled over their heads.

"Will someone—?"

Another arrow shot past, this one in the opposite direction. It hit the Sandstrider in the stomach. He made it to the tree line before collapsing.

Afreyda got up and dusted herself off. There was a sour expression on her face. "You could not have waited one more second?"

"Sorry," said Megan, massaging her shoulders.

Eleanor shrugged defensively. "Communication breakdown."

Afreyda pouted. She pulled her sword—or what remained of it—out of her scabbard. The blade was now no more than a foot long, its truncated end jagged and covered with gore. She wiped it clean on the ground and resheathed it.

"We're all safe," said Megan. "Let's be grateful for that, huh?"

Loretta stepped forward, her children clutching her legs as if trying to drag her back to the shelter of the crowd. "Are we? Safe?"

"The guns have stopped firing," said Eleanor.

They stared westward, in the direction of the battle they had fled. Nothing but trees and river and the deepening glow of the setting sun. The forest was keeping its secrets for now. "I wonder who's won?" said Megan.

"I think we can guess it's not us," said Damon.

"Not if the men showed your levels of cowardice."

"A coward is what an idiot calls a pragmatist."

"Should we stop here tonight?" asked Loretta.

The stress that had been piling up and up on Megan for the past day made her snap. "Why do you keep pestering me? Can't you think for yourselves? Leave me alone for a minute?"

Loretta took a step back, her face reddening. "I'm sorry. I know—we know—what you've done for us."

Megan sighed and looked away, ashamed at her outburst. The sun was sinking fast. There was half an hour of light left, if they were lucky. "I don't know. We probably should stay. What does everyone think?"

There was a murmur of ascent from the crowd. They'd been walking for two days straight now, and the exhaustion showed on every face. "Let's go see if there's anything we can salvage," said Eleanor.

They spread out. Afreyda stomped off on her own. Megan pulled on her dry clothes and fingered the ragged remains of the tip of her ear. The skin was still tender. She should put some more of Lynette's ointment on it.

Everyone gave her a wide berth. She ended up scavenging with Damon, who over the time they'd spent together had worked up an immunity to her anger, even when it was directed at him. Especially when it was directed at him.

"I see no one's thanking me for *my* efforts," he said, sorting through a pile of firewood no one had got around to burning. "I almost got myself shot and blown up out there."

Megan sighed. "Fine," she said. "Thanks for the quality taunting."

"You're in a mood, aren't you?" said Damon, piling logs into Megan's outstretched arms.

"You're putting everything I've been through down to a *mood*?"

"I've been through it too. So has everyone else."

"I know that," said Megan. She backed up a step before Damon could burden her with another log. Her arms felt numb enough as it was; any more weight and they'd drop off. "But why do I have to do their coping for them?"

"They think you know what you're doing. Don't let on you don't. We'll have a panic on our hands."

"I feel like a fraud."

"You say that like it's a bad thing."

Megan shook her head. All frauds were found out in the end. And she feared she'd be found out quicker than most.

Dawn broke with a sense of calm renewal and a debate over what to do. Everybody argued with everybody else, relying on volume rather than logic to put their point across. Some wanted to find the army; some wanted to go south to Cheetham; some wanted to return west, to Eastport, to protect their property from Sandstrider looters; some wanted to head north, all the way to New Statham; a few wanted to remain at the camp and pray for guidance; one man suggested his great-aunt's small-holding on Ainsworth's east coast, but when pressed admitted he hadn't spoken to his great-aunt in four decades and conceded she might not be alive or, even if she was, happy to receive so many visitors.

New Statham won out, its thick walls having the allure of a mother's arms. They followed the tracks made by the army, reckoning at some point they would inter-sect the northern road. This was the most likely route for the army itself to take, assuming they were retreat-ing and not regrouping for another attack. It wasn't the wildest assumption ever.

It was a weary journey, made worse by the bitter taste of defeat and the feeling of helplessness that permeated the travelers. There was none of the nervous energy that had powered the march down, just a sense of foreboding that the next corner rounded or hill crested would reveal their doom. Some dropped out, declaring they lacked either the will or the energy to continue. Megan gave up trying to motivate them.

She caught up with Afreyda, who was striding along way out in front as if she had an important meeting to get to. "We didn't mean to fire so early," she said. "We weren't sure what we were doing. If the Sandstriders had got across the bridge . . ."

Afreyda waved at the line straggling behind them. "You would sacrifice me for them?"

"I said—"

"Would you?"

The ground sloped upward. Megan's shins began to ache. "I suppose I would," she said, mentally squirming. Afreyda pouted. "I don't know. I feel responsible for them for some reason. Something I picked up from Eleanor. I guess you must be the same, being a princess and all."

"You had to be noble to enter the court. My father spent too much. He was trying to impress people who would call us scum even if we had bought an imperial title. It does not matter now. I am what I was born, and those who despise me can do so for what I am, not what I pretended to be."

"Sounds like a nice place."

"It is," said Afreyda, her eyes burning. "It is the most beautiful place in the world. The palace is as big as a city. The walls are lined with gold so pure it shines without the sun. The fountains glitter like the stars. It is never cold, never rainy, there is food at every corner."

"And the people?"

"Bastards to a man."

They reached the top of the hill. Movement in the plains stretched out before them caused Megan to throw herself on the ground and drag Afreyda down with her.

"I do not think this is—"

Megan shushed her and pointed. Half a mile or so away, a small group of figures could be seen loitering on the road that cut through the tall grass. Sunlight flashed off metal: arms and armor. Soldiers.

Megan waved to the crowd behind them, pushing her flattened hand to the ground. Damon spread his arms and mouthed, "What?"

"Get down and keep quiet," Megan hissed.

"Right!" Damon shouted.

Megan rolled over so she was lying prone and turned her attention back to the distant men. "Are they on our side?" asked Afreyda.

"I don't know," said Megan. They were too far away to discern uniforms. If this was what was left of the army, then there was no doubt who had won the battle. On the other hand, they could be one of the witches' gun crews looking to meet up with their compatriots.

She shielded her eyes. The men flitted around, obscuring one another and sometimes disappearing from view, making it difficult to get a head count. She estimated a good dozen of them. Although some of the refugees had raided the weapons of the dead witches, and a few others had armed themselves with stout branches, they couldn't cope with that many trained soldiers.

"Probably best we don't draw any attention to ourselves before we find out who they are."

Afreyda cleared her throat. Half their party was arranged along the ridge. They were gawking at the far-off soldiers, peering over each other's shoulders and exchanging wild theories.

Megan shooed them back. "If they're witches, I'm pretty sure their guns can reach us from there."

A beaten retreat left Megan and Afreyda with the top of the hill to themselves. "I do not think guns can shoot this far," said Afreyda.

"They don't need to know that."

A flash of copper hair heralded Eleanor's arrival. "What've we got?"

"I'm not sure," said Megan. "We'll have to go take a closer look." There was silence. "You want me to go?"

"I was thinking of someone a little more expendable."

"Don't think I don't know who you mean," said Damon, a safe distance behind them.

"It's all right," said Megan. "I prefer to be doing something rather than waiting."

Afreyda pulled a knife out of her boot and tested the point. A drop of blood welled up on her thumb. "I will come with you."

"You don't have to."

"There is no river here."

Megan nodded. "We'll need you to cover us if things go wrong," she said to Eleanor.

"Do not shoot at us," added Afreyda.

"Is she *still* sore about that?"

"It's custom where she comes from that friends don't try and kill each other."

"How terribly civilized."

They set off down the hill, keeping low in the tall grass. The fields were peaceful, free from squabbles and moans, the only sounds the creak of leather as Afreyda's armor shifted around her body. Would it be so bad if they left everybody behind and kept on going?

They stopped to rest. Afreyda poked her head up. "Anything?" whispered Megan.

"Too much sun," said Afreyda huddling back down. "And I never thought I would say that in *this* country."

They set off again, switching to a crawl and swinging west so they could approach the soldiers from the south and observe them without being blinded. Whatever Afreyda's opinion of the weather, Megan found it hot going. Her knees hurt, her palms stung and certain crevices were getting very sticky.

She peered over the top of the grass. Deserted plain stretched out before her. "Uh-oh."

"What?" said Afreyda, looking up. "Where are the soldiers?"

The point of a sword jabbing into Megan's neck told her exactly where they were.

"We spotted you a mile off," said a man's voice from behind them. "Creeping up on us, were you?"

"Of course not," said Megan. "I dropped a . . . a . . ."

"Needle?" said Afreyda.

Megan swallowed a retort. "Er, yeah, needle."

"And you're searching through hundreds of acres of grassland to find it?"

"We had the afternoon free."

"Why don't you ladies get up so I'm not talking to your asses?"

Afreyda flashed Megan the blade she had hidden against her forearm. Megan nodded, licked her cracked lips. She slid her hand down to grip the dagger stuck in her belt. They just needed enough of a strike to give them a head start. Armored soldiers couldn't move very fast, especially with blood in their eyes.

"Promise not to scream?" she said.

"Why would I scream?" said the soldier. "You're not going to turn out to have beards and one of those warts that—"

Megan kicked backward, smashing her boots into the man's knees. As he howled and cursed, she flipped to her feet, pulled her knife out and whirled around. The edge was inches from its target when she recognized the uniform of a soldier of the Faith. She pulled her hand back, overbalanced and tumbled into the grass.

Chuckles greeted her pratfall, a little uncalled for considering she had just saved the man's face. She sheathed her knife and picked herself up. The soldier was hunched over, massaging his kneecaps. Afreyda had her arm raised, debating whether to strike.

"Put the knife down, love," said the soldier. "We're all friends here. Probably." He raised his voice. "I got them, sir!" Other soldiers, scattered across the plain, converged on their position. They couldn't have spotted them that well if they were spread out like that.

As he drew closer, Megan recognized their commander. "Lieutenant Aldred!"

"Is Eleanor with you? Is she all right?"

"*She's* fine."

Aldred got the hint. "How are you?"

"Can't complain," said Megan. "Well, I could, but no one'd listen. There're others with us as well. They need your protection." She indicated the soldiers. "Is this all that's left of the army?"

"Everyone else is retreating to New Statham. We think they are anyway. Communication's a bit sketchy. We volunteered to stay behind to direct any stragglers."

"We've got plenty of those."

They reunited with the others. The refugees immediately looked to Aldred for guidance, which filled Megan with both a sense of relief someone else now bore her burden and annoyance she had been thrown over at the first sign of a replacement. Who cared for a grubby girl now heroic, manly soldiers were here?

A couple of soldiers stayed behind to look out for other survivors while the rest of the party set off to catch up with the remnants of the army, a day's march ahead. Aldred filled them—well, Eleanor—in on what had happened. After bloody hand-to-hand fighting in the forest, the army had regrouped at a point unreachable by the witches' guns and held a defensive line while the civilians were evacuated across the river on boats brought up from Eastport. The bulk of the people were moving back north but there were plenty of others—both soldiers and civilians—who were chancing their luck in other directions.

Nightfall revealed the fires of the army's camp, which had been set up on the edge of a copse. Their proximity gave Megan and the others the strength to keep going, a final push to claim the illusion of sanctuary, even if the cloudy sky caused stumbles on the bumpy road and the need to pick someone up every few seconds.

The glow of a lantern bounced toward them. "Halt! Who goes there? Friend or foe?"

"Shall we say 'foe' for a laugh?" said Damon.

"You want to get us killed?" said Megan.

"I didn't say we'd maintain the pretense."

"I'm Lieutenant Aldred of the Tyldesley regiment."

Their interrogator waddled forward with the bow-legged gait of someone who had spent a lifetime on horseback or the past week with an unfortunate bowel complaint. "Sergeant Merton, sir, of the—" a cough obscured his next word "—regiment."

"Sergeant? I only see two stripes."

"T'other got ripped off in battle."

"On both arms?"

"Yeah, weird that," said Merton. "You know how long I waited for 'em? You ain't got any have you, sir?"

"Any what?"

"Stripes, sir. For field promotions and the like."

"Where can we set up?" said Megan, stepping into the lamplight. "We've got a lot of tired and hungry people here."

Merton frowned as he examined this interloper to the conversation. He raised an eyebrow at Aldred, who nodded. "Anywhere you like, miss. No one's standing on ceremony. Avoid the tents though. The priests got those."

"Some of them made it out of the palace?"

"Aye."

"I can't decide," said Damon. "Is that proof for or against the existence of God?"

"Show some respect, boy."

"Yes, corporal." There was a sharp intake of breath. "Sorry. Sergeant."

Merton led them to one of the fires. There was immediate jostling for its warmth—with everyone claiming they deserved priority because they were young, old, wet, a mother, arthritic, or armed—so much so that they had to get another one going. Another argument broke out about the food rations. Aldred dispatched a couple of his men to the interior of the camp. They returned with a roasted boar, which shut everyone up, for the moment at least.

Afreyda shivered and inched closer to the fire. "You're still cold?" asked Megan, sat next to her.

"I am always cold here."

Megan remembered winter nights at the mill, when the wind would blast cold air through gaps in the walls and she and Gwyneth would shiver in the dark. She did what she did back then. She huddled in close to Afreyda and wrapped an arm around her. Afreyda tensed. Megan thought she was going to pull away. Practicality won out over standoffishness. Afreyda huddled in and rested her head against Megan's shoulder.

"Do you ever think about going home?" Megan asked. "Diannon merchants sometimes make it to East-port, New Statham, even. They might take you back."

"All the time. But I cannot. Not until the Emperor is dead."

"Is that likely anytime soon?"

"Not if I am not there to kill him."

"No one else likely to do the job?"

Megan felt Afreyda shake her head. "Everybody hates him, but they hate each other more. They fear what they will lose if he is not there to hold things together."

"How did you manage a rebellion?"

"Badly," said Afreyda.

They sat contemplating the flames and the popping wood and the murmur of conversation. It was only when Megan caught the sounds of gentle snores did she realize Afreyda had dozed off. She kissed her fore-head and stroked her hair, enjoying the brief moment of tenderness.

Twelve

Damon clinked the dice in his pocket and wandered the camp, looking for action. If there were priests around, there was a chance they had some booze with them, and where there was booze there were people who thought they could beat the odds. You could never beat the odds. Especially when they were being fiddled.

He flitted from fire to fire, keeping his head down whenever he saw someone he thought might recognize him. A scream of agony ripped through the camp, reminding him not everyone had got away in one piece. An arrow being pulled, he guessed, or an amputation to which consent had finally been given.

The few tents were huddled in the middle of the camp. They had been ordinary soldiers' billets on the way down; returning, they were ecclesiastical palaces. A few priests were gathered around a nearby fire, sharing a bottle. Damon straightened his clothes, affected a look of boyish innocence and took a step toward them.

"I wouldn't bother, boy," said a voice behind him.

Damon turned to see Father Galan sat in the doorway of a tent. At some point he had found new robes and reshaved his tonsure, though such efforts had been in vain considering the splatters of mud and what looked like dried blood. A bottle sat between his legs: spiced spirits, judging from the eye-watering whiff that made it to Damon's nostrils.

"I don't know what you're talking about, father."

"I'm sure you don't," said the High Priest. He proffered the bottle. Damon shook his head. "What are you scared of?"

"If you want a complete list, it could take a while."

Father Galan shook the bottle at him. Damon gave in. It was probably the best offer he was going to get.

The alcohol burned its way to his stomach, taking the lining of his throat with it. Father Galan laughed at his spluttering. "We'll make a man of you yet, boy."

Normally Damon didn't mind people calling him "boy"—it lured them into a false sense of superiority—but considering the circumstances, it was patronizing. All were equal when you were fleeing for your life.

"How come you're not in ten thousand pieces, father?"

"I wasn't in the palace when it exploded."

"But it was your home," said Damon.

"It had been commandeered by the Supreme Priest and his cronies."

Eleanor would love the irony. "And they didn't even invite you to the shindig?" Father Galan's grunt in reply was noncommittal.

Damon beckoned for the bottle. The second slug wasn't so bad, possibly because the first had cauterized the wounds it had caused. "I guess this disaster leaves you one of the senior people in the Realm, if not *the* senior. Can't be many high priests left."

"I suppose."

"Shouldn't you be a-plotting then?" said Damon. "Isn't there power to be seized?"

"What's the point?" said Father Galan. "God has made his judgment. He favors the witches."

"Maybe He was passing judgment on priests, not the priesthood."

"What do you mean by that?"

"The Saviors granted power to the monarch, not the priests," said Damon. "Maybe God's decided it's time he had it back again. Or she."

"You're not telling me Endalay . . . ?"

"What would be the reaction if she did?"

"My brethren will not surrender power lightly," said Father Galan, "and they certainly won't give her the chance for revenge. The day she makes a claim for the throne will be her last."

* * *

Megan stared into the fire, contemplating the flames and trying to bring Cate to mind. It had been so long since she had seen her, and for so brief a time, she feared the images that came to her were inventions not memories. What would her daughter be doing now? Would she still need feeding during the night or would she sleep straight through? How much had she grown? Was she big and strong, or small and sickly? Was she alive or was she—?

"Room for another?" said Damon, squeezing in beside her.

"Shh," said Megan, comforting Afreyda, who mumbled in her sleep. "I just got her down."

Damon jiggled a bottle in front of her. "Drink?"

"I'll pass."

"Probably for the best."

He took a swig from the bottle. "You seen Eleanor?" he asked. At least that's what Megan thought he said. It was hard to make out over all the gasping.

"Not for a while."

"She with *him*?"

"I don't know," said Megan. "Probably."

"What does she see in him?"

"Apart from looks, charm and an actual sense of honor?"

"Hey," said Damon, "I have—"

"What? Please don't tell me you were going to say 'honor.'" Megan adjusted the sleeping Afreyda so she wasn't completely numbing her arm. "Look, do you really want my opinion?"

"Only if it agrees with mine."

"We've been stuck with each other for the best part of a year now. Don't you think if something was going to happen between you and Eleanor, it would have by now?"

"She might have been holding back," said Damon. "Out of respect for you."

"Me?"

"You might have got jealous."

"The incredulous look on my face tells you all you need to know about *that*."

It wasn't as if Megan didn't like Damon; she just couldn't see him as anything more than a friend and someone not to play dice with. She hadn't thought about a boy in that way since Wade and, considering how that had turned out, she wasn't mourning that aspect of life.

Damon ground out a groove in the dirt with his heel. "You know why we're going to New Statham, don't you?"

"The usual. Running and hiding."

"It because that's where everybody else is." He lowered his voice. "No point in being queen if you're stuck in some hovel in Baleyworth."

"Baleyworth? Isn't that the county with all the . . . ?" Megan trailed off, realizing that wasn't the key part of Damon's last sentence. "*Queen?*" She looked around for possible eavesdroppers. The circle was too wrapped up in its own thoughts to bother with them. "Where the hell did you get that idea from?"

"From her," said Damon. "Perfect timing. The Supreme Priest is dead and so are most of the high priests. Our countess gets to the capital, dispenses a little goodwill—"

"Goodwill?"

"Bribes. And before you know it, she goes all regal."

"How's she going to bribe them without . . . ?" Megan remembered the papers in Lynette's study. "She's named in Lynette's will, isn't she?"

"It's a toss-up between Eleanor and the cat."

"Lynette didn't have a cat."

"A toss-up between Eleanor and Eleanor then."

"It's never going to work," said Megan.

"I know," said Damon. "Father Galan was happy to confirm it."

"You told him?"

"I just floated the idea, see what his reaction would be. Don't worry, he's only interested in drinking. Some of the other priests might be a little more . . . proactive."

"They're going to kill her?" said Megan. Damon nodded. "They'll have to get in line."

Megan found Eleanor talking with Aldred among the officers and the sergeants. She dragged her away to a half-hearted chorus of catcalls and marched her through the camp and beyond its perimeter. The barest hint of a crescent moon hung in the sky, a shaving of silver laid out on sable. A few people were around even this far out—a patrol here, a potential suicide staring into the void there. No one gave them a second glance.

Eleanor stopped abruptly. "Before you give me a lecture you're not entitled to give, there's nothing going on between me and Aldred."

"I don't care about that," said Megan. She pulled Eleanor further into the gloom, more to prove a point than because she feared being overheard. "What I do care about is the disaster you're about to lead us into, your majesty."

"Ah . . ."

"What the hell are you thinking?"

"I thought you'd be pleased for me."

"*Pleased?*"

"I'm reclaiming my birthright," said Eleanor. "Don't you want to take what's yours from those who destroyed it? You want your home back, don't you?"

More than anything—to take Cate back to the mill and raise her there. But there were other things Megan wanted and could never have. To show her grandfather his great-granddaughter. To see her friends again. To laugh and joke with her sister and lie next to her hidden in wheat fields while the sun burned hot.

"You were never meant to be queen," she said. "This is all—what?—some technicality."

"It doesn't matter. The people need someone to lead them against the witches. The priests, what's left of them, don't have the will for the fight."

"And there'll be a fight all right," said Megan. "Once everyone knows who you are, the witches are going to come straight for us."

"And by that point I'll have an army between them and us. A real army. It's your protection I'm thinking about."

"Like hell it is."

Megan made to head back to the camp. Eleanor grabbed her arm. "We can send for Cate."

"What?" said Megan, trying to suppress the quaver in her voice.

"Once I'm established on the throne. It'd be the safest place, with us. With you."

Megan hung her head. "Don't do this to me."

"What? Give you hope?"

"This is what *she* did. Tried to buy me off."

"I am not your sister," snapped Eleanor.

"No? So you're not scheming for power because you're convinced you know what's best for everyone? Next you'll be claiming it's your God-given right."

"Well, technically . . ."

"What if someone stands against you?" said Megan. "What if there's someone you can't pay off? Are you prepared for a civil war? Are you prepared to kill the

Faithful? Are you prepared to break God knows how many of the Pledges?"

"You're talking hypotheticals."

"Oh, really? And what's your plan based on? A deep- and well-seated desire in the Faithful to see the monarchy restored? We've moved on. No one wants you."

There was a sharp intake of breath. A pregnant pause. Megan had let her mouth get away with her. But Eleanor needed to hear it, because if Megan if was thinking it, you could bet plenty of the Faithful were thinking worse.

"Thank you for your gratitude," said the countess, her voice brittle.

"You know I didn't mean it like that," said Megan. "I want—I need—Eleanor. Not a queen or even a countess. You."

"And you have me," said Eleanor.

But for how long? thought Megan.

Thirteen

Edwyn the Unifier had walked to the ends of Werla-via, converting the warring princes—sometimes, well, most times, at swordpoint—and dictating the Book of Faith. Nowhere in the book, however, did he provide any practical advice on how to avoid blisters and aching muscles and swollen ankles and feet you forgot were in agony until you rested a moment and the pain dropped to a recognizable register. Megan suspected in Edwyn's case "walked" was a euphemism for "rode in comfort in a well-appointed carriage."

People left them on the route: some wandered off on their own, claiming this way or that was safer; some remained behind at whatever town, village or staging post they tramped through; some died, of their wounds from the battle or simple exhaustion. Others joined them: refugees from Eastport, pathetically grateful to discover they weren't the only ones left alive; towns-people who at the first mention of the witches saw the attractions of defensive walls; deserters who declared themselves to be "advance scouts" and "reserve units."

They reached Hickton, the last town before the northern road climbed the Akram Hills then descended into the Stathian Plain. The hills weren't high but they were energy-sappingly steep, prompting mutterings among their number. Megan scowled at the complaints, even if they were the same ones she was making to herself.

They rested by the remains of an ancient watchtower that jutted out of the ground like a rotten tooth. Loretta's children, Isen and Audrey, weaved in and out of the scattered stones, energy regained as soon as they weren't required to walk. Megan fantasized it was Cate out there—hiding and being found, chasing and being caught, the consequences nothing more than laughter and a reversal of roles—but would she ever see Cate play? She pulled out the statuette of the Saviors she had bought in Statham and prayed she would. Megan let out a hollow laugh. If the witches were right, she was pleading with her own daughter to protect herself.

"You shouldn't mock the Saviors."

"What?" Megan looked around. Loretta was propped up against a chunk of fallen wall, looking disapproving in a manner only a mother could manage. "I wasn't . . . I was thinking of someone . . . something else."

Loretta pointed at the statuette. "The children used to have one of those in their room."

"Better made than this, I hope."

"Was it . . . was it your child's?"

"What?" said Megan. "No!"

"I'm sorry. I didn't mean to . . . I thought you might have lost someone."

"We've all lost someone." *But I will not lose my daughter.*

Loretta shouted at her children who were expressing their mutual affection by hitting each other. "I don't know what I'd do if they . . ." She cuddled baby Edwyn who, as usual, was slung across her chest. "I feel so helpless. I don't know how to protect them from all this."

"Knives usually work for me," said Megan.

"I don't even have one of those."

Megan slipped a stiletto out of her boot. Loretta looked warily at the proffered hilt. "I couldn't."

"It's all right. I've got plenty."

"Why?" said Loretta. "Who are you exactly?"

"Just a girl looking after herself."

Megan offered the knife again. Loretta hesitated, then accepted.

The road cut through desolate moorland, the fells undulating and interlocking like crumpled laundry. Wild grass and lilac-topped heather stretched out until it met low-hanging cloud that made Megan shiver just looking at it. It was a throwback to a primeval time, when life was at its most basic and uncomplicated.

Afreyda was a few yards ahead of Megan, trying to ignore the soldier who strode beside her. Judging by his hand motions, Megan assumed he was either trying to chat her up or describing the entrants of a misshapen-vegetable contest.

"Come on, love," said the soldier. "Don't be like that."

"I will be like how I want."

The soldier held up his hands in mock surrender. "Look, what's your name?" After a short hesitation, Afreyda told him. "Pleased to meet you, Afreyda, I'm Norvel. What say you and me leave this war behind and lose ourselves in each other's bodies? Got a nice place up in Kewley. The wife'll take good care of us."

"Wife?"

"You didn't think a good-looking guy like me was unmarried, did you?" said Norvel.

"I . . . I do not think your wife would want me in her home."

"It's all right. She doesn't mind foreigners."

Norvel changed approach. His hand drifted downward, hovered over her leather-clad behind, then went in for the kill. Afreyda swept his legs out from under him, paused briefly to bat the dust from her pants and resumed her journey.

"Could you teach me how to do that?" said Megan, catching up with her.

"I did not think you were interested in nonlethal forms of combat."

"Girl's got to experiment."

They were getting close to New Statham and the start of whatever schemes Eleanor had planned. Maybe the countess had already begun, promising favors to Aldred and his men, accumulating followers, people who would kill for her.

"Did you try to persuade your father not to rebel?" she asked Afreyda.

"It was not my place to question my father."

"Even knowing how much you had to lose?"

"To sleep in soft beds and fill our bellies with rich food and numb our consciousness with fine wine while the Emperor terrorized our people?"

"But an open declaration of war you couldn't win . . ."

"We thought we could win," said Afreyda. "We thought the populace would rise up against him, that his generals would mutiny, that people wanted justice."

"And they didn't?"

"Some thought they did have too much to lose. Others did not see how they would gain. They saw one ruler wanting to replace another."

There was wheezing and panting behind them. Damon hauled himself up the last of the immediate hills and drew level. "Have you noticed something?" he said, gasping. "Or, rather, not noticed something?"

"Like what?" said Megan. "Or not what?" She looked around. "I don't see anything."

"You're right," said Damon, "there's nothing. Where is everyone?" Megan motioned at the line trooping past them. "That's us. But why is no one coming from the opposite direction?"

"From New Statham?"

"This close to the largest city in the Realm? You'd expect there to be someone. There's always some guy being run out of town."

"We saw some New Stathians in Hickton," said Afreyda.

"That guy who accused you of stealing his purse, for one," added Megan.

"He *lost* his purse," said Damon. "I happened to find it a short time afterward. But he'd have left New Statham days ago. Has there been anyone since?"

"What're you trying to say?"

"They've sealed the city. They're not going to let us in."

"Why wouldn't they?"

"Too many people to feed," said Afreyda.

"Especially with an impending siege," said Damon.

"Siege?" said Megan. "The witches wouldn't come all the way up here."

Even as she uttered the words, she realized how false they were. "They crossed the Savage Ocean all the way from the Diannon Empire," said Damon. "Eastport to New Statham is a pleasure jaunt by comparison."

"A pleasure jaunt that wouldn't take them very long."

"No."

"Faster than, say, walking."

"Easily."

"Are you thinking what I'm thinking?"

"If I am, you're a lot kinkier than I gave you credit for."

Megan scanned the weary faces trooping past. "We need to find Eleanor."

She hurried down the line, her walk becoming a jog. There was no sight of the countess's distinctive hair. She was driven to calling out her name.

"What's wrong?"

Megan jumped. Eleanor was a mere six feet behind her, her hood up. Megan pulled her into the wild grass by the side of the road. "We're about to walk into a trap," she said. "Again."

"What kind of trap?"

"Well, not the good sort."

Damon found them. "You given her the news?"

"I'm not sure what either of you are talking about," said Eleanor.

"The witches are at New Statham."

"What? How did you reach that conclusion?"

"Put it this way," said Megan. "Where would we least like them to be?"

"We're predicting by pessimism now?"

"Where else were they going?"

"Nowhere," said Eleanor, "anywhere. They wanted to lure us into Eastport. They don't have the men to take New Statham, and without both the Saviors they wouldn't have the nerve."

Megan shivered at the thought of the role intended for Cate. "It hasn't stopped them so far."

"Besides, I'm not sure even the witches' guns can breach New Statham's walls."

"Which is nice if you're on the *in*side . . ." said Damon.

"We need to find Aldred," she said, "warn him what to expect."

"Clever guy like him? I'm sure he's already guessed."

He had, which shut Damon up. More than guessed, in fact. After checking there were only soldiers in earshot, he told them advance runners had confirmed the presence of the witches' fleet on the Rustway. New Statham had taken a battering until archers had taken out one of the gunpowder-laden ships with a volley of fire arrows, forcing the witches to retreat. For the time being.

"Why are we still headed there then?" asked Megan. "Instead of somewhere, I don't know . . ."

"Less idiotic?" said Damon.

Aldred's fist clenched beneath his gauntlet. Eleanor gave him a quick shake of her head. "We're going to relieve the city and attack the witches," he said.

"You can't take a bunch of civilians into battle," said Eleanor.

"The army'll leave the civilians at Kewley, then swing down the Rustway and join up with the New Statham garrison." Kewley was a summer resort on the south shore of Lake Pullar, frequented by the rich and powerful and those who needed a second home to house their self-regard. "The witches have set up camp south of the city. We'll rush them under cover of darkness."

"I like a plan where absolutely nothing can go wrong," said Damon.

Aldred's lip curled. "Remind me again why you didn't enlist?"

"I have an exemption warrant."

"On what grounds?"

"Forgot what I asked for now." Damon fished out a grubby scrap of parchment from which a wax seal dangled. "Ah, an ecumenical exemption."

"You got yourself excused from fighting in a religious war for religious reasons?" said Megan.

"My god is an ironic god."

Eleanor took Aldred aside, though not far enough that Megan couldn't hear what they were saying. "When were you going to tell me about this master plan of yours?" said the countess.

"It's not my plan, and it's not my place to inform civilians of military matters."

"I'm not a civilian, I'm . . ." Eleanor cut herself off. "It's going to be dangerous."

"I've faced the witches' guns before," said Aldred. "I'm not scared."

"But you haven't rushed headlong into them. That's . . ."

"Suicidal," Damon called out.

The army's capacity for keeping secrets proved to be no greater than their capacity for strategic planning. A rumor sprang up civilians were to be used as gun fodder, to distract the witches while the soldiers attacked from the rear—a rumor the curt dismissals of the priests and the senior officers did little to quell. There were calls to fall back to Hickton. Fights broke out over their provisions and the few horses they'd been able to requisition. Breaking a few heads soon restored a sullen order, but that didn't stop civilians peeling off to take their chances elsewhere.

As they trudged across the moorland peaks, the ragged host began to organize itself into platoons and companies, like disturbed sediment settling into layers. Megan and the others found themselves in the vanguard, overtaking soldiers burdened by packs and armor and an impending sense of doom. She could do nothing more than offer grim smiles of encouragement.

"This is lunacy," she said. "Who's going to protect us once the army's dead?"

"We could make a defensive wall out of the corpses," said Damon. "It'd get very smelly very quickly though. Plus you'd get bits dropping off, what with decomposition and everything. Maybe if it was winter, things'd hold together a little longer . . ."

"What is he talking about?" Afreyda said to Megan, frowning.

"He babbles when he's nervous."

"I'm always nervous. It's being around you that—"

"It's a good plan," interjected Eleanor.

"What?" said Megan, Damon and Afreyda with varying levels of incredulity.

"The guns are ranged weapons, slow to aim, slow to reload."

"One gun maybe," said Megan. "The witches have dozens, hundreds even."

"We'll have surprise on our side," continued Eleanor, giving no indication she had heard Megan. "Once you rush troops to the guns' positions, they'll be useless. It'll be a straight fight. And we have more men than them."

"Men who have just marched the length of the continent," said Megan. "Men who are in no fit state to fight."

"Maybe they need a queen to lead them," said Damon. "Gee up their spirits." Eleanor responded with a look that was in no way regal.

The hill they were climbing proved to be the final one. Megan caught her breath at the sight of the Stathian Plain stretched out before them, vast tracts of crops bathed golden by the sun. To the north shimmered the silver ribbon of Lake Pullar, seeming to hover above the green mattress of the woods on its southern shore. Over to the northwest lay New Statham, a smudge on the horizon at this range.

"What's that?" said Damon, pointing to a dust cloud in front of the city.

"It'll be guns," said Megan.

"Is it me or is it a bit coming-this-way-y?"

"Do you want to rephrase that in less technical terms?"

Eleanor stepped forward and shielded her eyes from the sun. "It's not guns," she said. "It's an army."

"But they're . . ." said Damon, jerking his thumb at the advancing column behind them.

"Not *our* army."

The witches knew they were here. They were coming for them. There would be no sneak attack. The witches would fight on their own terms. And it was going to be a massacre.

Fourteen

A call went around for everyone not to panic. Naturally, the "not" went unheeded. People started fleeing, both back along the road they had followed and out into the wild moorland, as if in hope the witches wouldn't follow them lest they get their boots dirty. Officers rushed along the lines, barking orders that bordered on threats. The troops shuffled into formation, but it was obvious from their faces they were one man losing his head away from a stampede.

"I guess we lost the benefit of surprise," said Megan. "What happens now?"

"We're going to attack," said Eleanor.

"Well, that'll regain the element of surprise," said Damon. "The witches'll recover pretty quickly though."

There was a swish of robes as Father Galan made his way to the front. He batted the worst of the mud off himself and held a hand up. The rebellious mutterings ceased, or at least dropped to an unintelligible level.

"Men of the Faith!" he bellowed. "Remember the second Pledge. God has delivered our enemy—His enemy—to us. It is our duty to destroy them. No one said this would be easy; God's work never is. You must dig deep within yourself and find the determination to wipe this abomination from the face of Werlavia. The Realm is depending on your courage and your fortitude."

"We're screwed," muttered Damon.

Father Galan made the sign of the circle and led the soldiers in prayer. "God, born of the eternal universe . . ."

Megan wasn't listening. Instead she was staring out on to the plain where the distant army gathered like storm clouds. *Are you down there, Gwyn? Does the scent of impending victory thrill you? Do you feel anything for the people who die fighting for you or against you, or do you think only of the power your child gives you?*

The officers started to organize the men into neat formations—four decades of not fighting had made the army very good at marching if nothing else. Megan caught Eleanor staring at Aldred, trying to keep the emotion from her face. He turned, bowed to the countess. She acknowledged him with the briefest nod.

Megan nudged Eleanor. "You should go over, say goodbye."

"He's busy," said Eleanor, wiping the corner of her eyes with her sleeves, "and we've got things to do. Time for Plan D."

"Running away?" asked Megan. The countess nodded. "What were plans A to C?"

"Variations on a theme of running away."

Eleanor set off down the hill. "Speaking as an amateur enthusiast on the art of skedaddling," said Damon, "I can't but wonder if she's going the right way."

"Plan D incorporates part of Plan C," said Eleanor, craning her neck around. "We're still heading for Kewley."

Megan pushed through the wild grass and caught up with her, kicking up gravel as she skidded on the road. "And after that?"

"We cross Lake Pullar and head north."

"How far north?"

"North as you can get."

"The Kartik Mountains?" Megan mentally shivered. They'd spent the winter in their shadows, while she had been pregnant with Cate. She'd never been colder.

"North-er."

"You've got be kidding me."

Damon drew up beside her. "We're headed for the Snow Cities? They'll slaughter us before we can say *diné katullá mi sitúpa*."

"What?"

"It's Hilite for 'Please don't slaughter us'."

"You speak the language?" said Megan.

"What else was I going to study in the seminary? Divinity?"

"What is the problem?" asked Afreyda. "Mountains make good defenses. We can find safety on the other side."

"They don't exactly like us in the Snow Cities," said Damon. "I think it's our habit of trying to invade and convert them to the Faith. Pisses them off a bit."

"Like you did to the Sandstriders?"

"Uh-huh."

"And the True?"

"Well . . ."

"I think I see a pattern," said Afreyda.

"I'm not responsible for the Realm's foreign policy," said Damon. "Not that we view anybody else as foreigners, really. Which might be the problem."

Footsteps crunched on the gravel behind them. Loretta was leading her children and a pack of civilians down the hill after them. Many of those following her had been with them since they crossed the Speed at Clibbur Point.

"Please wait!"

"What?" said Megan. It took her a moment to realize the implications of Loretta's plea. "You want to come with us?"

"Are you crazy?" said Damon. "We're going from certain death to certain death with frosty bits." He looked to Megan. "Are *we* crazy?"

"He's right. We can't keep you safe. Stay with the army, run back to Hickton, go anywhere rather than with us."

Loretta clutched baby Edwyn tight to her chest. Her gaze flicked over Megan's shoulder. Megan didn't need to turn to know what had caught her attention. "You've protected us so far."

"We . . ." Megan swallowed. "That was luck, nothing more."

"Luck is how God expresses His favor."

"Ah, theological arguments," said Damon. "Can't argue with them. Possibly why they're so popular."

It was superstition, nothing more, a blind belief that what had happened before would keep on happening. "I can't stop you from coming with us," Megan said to Loretta. "You have to look after yourself though. I can't promise to be there for you." That was a lie. She would be—she couldn't live with herself if she wasn't. The burden she thought she'd offloaded returned with spine-crushing vengeance.

They headed up the Kewley road, which was well-maintained and largely level, with deep grooves worn into the stones from decades' worth of carriages. Megan found herself hurrying everyone along, as if she could propel the others to their destination by a light hand between the shoulders. She kept looking back, but trees and the lie of the land obscured the view.

There was a rumble of gunfire, not as distant as Megan would have liked. "It's begun," she said. Eleanor nodded and pursed her lips. "There's nothing you can do. One more archer won't make a difference."

"That was never an option," said Eleanor. "I have to keep you safe."

"Me? I'm not important. Not once I gave birth to—"

"You are to me."

They continued on, adrenalin never quite managing to cancel out tiredness. Fields gave way to orchards. Behind them, smoke crept above the horizon, dirtying the sky like ink dripped in water. The primeval noise of the battlefield—a mix of anger, fear and pain—refused to be outrun.

They approached the outskirts of Kewley. Here was where those who couldn't afford a lakeside view resided—those whose job it was to hide all the bad things in the world from the rich. There were cabins and cottages, with gardens as neat as architectural diagrams. Someone somewhere was baking bread. It used to be the smell that greeted Megan when she woke, that banished the nightmares and told her her grandfather was nearby.

Pale faces appeared at windows, dogs barked in a show of bravado, a gardener threw down his hoe and dashed for shelter. "Not the welcome I was hoping for," said Eleanor.

"What now?" said Megan.

The sounds of battle were getting louder. Had the army broken through the witches' guns?

"We find some supplies, then . . ." Eleanor turned around slowly, as if trying not to attract attention. There was a distant look in her eyes. "Then we . . ."

The battle wasn't just getting louder; it was getting closer. "Down!" yelled Megan.

Some threw themselves to the ground as the earth exploded, others screamed and panicked, rushing this way and that. One woman even dashed across the gardens, toward the spot where the gun had impacted. A second shot, smashing into the ground fifty yards closer, made her collapse into gales of sobs.

Megan swore and sprinted over to her, instinctively keeping low even though rationality told her crouching a bit was hardly going to save her from a high-speed metal fist. She tugged at the woman, urging her to her feet. The woman shook her head and huddled in on herself.

"Come on," said Megan, forcing her hands under the woman's armpits and heaving. "The witches'll be here in a few minutes."

"Let them take me. I'd rather be dead and with God than here and scared without hope."

Megan tried to drag her, but the woman was heavier than she could bear without help or cooperation. Eleanor called her name and gestured toward the town. Megan gave the woman a final yank. She refused to budge. Megan abandoned her and dashed back to the others.

Soldiers in the brown uniform of the Realm appeared out of the orchard and headed toward them. They were moving at pace; some had even discarded their armor to help them go faster. Megan doubted they were doing so because they were eager to find the nearest pub in which to celebrate their victory.

She intercepted the guy at the front. He had a scar across his cheek that wept fresh blood. "What happened?" she asked. He gave her a blank look and swatted her aside.

The other soldiers followed him, charging into town. More burst out of the orchard and headed after them. One stumbled and sprawled to the ground. Megan was about to scream at the others to help him up when she saw the crossbow bolt sticking out of his back.

Eleanor grabbed her hand. Now it was Megan's turn to be urged on. She stumbled alongside the countess for a few steps before jerking to a halt.

"Wait! Where're Damon and Afreyda?"

"I sent them on to the marina," said Eleanor. "That's where we should—get behind me!"

A witch was poking out of the distant trees, aiming a crossbow. Megan threw herself to the road. A crossbow bolt whistled over her head. Eleanor notched an arrow and let fly. Megan looked up. The soldier staggered away, an arrow sticking out of his shoulder.

More soldiers from both sides poured out through the orchard. Megan ran after Eleanor as she hurried into town, struggling to keep up with the long-legged countess. Citizens overburdened with valuables floundered in the streets, knowing they had to run but not knowing where to. The witches' guns were getting closer: one hit a cottage roof, which erupted in a shower of splinters and thatch that fluttered to the ground like burned snowflakes.

Someone grabbed Megan's arm. She flailed and turned around to curse her assailant, only to find Loretta trembling there. Edwyn was screaming at her chest, demanding the war pause so he could nap.

"They're gone," jabbered Loretta. "I looked everywhere but I can't find them. I told them to stay with me but they ran off. They always run off. You think they'd have learned by now, but no . . ."

"Calm down," said Megan. "Where did you last see them?"

"That way," said Loretta, pointing down an alley.

Megan dithered. Eleanor had vanished into the crowd. No matter, she'd soon find them again: just follow the panic. "All right. Come on."

She dashed down the alley, calling out the children's names. Where would you hide if you were a scared kid who'd experienced more battles than a hardened soldier? She bounced between walls and fences, jumping to look over them. No telltale motion, no giveaway whimpering.

Loretta followed, her baby's cries wavering as her motion bounced him up and down. "There!" she shouted. "They're down there!"

"What?" said Megan. "Where?" Loretta pointed at the side of a building. Cellar doors gaped open. "I didn't—"

"I saw them!"

Megan peered down into the darkness. She recalled another cellar, where the landlord of an inn had eviscerated a boy in imitation of what some crazy priest had dreamed were the witches' rites. No smell of blood this time, just mustiness and a whiff of spoiled food.

"Isen!" she called. "Audrey!"

No answer. "They're too scared to answer," said Loretta. "We need to go down."

Megan wasn't sure where this "we" had come from, but she poked out an experimental foot. The steps were solid enough. One of the advantages of living in a well-to-do town. You wouldn't want a vintner breaking his neck restocking your wine cellar.

The cacophony of battle became more and more muffled as Megan descended. By the time she got to the bottom, it was just a murmur, a background noise you could convince yourself didn't matter. It was pitch black, the light from the outside restricting itself to a narrow rectangle as if afraid to venture further.

"Isen, Audrey," she said in what she hoped was a soothing voice, "I'm here with your mother. Everything's going to be all right."

Something smacked into Megan's head and sent her sprawling.

Fifteen

The world flashed strange colors. Damp flagstones scraped Megan's palms. Her stomach convulsed. Bile scorched her throat and spattered on to the ground. She tried to push herself back up, but another wave of nausea hit her.

What had happened? Footsteps scampered in the darkness and an undersized foot kicked her in the mouth. Sparks flashed in front of her eyes. She tasted blood.

"You killed my daddy!"

Megan struck out blindly, but only swatted musty air. Two sets of small fingers grabbed her wrists and forced them together. Twine bit into her skin, gripping her in a scratchy embrace.

"That's it, Isen," said Loretta. Her distress had evaporated. "Like I showed you. Nice and tight."

"What the hell?"

"Don't swear in front of my children."

Megan wriggled, struggling against her bonds. Her elbow hit bony flesh. There was a pause, then a wail filled the cellar.

"Mommy!"

"Shush, Isen," said Loretta. "Here, hold your little brother a moment."

The lightning flashing around Megan's brain subsided. She struggled to her feet, an awkward procedure with her hands restrained. Silhouetted against the column of light streaming down from the outside, she saw Loretta hand her baby over to her son.

"I'm getting out of here," she said, stumbling toward them. "I don't want to hurt you, but if you try to stop—whoa!"

Loretta had tucked Isen behind her and produced a knife: the stiletto Megan had given her. Megan found herself backtracking as Loretta stalked toward her. She thudded into a pillar. Slivers of rotten wood crumbled against her arm.

"We know who you are," whispered Loretta, holding her knife up to Megan's face. The razor-sharp blade was a slash of silver in the black. "We know what you did to us. You're responsible for all this."

"I . . ." Megan choked off her denial, not sure what she should be denying. Cate—did she know about Cate? The questions she'd asked: had she been pumping her for information? "I don't know what you're talking about. I've done nothing but help you. You'd be dead if it wasn't for me."

"Trying to salve your conscience?" Loretta's breath was hot and humid against Megan's cheek. "The witches wouldn't have come back to the Realm if it wasn't for you. My husband would still be alive. My children would still have a father."

Megan forced herself to be calm even though her heart was racing. "I don't know what you've heard," she said, trying to sound conciliatory, "but none of this was my fault. You have to—"

The knife flashed through the air. Megan cringed as it stuck into the pillar by the side of her head. "It's your fault he's dead!" screeched Loretta.

"Killing me won't bring him back."

"No, but giving you to the witches will keep my children safe."

"What?"

Loretta tugged at her knife, trying to dislodge it from the pillar. It had embedded itself with some force in the wood. "They'll soon be here," she said, grunting with exertion, "and when they are, you're theirs." Her other hand came to help the first. "They'll give me anything I want."

"I'm sorry."

"Thought you said it wasn't your fault."

"No," said Megan, "but this is."

She smashed her forehead against Loretta's nose. Cartilage cracked. Warm blood spurted on to her face. Loretta hollered and reeled backward.

Megan launched herself at the exit. Isen screamed and ran at her. She shoulder-charged him out of the way, wincing as his puny frame smacked into the flagstones, suppressing the urge to stop and check on him.

She reached the stairs. The world darkened. Someone had stepped in front of the exit. No, more than one someone.

A child squeezed between their legs. Loretta's daughter, Audrey. "There she is, sir," she said, pointing down. "The girl you're looking for. Megan."

Megan backed off, wrists twisting in vain as she tried to escape her bonds. Audrey skipped down the steps into the cellar, leading the witches in single file as if doing nothing more than showing off a painting she had done. The witches, three in total, were grim, grimmer even than men threatened with children's art, the clomp of their heavy boots echoing around the enclosed space like the thump of a funeral drum.

Megan recognized the lead—the witch captain, Tobrytan. He bent down to Audrey. "You've done well, little one." He pointed to Loretta and Isen, huddled against some barrels. "Is that your family? Go on over to them."

He turned to Megan. "Where is the Savior?"

"I'll die before I tell you."

"You know how many times I've heard that promise?" said Tobrytan.

"A few?"

"You know how many times it's been kept?"

"No."

"Never."

Megan swallowed. *I'm going to be the first one*, she thought, *because I really don't have anything to tell you.* He would never believe her though, not until he'd tortured the denial out of her.

"Isn't there some proscription about hurting the mother of the Savior?"

"No."

Megan rolled with the anticipated blow—a contemptuous backhand—and collapsed to the floor in a controlled fall. She curled up, not solely as protection from the next blow, but so she could reach the knife in her boot. Her fingers touched empty leather. Damn: she'd given that knife to Loretta. She checked the other boot. *There we are.*

"After everything you put me through, you think I'm going to talk after one little slap?"

Tobrytan hauled her to her feet. Hands hidden behind her back, she started to saw away at the rope binding her wrists. Damn, the little bastard had done a good job, and a stiletto wasn't the best blade for the job.

What she needed was something with teeth—
something like the serrated dagger Tobrytan had just
pulled out.

Alarmed, she scrambled backward. "Don't worry,"
said Tobrytan. "I'm going to put off hurting you. Your
sister wanted to watch anyway." He turned to Isen.
"Come here, little boy." Isen shook his head and buried
himself in his mother's arms. "I said *come here!*"

Reluctantly Isen broke away from Loretta, who
started to sob and sidled across the cellar toward
him. Tobrytan grabbed the boy as soon as he was in
range and dragged him close. He held the dagger to
his throat. Loretta screamed and dived for him. One
of the other witches intercepted her and sent her
sprawling.

"Why do you think I care what you do to him?" said
Megan, her sawing becoming ever more frantic. "They
sold me out."

"Where is the Savior?"

"Even you wouldn't hurt a child."

Tobrytan ruffled Isen's hair with his knuckles. "What
is the first Pledge, little one?"

"The . . . the what, sir?"

"The first Pledge of Faith. What is it? You look like a
clever little boy. You must know it."

"I pledge . . . I pledge to obey God and . . ."

"Go on."

". . . and His priests. Sir."

Tobrytan sneered at Megan. "The boy is not True." He rested the sharp blade against Isen's throat. "It doesn't matter if he lives or dies."

"He's a child. He doesn't know what he is. He does what his parents tell him."

"Then his parents condemn him."

"No!"

The rope came free. Megan flew at Tobrytan. He shoved Isen aside and brought his arms up to defend himself. Megan drew her arm back, prepared to thrust.

An almighty crash filled the air as the ceiling collapsed.

Megan waited until the last thud had subsided before she moved her arms from her head. Dust danced in the crisscrossing beams of light streaming from above. Planks and timbers stood at haphazard diagonals all around her. A smashed wine barrel glugged out its contents. A child began to wail. Hard to tell if it was a boy or a girl.

"Idiots!"

Tobrytan. Megan couldn't see him. The thought did remind her why she shouldn't be there. She looked around. A ceiling beam now led all the way up to the ground floor. She reached out, shook it. It seemed well jammed into its current position. She scrambled up it on all fours, hopped across a scrap of undamaged floor-board and threw herself outside.

The world swam as she sucked in fresh air, but she felt a little better. The ground trembled as guns fired nearby. All right, not that much better. The crying continued from below. Two distinct voices now. Megan hesitated, wondering whether to go back and help. No, she'd done enough, considering what they'd done to her. And her staying might put them at risk.

She stumbled around, trying to get her bearings. Which way had they come? She heard a commotion to her left. As good a direction as any. She hurried toward it. A mental alarm warned her the cause of the commotion wasn't necessarily friendly. She pressed herself against the wall. Figures dashed past the end of the alley. They didn't look like witches.

The crowd caught Megan as it surged along. They reached the marina. Out on the lake, some boats had already cast off, their sails billowing in the wind. People shoved and clambered over each other as they fought to get on to the remaining vessels. Some soldiers used their authority to impose some kind of order; others pulled rank to move themselves to the top of the evacuation list.

Someone barged Megan as they dashed past, almost knocking her into the water. She teetered on the edge before someone else dragged her back.

"You're not that good a swimmer," said Eleanor. Her brow wrinkled in concern as she took in Megan's appearance. "What the hell happened to you?"

"The witches have reached the city," said Megan. "Where're the others?"

"I assume they're waiting for us."

"You assume?"

"I was too busy looking for you to worry about them."

They rushed from jetty to jetty searching for Damon and Afreyda, pushing their way through the crowd who, fearful someone was stealing a march on them, pushed back. Palms slapped cheeks, elbows jabbed ribs, feet kicked ankles. All the while, guns boomed, masonry fell and steel rang upon steel as the witches' vanguard met the Realm's rearguard.

They reached the last jetty, where a harassed corporal was trying to control the boarding of a luxury yacht. "They're not here," said Eleanor, having to raise her voice over the hubbub. "They must have already sailed."

Megan shook her head. "They'd wait for us."

"Really?"

"All right, Damon might not, but Afreyda would."

The lake erupted into a wall of foam that saturated everyone on the pier. When the deluge abated, they saw that a boat that had just cast off had a hole gouged in its stern. It was taking on water. The crew started to turn it back to shore but some of the passengers took matters into their own hands and threw themselves overboard.

The gunfire had thinned the crowd, both by encouraging the lines for the outgoing boats to move even faster and panicking some people into fleeing further down the shore. There was still no sign of Damon or Afreyda. Megan clattered down the jetty calling their names at the top of her voice. A couple bustled by. She grabbed them.

"Have you seen my friends?" she asked. "A man with blond hair and a girl with dark skin?" They shook their heads and pushed past her, whether they hadn't seen them or weren't willing to delay unclear.

None of the other refugees had seen Damon or Afreyda either; some at least had the decency to look sorrowful when they gave her the bad news. Eleanor had gone in the opposite direction, but a shake of the head indicated she was having no more luck than Megan.

The thunder of guns was becoming deafening. Another couple of balls crashed into the lake, sending water cascading over the jetty. Out of the corner of her eye, Megan saw the corporal urging her back to the pier. The yacht, low in the water, was getting ready to leave. She looked down the length of the marina. All the others had left. It was their last chance.

She rushed to the jetty, almost colliding with Eleanor in the process. "They must have got on one of the other boats," shouted the countess.

"You sure?"

"We can rely on Damon's instinct for self-preservation. We'll see them on the other side."

The last of the refugees—an imperious woman, all bosom and gaudy jewelry—was arguing with the corporal, trying to persuade him to let her take on board a massive trunk her two servants were straining to carry.

"We can't afford to take on any extra weight, ma'am."

The woman was shrill with indignation. "This crockery has been in my family for generations. The teapot was a wedding gift from Edwyn the Fourth himself."

There was a shout behind them. The pier rattled to the thud of footsteps. It was Aldred and three of his men. One of them—Norvel, the soldier Afreyda had seen to—had a bandage wrapped around his head and a bloody patch where his eye should have been.

Eleanor moved to embrace Aldred, but he held her off. "We need to get out of here," he said. "What's the hold-up, Corporal . . . ?"

"Corporal Eddy, sir." He waved at the woman and her luggage. "Too big."

"It's probably a bit too late to get her to diet."

"The luggage, sir."

Aldred motioned to his men. They grabbed the trunk from the servants and heaved it over the edge. It hit the water with an almighty splash that had everyone ducking.

"What!"

"It's all right, ma'am," said Eddy. "Porcelain doesn't rust. You'll be able to retrieve it when we come back." He started to unwind the rope securing the yacht. "If we make it back. All aboard!"

They leaped across to the yacht. There wasn't much deck space left, and Megan clattered into a group of people. She muttered an apology that was gracelessly received.

Eddy finished unwinding the rope and threw the coil on to the deck. The boat began to pull away like a dog let off its leash eager to join its pack, albeit a very fat and arthritic dog. Alarmed, the corporal launched himself off the jetty. He misjudged his jump and smacked into the boat's hull. Aldred's men caught him before he slid into the water.

The yacht picked up momentum and cleared the marina. Back in Kewley, a glow licked the rooftops of a villa as a fire started up. Two figures emerged from town, rushing toward them and waving frantically. Too late now. They'd have to take their chances with the witches.

The two bolted down the jetty. A claw squeezed Megan's heart as she recognized Damon and Afreyda pleading for them to come back. She shook Eleanor and pointed. "We have to turn the boat around!"

"What . . . ?" The countess looked out, back to shore. "They'll have to swim for it. We're not going to get this—"

"Afreyda can't swim!"

The expanse of water between the jetty and the boat was growing ever larger. Megan threw her cloak off and began to tug at her jerkin. "What are you doing?" said Eleanor.

"I'm going back there. I'll bring her across."

"Are you crazy? You'll never catch up with us, even if you didn't have to drag another person along with you."

Black-armored soldiers poured out of the town like flies bursting from a corpse. "We can't leave her to Damon," said Megan. "He can barely doggy—"

Booms cracked across the lake. Water erupted in a wall of spray. By the time it settled, Damon and Afreyda had disappeared.

Sixteen

The boat cut through the lake with a hiss. On deck, some congratulated themselves on their escape and convinced themselves they had won a great victory; others, realizing what they had lost, stared back over the water with the faraway gaze of the grieving. Megan was among the latter, hanging over the bulwarks, hoping beyond hope some ship would appear on the horizon and Damon would wave at her with a cocky grin while Afreyda stood stoically beside him.

Eleanor slipped in beside her and placed a hand on her shoulder. Megan pulled away. She still blamed the countess for refusing to turn back, even though she knew to have done so would have been presenting themselves to the witches. Eleanor took the rejection with good grace and leaned on the side of the ship. Her hair blew in her face like flames licking a marble statue.

"The fleet's heading east," she said. "They'll dock at Stratton and the army'll take the road across Gerland to Janik. And stop playing with your ear. You'll make it bleed."

Megan hadn't realized she was. "How long will it take us to get back to Kewley?"

"What?"

"We have to go back for them," said Megan. "Damon and Afreyda."

"I'm not taking you back there. The place is crawling with witches."

"Who says I need you to take me?"

"Megan, think about what you're saying. You're going to walk back into Kewley and do what? Wander the streets calling their names as if you'd lost a pair of puppies?"

"You went back to Eastport for *your* friend. Would it help if Damon and Afreyda had a fortune?"

"We have no choice."

"You can't get to be queen if you're dead, huh?"

"This isn't about that," said Eleanor. "This is about keeping you safe."

They were abandoning their friends and running. It was pathetic and cowardly and absolutely their only choice. Eleanor might claim it was her duty to keep Megan safe, but in reality it was the other way around. The countess was her only sure link to Cate; Megan had to keep her alive. She could ask for the information, of course, and Eleanor might even give it to her, but then Megan wouldn't be able to resist going after her daughter. And if she did that, who knew who'd be following in their wake?

The boat hit a swell, throwing Megan along the bulwark into Eleanor's arms. She allowed herself to be held for a moment, fighting the urge to huddle in the countess's embrace and lose herself to the despair. She broke away, straightened, directed her attention from south to east, away from Kewley and the friends she had abandoned.

"Is it safe in Janik?" she asked.

"It's up in the hills," said Eleanor. "Pretty defensible. We're not going there though."

"We're not?" said Megan.

"We're going to Hil."

The largest of the five Snow Cities. "What makes you think they'll give us sanctuary?" asked Megan. "Why wouldn't they kill us on the spot or let us freeze to death on the mountains?"

Eleanor pressed against the bulwark as a passenger squeezed past. "I have family there."

"You what?"

"My aunt is married to the Lord Defender or Lord Decapitator or whoever makes sure the brutes don't kill each other."

"You've never mentioned her."

"I've never met her," said Eleanor. "My mother's father, Lord Kalvert, married her off as a prelude to sealing an alliance. Well, that was the plan. The first war against the witches broke out shortly afterward. My grandfather went the way of the rest of the Kalverts."

"Why don't we stick with the army?" asked Megan.

"It'll be safer over the mountains."

"How safe?" She lowered her voice. "Safe enough for . . . ?"

"I don't know," said Eleanor. "Maybe."

Megan tried not to let hope overwhelm her. Eleanor had made similar promises about New Statham. "We could go for her on the way. It wouldn't be too much of a diversion, would it?"

"She's hidden, safe for now," said Eleanor. "I don't want to risk that if I don't have to. Besides, we don't know who here we can trust."

No, not after Loretta. Megan looked around at the passengers—some forcing humor, some giving in to grief, others dead-eyed in shock. How many of them would be prepared to give up her child to save their own? Wouldn't it be something Megan would be prepared to do, if it ever came to a last desperate choice?

Eleanor let the wind blow the hair from her face, then tied it up. "We need to get as much of a head start as possible. We can sail all the way up to Aedran and head north from there." She slipped a knife from her belt. "Time to persuade the skipper to change course."

Megan grabbed her wrist and pushed the blade out of view. "And if he won't? You'll kill him?"

"Not necessarily."

"Is that what we've come to?"

"When did you get squeamish?" said Eleanor.

Megan held her gaze. Eleanor sighed and sheathed the knife. "All right. I'll smile and ask nicely."

It turned out the smiling was for Aldred's benefit and she had asked him nicely to threaten the skipper on her behalf. The passengers raised a commotion when they realized they were leaving the rest of the fleet behind, which Aldred and the men under his command quieted with a show of weapons. As no one was hurt, Megan restricted her complaints to a scowl Eleanor pretended not to comprehend.

Aedran was at the northern point of Lake Pullar, a small town given to fishing and coordinating the trade of the local farmers. It was late evening when they reached it. A mob gathered on the dockside to greet them, their torchlight guiding the boat to a jetty. They wielded a variety of weapons: axes, butcher's knives, gardening implements brandished in a way that suggested a floral border wasn't on the agenda.

Megan, Eleanor and Aldred hopped on to the pier. The crowd made no effort to let them pass. "You're not welcome here," said a spokesman.

"Please," said Megan. "We've been traveling for days. Some of us for weeks."

"Another day or two that way—" the spokesman pointed out to the lake "—won't bother you too much then."

Aldred drew his sword. "I've had enough of this." In response, the mob raised its weapons, which made up in quantity what they lacked in quality. In response to that response, Aldred's quartet of soldiers leaped over from the yacht and brandished their swords.

The crowd shuffled back a step but kept its shape. "Take your war elsewhere."

"It's your war, too," said Megan. "Or have you opted out of the fifth Pledge?"

An approaching voice sounded out from beyond the crowd. "Don't think to lecture us on the Faith, child."

An aisle formed to admit a priest. He was old—in his sixties perhaps—but he strode toward them with a surety of purpose. Straggly white hair dangled from his bald pate like ragged curtains. A deep scar down his left cheek made his face look as if it had come in mismatched pieces.

"It is your duty to help us, brother," said Megan.

"It's *Father* Broose."

"This place has a High Priest?" said Eleanor, a note of skepticism in her voice. Even from where they stood, the town was small enough they could see from one end to the other.

"It does now," said Father Broose.

"Isn't that taking self-promotion a little too literally?"

"I have a duty to keep the Faithful under my protection safe. We have no quarrel with the True, no weapons." Eleanor exaggerated an examination of the sharp implements pointed in their direction. "No weapons of war. The True have no reason to harm us. If we shelter *soldiers*—" the word was pronounced with the contempt usually reserved for taxmen, murderers and poets "—they soon will have."

"One night," said Megan. "That's all we ask."

"And tomorrow?"

"We leave."

"For . . . ?"

Megan looked to Eleanor, unsure how much to reveal.

"Hil," said the countess.

"You're going to the Snow Cities?"

"Only one of them. We weren't planning on a tour."

Megan stepped forward. "We can pay, father."

"You think gold makes a difference?" said Father Broose.

"I dunno," said an unidentified voice.

A titter rippled through crowd. Father Broose scowled, realizing he was losing his followers to the twin attractions of cash and mocking people. "Why am I negotiating with a slip of a girl anyway?"

Because everyone else is waiting to see if I get the pointy end of something, thought Megan. "We are negotiating then?"

"We—"

"What harm can one night do? The witches are hundreds of miles away."

Father Broose folded his hands across his belly and deliberated. Aldred whispered something to his soldiers, who closed around him. Eleanor wandered up the jetty: a nervous stroll or finding the best place from which to fire her arrows? Megan gripped the knife she had stashed in the back of her belt. She didn't want a fight, but she might have to cut her way out of the middle of one.

After an eternity, Father Broose spoke up. "Very well. One night."

Megan and Eleanor found a room in one of the inns, which cost them the price of a small palace. While they lined up for hot water, Megan fretted about Damon and Afreyda. Would they have made it out of Kewley? Surely a stealthy duo would succeed where a lumbering army had failed, and it wasn't as if Damon had no experience of fleeing. She prayed for their safety to God and the Saviors. She also asked Afreyda's ancestors to look after their daughter, hoping they wouldn't be offended by the lack of candles.

It was night by the time they got to wash. The landlady of the inn provided some food, which they took out to Aldred and his men, whom Father Broose had insisted stay on board the yacht. They made their way along the cobbled path by the lakeside, Eleanor lugging a pot of stew, Megan trying to keep a stack of wooden bowls from clattering to the ground. Shuttered windows tantalized with glimpses of carousing; walls muffled raucous laughter that tipped into bitterness; people staggered into dark alleys in ones and twos to answer various demands of nature. Everyone was trying to forget what had happened, clinging on to the life they had been granted.

As they reached the shoreline Father Broose stepped out to block their path. "Reduced to a soldier's strumpet, my lady?"

"Why does everyone use my titles as a term of abuse?" asked Eleanor.

"Something you might want to bear in mind," muttered Megan.

Eleanor flashed her a dirty look, then turned to Father Broose. "You know who I am?"

"I was at your parents' wedding in Statham," he said. Ceremonies held in Statham, where the Saviors appeared to the Unifier, were held to be the most auspicious, which meant only the richest could afford them; the locals had to troop up to New Statham if they wished to marry, name their children or bury their dead. "What a grotesque extravagance that was."

"Lot of priests in attendance, were there?"

"I was only an acolyte back then. I was ordered to attend."

There was a pause, then Eleanor asked, "What was she like? My mother?"

"Prettier than you," said Father Broose. He chuckled at Eleanor's scowl. "Maybe the prettiness of youth. Maybe something else." He shrugged. "It was a long time ago, before the True and all the wars."

"You called them the True," said Megan. "The witches."

"That is their name."

"Their name for themselves, not ours."

"And? I remember the True before my esteemed colleagues came up with their childish propaganda."

"You don't think we should be fighting them?"

"Do we fight all those who don't share our beliefs? Is that why you're going to the Snow Cities, to convert the pagans? God will punish those who reject Him in the afterlife. I concern myself only with the—"

"Shush!" hissed Eleanor.

"Is that your reaction to a well-reasoned argument?"

"There's a boat coming in."

"I can't—"

"What part of 'shush' do you not understand, father?"

The three stood stock still, holding their breath. There it was: the faint slap of oar against water. The skeleton of a small sailboat glided into the far end of the docks like a wraith flitting between shadows.

A drop of sweat trickled down Megan's spine. "Are you expecting anyone, father?"

"At this time of night? You? Any stragglers?"

Eleanor placed the pot of stew on the ground and unstrapped her bow. "They would have gone to Stratton."

The boat came to a halt. A slender, hooded figure hopped out on to the jetty. Father Broose hollered a hello. The newcomer craned his neck to look at them, but made no effort to return the greeting. Even in silhouette, Megan detected an insouciance to his stance. Eleanor fired. Only after the arrow speared into the water, well short of him, did the figure scamper down the jetty for the cover of the buildings.

The bowls slipped from Megan's fingers and hit the ground with the clatter of a distressed xylophone. She drew a knife and made to give chase. Eleanor grabbed her arm and pulled her back.

"Not on our own."

She hollered in the direction of their yacht. Five shapes detached themselves and rushed over. Aldred and his men.

"What is it?" he asked.

"We have a spy," said Eleanor.

"Are you sure?"

"Well, short of him holding up a sign saying: 'Spy here, please have your secrets open for inspection,' I'd say so."

The soldiers drew their weapons and dashed around the lakeside to the far jetty. Aldred jumped down to the boat tied up there. He stretched out the canvas that had wrapped itself to the mast.

"Black sails," he said. "Someone didn't want to be spotted."

"Told you it was a spy," said Eleanor.

"Or a fashion victim," said Megan.

Aldred clambered out of the boat. "We need to spread out and look for him. You—" he indicated the one-eyed soldier, Norvel "—escort the women back to their room."

"Like that's going to happen," said Megan. She strode down the jetty and banged on the door of the nearest building. "Everyone out!"

The others hurried after her. "What are you doing?" demanded Eleanor.

"You said we couldn't do this on our own. We can either creep around in the dark while this spy picks us off one by one, or we can get the whole town looking for him."

Townspeople and refugees surged through the town, filling the streets like floodwater. They searched every narrow alleyway, every abandoned outhouse, every dank cellar, every dusty attic. The spy was nowhere to be found. If it wasn't for the evidence of the boat and the corroboration of Eleanor and the others, Megan would have thought she'd imagined the whole thing.

Everyone drifted to the town square, which was littered with moldy cabbage leaves and rotten carrots from past markets. The landlord of the inn next to the temple—there was a man who knew his customers—hoisted out some barrels and began selling cider at an exorbitant mark-up. People started drinking, forgetting why they were there. Smoke drifted on the air as if someone had got a barbecue going.

"He must have already left," said Megan.

"If you're going to scarper, why not sail?" said Eleanor. "That boat of his looked pretty fast."

"You think he's still here?" Megan looked at the crowd milling around the square. "He could be anyone."

"We could always ask everybody if they're a spy," said Eleanor. Megan clambered on top of one of the cider barrels. "I wasn't serious!"

The landlord grabbed Megan's ankles. "Get down from there. You'll spoil it."

"It's cider," said Megan, shaking him off. "Muddy boots can only improve it." She cleared her throat. "Hello!" she shouted. Everyone ignored her.

She bent down. "How do I get their attention?" she asked Eleanor.

"Flash them?"

"Seriously?"

Eleanor whistled. "Free beer!" she yelled. The landlord almost keeled over in shock. "But first . . ."

Megan took the prompt. "We need everyone to hold hands with someone they recognize." There was a mumble of discontent. "We need to make sure the spy isn't one of us."

The people began to coagulate, reluctantly at first, then with more vigor as Father Broose strode through them, clapping his hands and exhorting them to group up. Megan stayed on the barrel, keeping an eye on the perimeter and watching for anyone sneaking off. So far, the promise of free booze was keeping everyone in the square.

One old man pulled away from another who was trying to grab his hand. "Get off me! I don't know you."

"Sure you do, Frank."

"Never seen you before in my life."

"We're brothers."

"News to me."

"*Twin* brothers."

Father Broose stepped in to sort out the family dispute.

Everyone had now got into clumps. There was just one person left on her own: a young woman with black hair, a boyish figure and an increasingly alarmed expression. She darted from person to person, tugging at their sleeves and imploring them to vouch for her.

Megan hopped off the barrel and approached her. "Who are you?"

The woman swallowed and shrank into herself. Her eyes darted around as if looking for permission not to answer the question. "I'm not a spy."

"What's your name? Where're you from?" Her skin was a few shades darker than Megan's olive. Not the complexion of someone from this far north.

"Clover. I was a serving girl in Eastport."

Megan considered the woman. She could be mistaken for a man at range. Her woolen shirt and pants were anonymous enough. She wore no hood or cloak, but they could have easily been abandoned.

Aldred and his men formed a circle around Megan and Clover. "Does anyone know this woman?" he demanded. "Well? Anyone?"

No one was looking at him. They were all staring at the temple, eyes wide, jaws slack. Wisps of smoke were seeping through the gaps in the temple brickwork. The building was on fire.

Father Broose barked orders. The crowd jolted out of its rapture. Some citizens rushed into the temple, wielding cloaks they'd ripped off their backs or, more often, other people's backs. Others grabbed buckets and pots and anything else that could hold water and formed a chain down to the lake. One enterprising man—a connoisseur, Megan assumed—grabbed a half-full barrel of cider and heaved it through a window.

Megan joined the water chain, passing vessels up and down the line until the action numbed her. Her palms were raw, her shoulders throbbing. The guy next to her failed to pass her one bucket properly. It tipped, drenching her feet. If she'd had the energy, she would have clobbered him over the head with it.

Eventually Father Broose sounded the all-clear. One tower and the cellar under it had suffered fire damage; the rest had escaped unscathed. They were lucky they'd spotted it in time. Any normal night and most people would have been tucked up indoors.

Exhausted, the crowd dispersed to their homes, whether permanent or temporary. Megan found Eleanor and rested her head against the countess's shoulder. "I need bed," she said.

"Aren't you forgetting something?" said Eleanor.

"I think I'll be able to sleep through even your snoring."

"The spy."

"He came, he inflamed, he ran off," said Megan.

"You think he came all this way to burn a single temple?"

"The witches want to scare us, make a point."

"Maybe . . ." Eleanor squeezed Megan's shoulders. "Aldred's got his men watching the docks and the roads."

"Ooh, a cordon of five. No one's going to break that."

"Four. Aldred's placed that . . . wait. What happened to the girl? Clover?"

"I don't know," said Megan. "I lost track of her in the confusion." She looked around. The square was deserted. "How could she have started a fire when we were busy accusing her?"

"It began in the basement," said Eleanor. "It could have smoldered for ages before spreading. If she is a witch spy, she's seen your face."

"And if she knows who I am," said Megan, horror creeping over her, "she'll be wanting to get the news back to Gwyneth."

"Fastest way'd be by carrier pigeon." Eleanor spun on her heel. "The temple."

Megan made the sign of the circle as they crossed the temple threshold. Water sloshed around her feet. The smell of charring brought back unwelcome memories, of finding her grandfather dead and her home a burned shell. Above their heads, tiers of seating stepped down, the underside of the seats in the bowl of the interior. Megan thought she heard people up there, but it was only the timbers creaking, recovering from their trauma.

"I don't understand," she said. "Why burn the temple if she needed the birds?"

"It was only a small fire," said Eleanor, "and she probably wouldn't have realized she'd need them so urgently at the time. Not until you climbed on high and showed yourself off to the world."

"Someone had to do something."

"It doesn't always have to be you."

But it did. "Where're these pigeons going to be then?"

"Why would you expect me to know something like that?" asked Eleanor. Megan shrugged. "However, if I was a guessing girl, I'd say the opposite tower to the one that got set on fire."

"But you said—"

"She's not going to *willfully* cut off an option, is she?"

They hurried around the temple, their footsteps echoing off the walls, their shadows dancing as they passed the lanterns that lit the perimeter corridor. Father Broose was sprawled at the bottom of the staircase that wound its way up the far tower. Blood was trickling from his ear. Beside him, a wine bottle bathed in its own contents.

Eleanor pressed her fingers to his throat. "He's got a pulse," she said, keeping her voice low.

"Looks like we were right."

"I don't know. Lots of reasons someone might want to clobber a priest." Eleanor went for her bow, considered the narrow steps and drew her sword instead. "Stay behind me."

"You're expecting me to object and insist on leading, aren't you?"

"It'd be nice if you at least made the offer."

They tried creeping up the stairs, but the ancient risers squealed like a cat disturbed from its sleep, so they dashed up them instead. Or, rather, they tried to dash up them. After the night's exertions, they barely made it up a story before they were reduced to wheezing wrecks.

"If she puts up the slightest fight," gasped Megan, "we're dead."

They took it more slowly, and by the time they reached the top they'd regained a little of their breath. A trapdoor streaked with bird excrement blocked their path. They crouched under it. Above their heads came cooing and the fluttering of wings. Eleanor reached up and gave the trapdoor an experimental push. It rose an inch. The bird noise got louder. "Ready?" she mouthed. Megan nodded.

Eleanor flung the trapdoor open and threw herself into the loft above. Megan scrambled after her but tripped over the last step in her haste. Clover whirled around, catching an ink bottle with her elbow. It glugged its contents over the rickety table at which she'd been writing.

She had a pigeon clutched in both hands, its head bobbing back and forth as if to some private beat. Eleanor swiped at it with her sword. Clover pulled the bird out of the way and rolled across the attic. The other birds batted their wings against the cages, calling out in alarm.

Megan picked herself up and charged across the loft. Clover had far less distance to cover. She reached one of the open windows and threw the pigeon out. It flailed, then found its rhythm.

"It's too late, Mother," said Clover. "We're coming."

Seventeen

Eleanor shoved Clover aside and drew her bow, but by the time she fired the pigeon was lost against the night sky and the arrow arced harmlessly over the town. Clover slipped a hand under her shirt and produced a knife. She lunged for Eleanor. Before Megan could shout a warning, Eleanor twirled her bow and cracked Clover under the chin. The spy staggered. Megan leaped on her and smashed the knife out of her hand.

Clover went limp, offering no resistance. Megan let her go and took a step back. Clover knelt. She made the sign of the star-broken circle above her heart and dropped her head. Loose shutters banged against the tower walls. Birds continued to coo in agitation. Wind whistled in through the windows, chilling Megan's sweat-lined skin. She knew what she had to do, but could she?

Eleanor placed her bow on the floor and picked up the sword she had abandoned. She took a step toward Clover and raised the blade.

"Those who deceive you will not win, Mother," said Clover. "We shall find the Savior and the world will be healed."

"Leave my child out of this."

Clover looked up. Moonlight swam in her damp eyes. "He was a gift from God. It is your duty to share him with the world. When he leads us, the dark will dissipate and there will be no more suffering."

There was no show to Clover's words, no priestly declamations. They were simple, matter of fact, seductively so. One could almost believe they were as true as claims that night followed day or rivers ran into the sea. *Is it what you want, Gwyneth, or what you exploit?*

There was a wheezing, groaning sound. Father Broose hauled himself into the loft and collapsed in a heap against the wall. He scraped flakes of dry blood from his ear with his fingernail.

"I seem to have the hangover from the wine without the preceding benefits." He took in the scene. "You found your spy. Why does she still have her head?"

"You're very bloodthirsty for someone who doesn't think we should be fighting the witches," said Megan. "Have matters changed now the war isn't just happening to other people?"

"My head is still woozy. I thought you sounded disrespectful."

"I'm sorry, father. We should try her properly." *And absolve me of the responsibility of killing her in cold blood.*

"I already have," said Father Broose, the only judicial authority for miles around. "She's guilty."

"I don't think you're that impartial in this matter," said Eleanor. "It was you she hit, your temple she tried to burn."

"Fine, release her. Once the mob discovers who she is, they'll carry out the sentence. Only they won't be as clean as a sword."

Why couldn't Megan execute Clover? Because her angelic features reminded her of Afreyda? Because Megan didn't have the courage to strike without fear coursing through her veins? Because she secretly thrilled at the idea of someone revering her?

"I won't let them harm her," she said.

"I'm sure they'll respect your authority."

The priest was right. The only person she had any power over was her enemy. "They'll respect yours though, father."

"You wish me to take her into custody?" said Father Broose. "There are no dungeons in Aedran."

"That's all right," said Megan. "We're not stopping. Any of us."

"I am not leaving."

"The witches are on their way, father. Do you want to trust to their mercy?"

"Those who do not accept the way of the True must perish," added Clover.

Father Broose scowled. "I'll start organizing the evacuation at sunrise." He headed for the trapdoor. "I'd advise you to tie her up."

Eleanor ripped a strip off Clover's shirt. Clover remained meek as her wrists were bound. "Why did you spare me, Mother?"

In the end, the answer was simple. "Because Gwyneth wouldn't have."

Dawn brought frantic activity as people flung everything that could be carried on to anything that could carry, from boats and pack animals to handcarts and their own backs. Destinations were picked with varying degrees of certainty and viability: the villages of relatives and long-forgotten friends; over to Janik, where the remnants of the priests' army was heading; the faraway counties of Percadia and Levenshire, which gained mythical status as sanctuaries in a few short hours; sometimes simply "east" or "west." Wherever the witches weren't had to be better than somewhere they were going to be very soon.

Megan had wanted to leave at first light. Father Broose persuaded her not to. Some townspeople and some from the yacht had opted to flee for the Snow Cities, and surely it was best they stick together? Megan knew what that meant. He needed their protection, or rather that of Aldred and his men. She couldn't refuse him—she owed him for Clover; she owed them for dragging them into this.

Aldred called Norvel forward and handed him the reins of a horse. "I want you to stay here, keep an eye out for the witches."

"Not funny, sir," said Norvel, his hand going to the grubby bandage around his head, which still wept blood.

"Give it a couple of days, then catch up with us."

"And what about the . . . supplies, sir?"

"Everyone'll get their share."

They streamed out of Aedran, a couple of hundred people picking their way along the overgrown path that led north. Running from the witches: an all-too-familiar process for Megan. But she'd never run to the unknown before. Even if they did make it to the Kartik Mountains, who knew what kind of reception they'd get? The Realm wasn't exactly awash with tales of the Snow Cities' hospitality. Tales of their brutality, cruelty and even cannibalism—they were legion. Megan really hoped Eleanor knew what she was doing.

She kept Clover close to her and Eleanor. People had jeered and spat at her and called for her to be strung up and her insides ripped out, but no one was willing to be the first to break Father Broose's command or test if Megan's knives were strictly for show. Clover bore all this with the stoicism of a penitent. Only the flicker of an eye or the twitch of a cheek told Megan she hadn't retreated to the safety of madness.

As dusk was falling on the fourth day out of Kewley, they reached a farm and opted to camp there, commandeering the buildings. The farmer's wife fed them, albeit with all the hospitality of a prison warder. Then Father Broose placed a lacquered wooden box on the kitchen table. The sign of the circle was etched into its lid in now-fading gold leaf. He unlocked it and rummaged through a number of scrolls inside. He found the one he was looking for and laid it out on the table. It was a map.

"We have to make a decision," he said. "East or west."

"We're going . . ." Megan jabbed a finger upward.

"The Smallwood marshes are that way. We have to go around them. If we go east, we might find ourselves running into the True if they ride around Lake Pullar. If we go west, it'll take longer, but it'll be safer."

"Unless the witches ride around the other way," said Eleanor.

"It's further, and they'd have to cross the Rustway."

"And they wouldn't run into the remnants of the army between Stratton and Janik," said Eleanor. "They'll be coming as fast as they can. They might not be able to move their guns in time, unless they can find some ships to take them across the lake."

"Why?" asked Father Broose.

"They're heavy. You need a—"

"Why would they be coming as fast as they can?"

Eleanor glanced at Megan. "Um . . ."

"Are the True so eager to dispatch all their enemies?" Father Broose leaned in to Eleanor. "Or one in
particular?"

"I . . . My father led the first war against them and the
witches do know how to bear a grudge."

"Your presence is endangering us."

"No one forced you to come with us."

"You should surrender to them," said Father Broose.
"Sacrifice yourself for the sake of the people you
exploited over the centuries." Eleanor reddened. "Why
the council let you live is beyond me." His gaze flicked
over to Clover, who had been denied a seat and huddled in a corner. "Squeamishness always comes back to
haunt you."

Eleanor's hand drifted under the table. Megan feared
when she next saw it, it'd be hurling a blade in Father
Broose's direction. She slipped around the table and
placed herself between the two of them.

"We should go directly north," she said.

"I've already explained this, my child."

"You're telling me the marshes are impassable?"

"There are fumes," said the farmer's wife, who was
hovering by the stove with her husband. "Poison. You
won't make it out alive."

Megan examined the map. A thin line marking the
road led up from Aedran. It broke at the green smear
that represented Smallwood marshes, then continued
all the way up to the Kartik Mountains. The marshes

stretched east to west for what looked like a good hundred miles. North to south, though, seemed barely any distance. If it wasn't for them, they'd have a clear route to their destination. A few hours' journey versus days. Could they afford to waste that much time with the witches on their way?

She pointed at a sequence of red dots that bisected the marshes. "What's this?"

"The border," said Father Broose. "Separates Aedranshire from Baleyworth."

Megan understood now. "Aren't there customs posts between the counties?"

"To pay for the defense of the Realm."

That was working out well. "But there wouldn't be a post in the middle of an impassable marsh, would there?"

"It would be a bit of a punishment . . . Ah, I see."

"You have a route for smuggling, don't you?" Megan said to the farmers.

"Don't know what you're talking about," said the farmer.

"Not been used for years," his wife said over him. Her husband glared at her. She shrugged. "It's probably flooded by now. Fumed over."

"Fumed over?" said Megan.

"What happens when you have lots of fumes."

Megan looked to the table. "We're agreed then? We go through?"

"Because you said so?"

"I think you'll find that's how Megan defines agreement, father," said Eleanor.

The smell seeping from the marshes was insidious, as if the world was decomposing. The slimy vegetation looked infectious to the touch, as if it would cause you to molder away to a fungal sludge. The only sounds were the squelch of their footsteps and the bubbling of fetid pools. There had been dire warnings about not lighting torches lest the gas ignite, so the world was in a permanent gloom.

The farmer led them on, doubling back sometimes, other times shooting off at right angles. Only the hazy sun reassured them they were going in the right direction, but far more slowly than Megan had hoped. A few of the Aedran townspeople had refused to come along, citing reports of ethereal spirits that drained your will to live. Megan had yet to come across such ghosts. They weren't needed: the damp and the cold were doing their work for them.

Eleanor slapped her calf. "Something just hopped up my leg."

"Swamp toad," said the farmer. "Not dangerous. Good eating."

"Don't tell me . . ."

"You turn up unannounced, you get what you're given."

"I think I'm going to throw up."

"You don't like toad?" asked Megan.

Eleanor gave Megan the kind of look that could freeze volcanoes. "More anything with the word 'swamp' in its name."

"Too good for common food, are we?" said the farmer.

"Like you wouldn't believe," muttered Eleanor.

They reached a hill, an island of life amid the decay. There were a few rotten crates scattered around, remnants of the smuggling trade. Megan had a look in one. Whatever had been in it had decomposed to black mulch. A mulch that wasn't as static as she would have liked.

"We can rest here," the landlord said.

"How much further after this?" asked Megan.

"Another hour or two. Depending how much you dawdle."

The company collapsed on to the grass, which the horses set about converting to bare patches. It was good to feel solid ground, whether green or brown. Food was passed around, bottles opened. If she tried hard enough, Megan could almost fool herself into thinking this was no more than a camping trip.

"Have we got everyone?" asked Eleanor.

"Don't know," said Megan. "Is anyone missing?" Her yell was hollow. There was something missing from it, like a tune played on a cheap instrument. The swamp had swallowed the echo.

She received no response. "No one claims they're missing," she said.

Eleanor rolled her eyes. She pointed at the nearest tree, around which a group of people were sharing a flagon. "I'd better go see if I can spot any stragglers. You get lost in here, even the Saviors'll have a hard time finding you."

Eleanor shimmied up the tree and disappeared among the foliage. A few moments later, she made a sound that made Megan's heart sink.

"No . . ."

Eleanor dropped to the ground. "Cavalry squadron. Coming up to the entrance of the marshes."

"They might be ours," said Megan with an optimism she didn't feel. They were witches. Of course they were witches. Still hunting. And they always found her. "How'd they get here so fast?"

"I don't know," said Eleanor. "I'm sure if we wait for them to arrive, they'd be delighted to explain their itinerary."

There was much groaning at the interrupted rest, only partially quelled by the threat of impending death. "I don't see what the fuss is about," said Father Broose. "The swamp'll take the True."

"Good thing we haven't left a massive trail in our wake then," said Eleanor.

That spurred everyone on. They jostled each other down the hill, pushing and shoving as if a few yards gained on a neighbor would save them. One man plunged into the marshes without waiting for the farmer to show the way. A splash and a short-lived scream demonstrated the wisdom of that action. Aldred and a couple of his men went to drag him out. They came back empty-handed.

Progress was faster this time, but it brought carelessness. More and more people had to be reclaimed from the mud pools. One cart toppled over, its contents tipping out and sinking just slowly enough to encourage thoughts of salvage, but they had learned their lesson by now. Aldred cut the panicking horse free. It took four of them to calm it down, prevent it from galloping into the quagmire and suffering the same fate as its erstwhile burden.

It was getting hard to breathe. Flecks of light flitted in front of Megan's eyes. Were these the spirits the townspeople had feared? They didn't look scary, barely bigger than a grain of sand. She watched them dance for a bit. Eleanor rushed back and urged her forward.

The land became firmer, the paths wider, the air fresher. Megan's head cleared. They were going uphill, gently at first, then increasingly steeper. Reeds gave way to mossy rocks, mud path to gravel road.

They reached the top. In front of them the road disappeared into a distant line of trees. Behind and below them, the marshes stretched out, a thin mist sitting above them like condensed breath. The hill they had stopped at peeked out from the white. Tiny figures congregated on it. Men and horses.

"They're catching up," said Megan.

Gasps and prayers shot around the company. "You want to say that a bit louder?" said Eleanor. "Make sure you panic *every*body?"

"We have to take care of them."

"We won't win a direct fight," said Eleanor. "There are at least a dozen of them. Armed and armored."

"We won't have to," said Megan. She had realized what had caused her light-headedness the last half of their journey: the fumes the farmer's wife had mentioned were building up to dangerous levels.

"I knew this was coming," said Eleanor, shaking her head. "You can't resist, can you? What if they're on our side? What if they're coming to help?"

Megan looked at the refugees, exhausted and scared, then down on the marshes, where the mist was enveloping the advancing soldiers. Eleanor might be right, but could she take the chance, could she condemn the people to the witches' brutality? Maybe she should let someone else make the decision. She looked over at Father Broose. No, this was her idea. The witches were coming after her. She had to take the responsibility.

Megan scrambled on to one of the surviving carts. She rummaged around until she came across a stack of bottles. The glass was greasy to the touch. She uncorked one and sniffed. Olive oil. A small reminder of home.

She slashed strips off a blanket. Eleanor got the idea, tying the rags around her arrows and sloshing oil over them. They hurried over to a nearby outcropping. Eleanor notched one of her prepared arrows and held it out. Megan pulled out a flint and began striking it against her knife.

"Try and aim for halfway between here and that hill," she said. "It seemed thickest there."

"At this range, I'll be lucky to hit the ground."

Sparks rained down on the oil-soaked strips. They caught fire. Flames tasted the air. Eleanor aimed high and drew her string.

She yelped in pain and dropped the bow. Megan had to jump out of the way as the fire arrow tumbled to the ground.

"What the . . . ?"

Eleanor sucked her knuckles. "I burned my hand."

"You should have worn gloves."

"I know that *now*."

Eleanor pulled on the leather gloves she had stuck into her belt. She selected the second arrow and lit it from the smoldering remains of the first. Again she aimed, drew, gritting her teeth with the strain. The arrow quivered under the tension.

There was a deep hum. The arrow shot high in the air, slowed until it seemed to hover in the air like a hunting raptor, then dived, faster and faster, leaving an arc of fire in its wake.

The arrow disappeared into the mist. Megan feared she had miscalculated, that the stagnant waters had quenched the flame, then there was a *whoomp* she felt as much as heard. The whole of the marsh erupted into a sea of blue fire.

She didn't know if the screams she heard were real or imagined.

Eighteen

Wind whipped across the snow-capped mountains, reducing Megan's nose to a block of ice clinging to her face. Her body was expending so much energy shivering it barely had enough left to walk, but walk she must. It was either that or freeze to death on the rocks.

"This is the last time I let you pick our vacation destination," she muttered to Eleanor. Or rather tried to. Her lips were as compliant as two chunks of dead fish.

"I assume that was a complaint," said Eleanor. She seemed to be taking the cold in her stride. "It'll warm up once we get back to sea level." Megan pointed up the Kartiks and exaggerated her shivering. "Yes, all right, we do have to go a *little* higher . . ."

Their numbers had halved since the marshes, lost to the villages they had encountered along the way. Once they had escaped the witches, it was all too easy to forget the danger, to believe that sanctuary had been found and a weary journey was no longer necessary. Megan wished she could convince herself.

The road became nothing more than a smudge on the landscape as it climbed to the Arrowstorm Pass. There was no sign of snow up there at the moment; Megan assumed the weather was holding off until they got there. It was a route taken by many a would-be conqueror, and one usually retraced in short order. Those who held the mountains could pick off invaders with ease, and those they didn't, winter would defeat. Only the Unifier had ever made it through, proof of his divine favor if ever there was one.

An arrow skittered at their feet. The company gasped and took a step back. All except Eleanor. She regarded the arrow for a moment, then picked it up.

"This anyone's?" she asked. "No?"

She dropped it into her quiver. "Thanks for the gift!" she shouted into the mountains. "But we were hoping for something else."

The rocks shimmered. What had once been hard stone was now a squad of bearded men, clad in furs in irregular patterns of white, gray and black. Each of them had a bow trained on the refugees.

Father Broose bustled forward. "Do any of you savages speak Stathian?" An arrow whistled over his shoulder. He scuttled back to the safety of the crowd.

"Of course border guards speak the language of the people on the other side of the border," said Eleanor, retrieving the second arrow. "How else are they going to tell them to get lost?"

"Variations on a theme of 'Ug'?" said Megan.

Aldred brandished his sword. "Fire at us again and we'll—" His sword went flying as an arrow hit it.

"They're good," said Megan.

"This range," said Eleanor, "they weren't aiming for his sword."

She took a few steps forward and lowered her hood. The wind blew her hair out, a blaze of richness amidst the gray. "I am Eleanor of the house of Endalay, Countess of Ainsworth, Baroness of Laxton and Herth, First Lady of Kirkland, Overlord of the Spice Isles and Defender of the Southern Lands." She licked her lips. "I'm also the granddaughter of Lord Kalvert, heir to his lands, titles and treaties made in his name. I've come to pay my respects to my aunt, Marian, consort to the Lord Defender of Hil." She affected innocence. "You didn't get my letter?"

"Lady Marian is dead," shouted down one of the Hilites.

"I've come to pay my *last* respects to my Aunt Marian."

"She's been dead thirty years."

"Ah . . . Sorry?"

Two of the Hilites had a conference. The others remained still, their arrows trained on the company. They could pick off Megan and those at the head of the line in a few seconds flat, and that was just counting the ones they could see. She assumed there'd be more men hidden, waiting for the order to strike.

"You're allying yourself with the Snow Cities?" Father Broose said to Eleanor. "You're exploiting the war to stage a coup?"

"Hypocrisy is a vice that afflicts other people, isn't it, father?"

Megan pulled her aside. "Are we? Is this what it's all about? Have we come here so you can recruit an army to put yourself on the throne?"

"You're being silly," said Eleanor. "This is to get you and everyone else to safety." She looked up to the conferring Hilites. "Or to get us killed."

The Hilites made their way down, jumping from rock to rock with the assuredness of goats. This had to be a good sign, surely? Megan remembered tales of the wars against the Snow Cities, where the pagans would rip the throats of their enemies out with their teeth. She pulled her collar up.

The Hilites reached them. "Lady Rekka is now consort of the Lord Defender," said one of them.

"Am I related to her?"

The Hilite slid one of Eleanor's locks over his gloved finger. "Definitely," he said. "She is the daughter of Lady Marian and Lord Rokert."

Eleanor's brow crinkled. "Wouldn't that mean she married her own father? Not that I want to cast cultural aspersions."

"There've been a few Lord Defenders since Rokert. Vegar is the current one."

"And Rekka's not related to him?"

"Only by marriage." The Hilite looked down the line at the waiting company. "I'm Willas, captain of the guard. Who are all these people?"

"My retinue. This is Megan, my lady-in-waiting."

"The hell I am."

"I say 'lady' . . ."

Willas frowned. "You have a very large staff. Don't the priests rule in the Realm?"

"I think we're all agreed what a bad idea *that* was," said Eleanor. "Aren't we, father?" Father Broose scowled.

Eleanor swept her hand up toward the road. "Well, captain, shall we?"

Willas stepped away for another conference with his colleague. Megan pulled Eleanor aside in imitation. "Do you reckon they're going for it?"

"They were quick enough to accept my aunt's dowry. The least they can do is offer us a cup of tea and a bed for the night."

"And if they don't?"

"That's Rekka off my Saviors' Day list."

"Seriously."

Eleanor gave a little shrug. "We go back, I suppose. Strike out on our own and lose ourselves in the forest."

"Abandon everybody?"

"Might be better for them in the long run."

The conferences ended. "I'll have to ask you to surrender your weapons," said Willas.

Eleanor unstrapped her bow and quiver and thrust them at an unprepared Willas. "They were getting heavy anyway." She pointed up the mountain. "This way?"

They turned off before they got to the pass. Willas led them through a passage in the rocks just wide enough to accommodate their carts. The sun barely penetrated the gap, leaving the world in a half-light. At least they now had some shelter from the wind.

Megan got the impression the rocks were moving: that they were being watched. There was the patter of displaced gravel; the slap of leather; the scrape of metal on stone. Every time she thought she had a fix on a sound it disappeared.

"Was this a good idea?" she whispered to Eleanor.

"I think not marching into somewhere called the 'Arrowstorm Pass' eminently sensible."

"How do you know they aren't going to leave us here to die?"

"My family couldn't have pissed them off that much," said Eleanor. "Well, probably not. Anyway, if they wanted us dead they could have done it out there."

"This way's tidier. Doesn't leave corpses littering the mountains."

"You're in a happy mood."

"I'm waiting for everything to go wrong."

The passageway came to a stop at a wall of stone. The company halted, each person using the one in front as a brake. As Megan was at the head of the line, she found herself shoved into the wall.

"And so it begins," she said, peeling herself off the rocks.

Eleanor tapped Willas on the shoulder. "Um, captain, there seems to be a . . ."

"I'd step back if I were you."

There was a deep rumble, as if the mountain was clearing its throat. Megan and the others scrambled back. The wall split. Twin doors of stone-plated wood oak inched outward, like the jaws of a predator opening.

She pointed at the widening gap. "We're going through?"

"You don't want to go over," said Willas. "It's freaking freezing, even this time of year."

The sun reflected off the swinging doors, sweeping a band of light across the passage walls. Arrow slits were chiseled into rock face. Megan bent down and peeked into one. Someone winked back at her from the other side. She gave him a bemused wave.

The doors were open, exposing a maw that led deep into the mountain. Willas urged them forward. Megan took a tentative step over the threshold. She held her breath, scared to wake the monster. Lantern light glinted off the teeth of huge cogs, black and shiny with grease; a series of levers, each of which reached Megan's shoulder; and a group of men, panting and sweating with exertion.

"There's nothing symbolic about this," said Eleanor, peering down the tunnel that led into the darkness. More lanterns spaced at regular intervals marked the way, but they could combat no more than a fraction of the void. "How long will it take us?"

"Couple of days," said Willas. "We sent a bird over to Hil. They'll be expecting us."

"I assume we can get the horses through?"

"You'll have to walk them."

They advanced, their footsteps echoing until it sounded as if there was an army down there. Behind them, the doors slammed shut with the finality of a tomb being sealed. A feeling of security settled on Megan. *Try and get through there*, she gloated at the absent witches. Then she remembered who else was on the other side of the barrier—Damon, Afreyda, Cate—and her triumph dissipated.

* * *

It was a dead, cold underground. Unlike on the surface, where the wind seemed to be actively trying to rob every last scintilla of heat from your body, here the cold just *was*. Occasionally Megan would loiter by one of the lanterns, hold her face to the hot glass as close as she dared until someone bustled her along and claimed the prize for themselves.

"How long did it take you to dig this out?" she asked Willas.

"A while."

"Mines, I'm guessing," said Eleanor. "Some natural tunnels."

"Are you assessing our defensive capabilities, my lady?"

"Not in the way you think."

Hidden from the sky, Megan lost all sense of time. Was it day or night? She tried counting her strides, but it soon took longer to say the number in her head than it took to take the corresponding step and she abandoned that idea. Hours, minutes, seconds—they didn't exist down here. Like in heaven. Or hell.

They emerged into a vast cavern. Megan's head swam as she looked up. Stalactites, slick with water, drooped from the ceiling, giving the impression the rock was slowly melting. If it was, Megan and her descendants would be long gone when the mountains met their end. Only God would bear witness.

"We can rest here," said Willas. "It's drier this way. Watch out for *Kolida*."

"For what?"

"In your language, the Pit of Certain Death."

Megan had been concentrating so much on what was above her that she had neglected to look down. A chasm stretched across the middle of the chamber. She shuffled to it and peered over the edge. It fell away into infinity. She nudged a stone over the drop with her toe. If it hit the ground she didn't hear it.

"You might want to put a fence around this," she said to Willas.

"The proposal keeps getting lost in committee."

Willas led them to the edge of the chamber, where there was a path across the chasm that wasn't as wide as Megan would have preferred. She looked straight ahead, staring so hard at the back of Willas's neck she could make out the individual hairs, trying not to obsess about her foot slipping on wet rock, of slipping over the edge, of falling forever.

Barrels of fresh water, sacks of dried food and bundles of firewood were stacked against the cavern walls. "No beer or wine?" said Eleanor. "It'd keep better."

"We used to, but people kept getting into drunken pissing contests over the edge of *Kolida* and, well . . ."

Tiredness claimed them. They ate a joyless meal, shivering in the dank, and tried to get some rest before another day's long march.

Megan found herself in a semiconscious state, where she could see everything going on in the cavern but could do nothing to prevent it. Witches crawled out of the pit, their armor like a scarab's carapace, their mouths mandibles. They swarmed over the refugees, snapping at their flesh and reducing them to skeletons. Megan tried to scream a warning, but no sound came from her mouth. The witches heard her though. Hundreds of heads snapped around. They hissed and streamed toward her.

She shuddered awake. Beside her, Eleanor, like the rest of their party, snoozed contentedly. There was one person still up though. Clover was by the pit, contemplating the abyss.

Megan unfolded her stiff limbs and went over to her. "Long way down, huh?"

"Yes, Mother."

"Don't call me that." *Only one person can call me that, and I can't be with her.*

"I'm sorry, Mo—" Clover squirmed as she rubbed her tied wrists against each other. "I mean no disrespect."

"You're allowed to disrespect me. Everyone else does. I'm nothing special."

"You are the mother of the Savior."

"I'm the mother of an ordinary little girl," said Megan. "You fitted the facts to fulfill some vague prophecy, and if that fitting involved mass murder, well, so be it."

"God has given you a gift. The greatest He could."

"No more than He gives any parent."

Clover rubbed her wrists again. The skin was raw under the bonds, pinpricked with spots of blood. Megan slipped a knife out of her arm sheath. She sawed through the cloth strips, which fluttered into the pit.

"Am I free to go?" Clover asked, massaging her abused flesh.

"If you think they'll let you through . . ."

"What shall I do then?"

"Well, not killing us would be nice for a start." Of course, to the best of Megan's knowledge, Clover hadn't killed anyone, which was more than she could say about the other party in this conversation.

They managed another couple of hours' sleep. After a quick breakfast, and an opportunity for Megan and Eleanor to knead the cricks and knots from each other's bodies, they set off again. They were going downhill now; just a slight incline, but a little relief for Megan's aching muscles.

A breeze kissed her face. The light in front of them didn't belong to yet another lantern but to the sun. The realization gave her energy, propelled her through the last yards.

She burst out of the mountains and found herself on a ledge. Beneath her, pine-covered hills plunged down to an inlet whose silvery surface mirrored the mountains surrounding it. Buildings lined the water's edge on three sides, small as children's toys at this range, plumes of smoke streaming from their chimneys. Everything looked so fresh, so pure. Megan felt cleaner just looking at it.

"You know," said Eleanor, "for a Snow City I was expecting more . . ."

". . . snow?" said Willas. "Give it a few weeks."

They picked their way down a zigzagging road cut into the forest. The trees here weren't the gnarled, bent things of home, spreading any which way they pleased, but stood straight and tall like a regiment on inspection. Birds flapped in their branches, sending down showers of needles. A deer gamboled into their path, stared at them with sad eyes, then galloped away.

A welcome party waited for them at the bottom, clad in luxuriant furs. No need to guess which one was Rekka. Her hair draped across her shoulders like beaten copper, her skin pale and unblemished. She looked to be the same age as Eleanor, give or take a couple of years, and not dissimilar from her cousin. Her features were sharper though, as if abraded by the harsh northern winds.

Two men stood either side of her. To her left, a hulking brute with an ornamental chain hanging around his neck and enough facial hair to fill a mattress. The one on her right was middle-aged, with steel hair that brushed his collar, a close-cropped beard and eyes that refused to rest.

Rekka broke into a wide smile that might not have been entirely forced and embraced Eleanor. "Cousin! I can't tell you how wonderful it is to finally meet you."

Eleanor looked a little overwhelmed by her enthusiasm. "I was in the neighborhood," she said, regaining her composure.

Rekka propelled the hulk on her left forward. "This is my husband, Vegar." The man took Eleanor's hand and kissed it, or rather rubbed it with his whiskers and said something indecipherable. "Sorry," said Rekka, "he doesn't speak Stathian. Except for the swear words."

She indicated the man to her right. "This is Secretary Fordel. He encourages the scribes and stops the cooks from stealing the silverware."

Fordel bowed. "Sadly I fear nothing will stop the cooks' pilfering."

"Yes," said Rekka, "it is so hard to get the staff these days." She peered at the company gathered behind Eleanor, who were taking in the sights with an air of bewilderment. "You, however, don't seem to have that problem, cousin."

"We're not going to cause any bother, are we?" said Eleanor.

"Of course not. We'll just have to be creative with the sleeping arrangements. Fordel'll sort it out. He likes that kind of thing."

They made their way into Hil, through well-maintained streets that led past cabins of stone and timber. People stopped what they were doing—cooking, sewing, reading, butchering, tanning, woodworking—to gawk at the visitors. Schoolchildren hung out of windows and pointed, jabbering among themselves in a language Megan didn't recognize. One red-headed little girl barreled out, took one look at Eleanor and burst into tears.

Rekka scooped her up and comforted her. "My youngest," she said to Eleanor. The girl objected indignantly. "Sorry, second youngest. She thinks you're a mountain ghoul come to supplant me."

"Know the feeling," muttered Father Broose.

"Local legend. Nothing to worry about."

A couple of men crept out of one of the buildings. They were more roughly dressed than the rest of the population and, unusually, were clean shaven. Hunching over, they headed not for Rekka and Vegar, nor Eleanor and Megan, but Father Broose. They knelt before him and made the sign of the circle. Megan was confused. Hil and the Snow Cities had fought bitter wars to keep themselves independent of the Faith and the Realm. What were they doing here?

"Pay them no heed," said Rekka, making shooing motions. "It's not as if they're electors."

The kneelers held their ground. "We have prayed for your arrival, brother," one said to Father Broose.

"Words we thought we'd never hear," said Eleanor.

The priest beckoned them to stand. "Rise, my children. You follow the Faith?"

"As best we can, brother."

"It's *Father* Broose."

"We do humbly apologize."

Eleanor turned to Rekka. "What's with . . . ?"

"The priest who came with my mother converted a few deluded people," said Rekka.

"Where is he now?" asked Father Broose.

"Dead. Alcohol problems."

"He drank himself to death?" said Eleanor.

"Someone hit him over the head with a beer barrel."

"A barrel?"

"They wanted to make sure," said Rekka. "He had annoyed an awful lot of people." The way she looked at the Faithful suggested the annoyance lived on.

"Brother Riley passed on much of his wisdom," said one of them, "but it is hard to keep the Pledges without a priest."

"If it pleases, my lady," Father Broose said to Rekka, "I would like to tend to the spiritual needs of these poor souls."

"If you must."

The Hilite Faithful led Father Broose away. "You're not a believer?" Eleanor said to Rekka.

"In a superstition fabricated to justify a warmonger's territorial ambitions?" Rekka turned to the refugees. "No offense."

No one thought it the right moment to take any.

One of the hot springs that bubbled up through the mountains was reserved for the Lord Defender of Hil; the only reason anyone would want the job, claimed Rekka. She invited Eleanor and her "little sidekick" to join her there. Megan was willing to overlook the belittlement to lose herself in the soothing waters, tumbling under the surface, cleansing herself of the distance and the sorrow.

She surfaced and squeezed her hair dry. Eleanor and Rekka sat in an alcove, submerged to their shoulders, drinking beer from crystal goblets. Rekka examined Megan like a housewife assessing a butcher's wares. Self-conscious, Megan sank down until the water lapped her chin.

"Where's the baby?" asked Rekka.

"What?" said Megan.

"I've had five children—some of whom I actually like—you can't fool me. I know what childbirth does to a woman." Rekka cocked her head at Eleanor. "You should have sent it to me. Am I not family?"

It's family we want to keep her from, thought Megan. "We didn't want to impose."

"No imposition," said Rekka. She took a sip from her glass. "I have staff."

"Why the interest in some servant's bastard?" asked Eleanor.

"Bastard maybe, but she's no servant and you brought no retinue. I know why you're here, cousin. You didn't bring greetings to my house, you brought a war."

"I brought the victims of a war."

"And its cause," said Rekka, fixing her sapphire eyes on Megan.

Megan shot out of the water. "What . . . ? I . . . ?"

"You could have given them what they wanted and stopped them tearing up the continent trying to find it."

"How did . . . ?"

"Fordel's *very* nosy."

Waves rippled out as Rekka stepped out of the water. Steam billowed from her as if her body was smoking. "Don't worry," she said. "This won't go any further." She turned to the gap in the rock walls that served as the entrance to the pool. "Vega!"

A young girl—another of Rekka's daughters, judging from her looks—scurried in and handed over a towel, which Rekka used to dry herself. "I'll leave the two of you to finish washing—" she looked to Megan "—or start washing. Don't forget the feast tonight."

Mother and daughter left. Self-conscious after Rekka's remark, Megan scrubbed her face with her hands and combed her hair with her fingers.

"Relax," said Eleanor, "you're fine."

Megan continued scrubbing anyway. "Do you think we can trust her?"

"Rekka? She *is* a Kalvert."

"And?"

"Of course we can't trust her. Devious to a woman. Had to be. Little land, no fortune. Just our wits and flawless skin."

"My heart bleeds."

"Don't play the surly peasant with me, Megan. Every social stratum has its winners and losers. Did everyone in your village own a mill and farmland?"

"My grandfather earned that."

"More than the soldiers under his command?" said Eleanor. "Or did they divvy my father's possessions up equally among them?"

Megan ducked her head under the water and stayed for a moment, working up the nerve for what she had to say. She surfaced. "You heard what Rekka said. We could bring Cate here. She'd be safe."

"I'm not entirely sure about that . . ."

"No one would have to know who she is. Rekka could arrange something. People would think she was another Hilite baby."

"We should wait," said Eleanor. "Make sure it's safe."

"How much more safe do you need it to be?"

"Don't let a bath and the promise of a hot meal blind you to the possible dangers. We don't know what Rekka's agenda is. Or the other Hilites' for that matter."

Rekka sent along a selection of her old gowns to the room Megan and Eleanor had been allocated in the Lord Defender's mansion. Eleanor had no problem choosing one that fitted; Megan, a good few inches shorter than the cousins, struggled to find one that didn't want to trip her up at every step.

"We could always take it up," said Eleanor.

"I'm crap at sewing," said Megan. "We always left that to Gwyn—to someone else."

"I'll do it."

Eleanor called for needle and thread and altered one of the dresses. Megan stared down at herself. Her cleavage stared back. "Do we have a shawl or something?" Eleanor found a scarf and draped it over Megan's shoulders.

There was a rap at the door. A guard stared into the middle distance. "Lord Vegar and Lady Rekka would be

honored by your presence," he said, like a child reciting his single line in the school play. Megan guessed
he spoke no Stathian and Rekka had taught him the
sentence phonetically.

"Thank you," said Eleanor. "We'll be along shortly."
The guard stared at her blankly. She shooed him away.

. They gave themselves a final check in the mirror.
Eleanor fluffed Megan's hair. "You know, once you're
cleaned up and out of stinking leather, you're quite
presentable."

"Don't you start," said Megan. "You stank just as
much as I did."

"I seriously doubt that."

Eleanor headed for the exit. Megan made to follow,
then had a thought. She grabbed one of her abandoned
knives and slipped it into its usual place in her boot.
Eleanor raised her eyebrows but didn't insist she leave
the weapon.

Rekka and Vegar escorted them to the grand hall, a
vast forest of pillars where the aisles between the tables
stretched as long as a road. The refugees and most of
the city were already here, seated on the long benches
or warming themselves at the great fireplaces that lined
the walls. Icy beer served from barrels helped to break
down the barriers created by the lack of a common
language.

One of the guards took a running jump and landed on a table, sloshing beer everywhere. A Hilite gave him the universal glare that questioned whether the object had spilled the subject's drink and whether the object would like a trip outside to discuss the matter further. The guard kicked him in the jaw. A cheer went up. The first brawl of the night.

"Stand for Vegar!" bellowed the guard. "Lord Defender of Hil, Marshal of the Armies and Chairman of the Council of Cities! Stand for Rekka, Lady Kalvert and First Lady of Hil! Stand for Eleanor, of the houses of Endalay and Kalvert, Countess of Ainsworth, Baroness of Laxton and Herth, First Lady of Kirkland, Overlord of the Spice Isles and Defender of the Southern Lands! Stand for . . ."

He pointed at Megan and gave Vegar a questioning shrug. Vegar whispered something to Rekka, who in turn murmured in Eleanor's ear. A reply made its way back along the chain of nobles. "Stand for . . ." He bent over. "Sorry, what was that?"

"It doesn't matter," said Megan.

The guard repeated his command, this time in Hilite. There was a mass scraping of wood. Everyone raised their drink—some of the refugees, who were making up for lost time, raised two—and shouted their names. Despite the botched introduction, Megan even caught her own name amidst the roar. She scanned the hall for its source and found Father Broose raising a drinking horn at her. Clover huddled by his side, eyes gleaming with either reverence or alcohol.

They swept down the hall to the high table. Although most gazes fell on Eleanor and Rekka as they slunk along like twin goddesses, some found their way to Megan. She pulled the scarf tighter.

Fordel was waiting for them with a tray of drinks. Megan snatched one and downed it. The bubbles in the beer fought back. She belched.

"Sorry," she said, covering her mouth. "Fizzy."

"It's the Lord Defender's special brew," said Fordel. "A little stronger than the regular stuff."

Megan made to put the empty goblet down and found her head swimming. "No kidding."

"Did you manage to find accommodation for everyone?" Eleanor asked.

"I thought we'd let everybody get dead drunk and sleep where they fall."

"Works for me."

They sat and ate. While Eleanor, Rekka and Vegar got the places of honor, Fordel led Megan down to the end of the table. They made small talk over a platter of bread and cured meats. It soon became apparent that none of their immediate companions spoke Stathian. Megan didn't think this a coincidence.

"Have you seen a lot of battles?" asked Fordel.

"Battles?"

"Between the True and the Faithful?"

Megan hesitated. Her instinct was to evade, dissemble, but these people were the closest to allies they had. Fordel probably knew everything anyway. Certainly he was aware of the most important thing—Cate's existence. "I was on the periphery."

"Must have been awful."

"Worse for the casualties."

"I hear the True have a terrible weapon," said Fordel. "Some kind of thunderous catapult?"

Megan nodded. "Guns. They brought them from the Diannon Empire."

"Diannon?" said Fordel, stroking his beard. "Interesting . . ."

"Why?"

Fordel answered her question with a knowing smile. "These guns, they're powered by a magical black powder."

"Are they?"

"I hear it can destroy ships."

"You hear a lot of things," said Megan.

Plates of salt-encrusted fish were brought out, tender white flesh that flaked in the mouth. Megan stuffed herself with it, then downed another goblet of beer to counteract the salt. When she caught Fordel's lupine smile, she asked for water and tried to sober up. She wasn't sure she wanted to tell him everything.

Megan changed the conversation. "The people of Hil elected Vegar their leader?"

"It was his turn," said Fordel with a shrug, "and he has a very beautiful wife. The electors were bored with Pálmar. In a couple of years they'll be bored with Vegar, and Pálmar will seem fresh and exciting." Fordel circled his fingers. "And so on."

"But you actually run the city, don't you?"

"That's a . . . wild conclusion. I merely handle the paperwork."

"So did the priests, until they took over the Realm." Megan peered at Fordel over her cup. "Do you want to take over here?"

"Against the will of the electors?"

"They wouldn't vote for you?"

"Yes," said Fordel, "but eventually they would vote against me and that would be tiresome. Better to surrender the trappings of power than power itself."

"What's so great about power?"

Fordel stared out into the hall, his focus alighting on a group of refugees who were being lectured by Father Broose. "Best it be in the hands of someone who knows what must be done."

Megan's stomach tightened. "If you hurt any of them, I'll hack your throat out."

"You misunderstand me. Many in Hil would prefer to hide, pretend the war in the Realm has nothing to do with us. And as for the other cities . . ." Fordel drank and let out a small burp he excused by placing a finger on his lips. "Someone has to make the decisions that will be the best for us in the long run. Easy short-termism is all too attractive when you have to appeal to a mob of scared electors."

"Maybe you need to explain things better to them?"

"And ask them to die?"

"Better than *commanding* them to die."

The doors at the far end of the hall were thrown open. A squad of guards marched down the aisle. Someone stumbled between them, but in the dim light Megan couldn't make out who.

Fordel sighed. "I was hoping they'd wait until after dessert at least."

"Huh?"

The guards reached the high table and parted, revealing their prisoner. Afreyda stood there, looking ready to drop. Her armor was shredded. Cuts and bruises marred her skin, some fresh, some beginning to heal.

Megan scrambled out of her seat, shoulder-charging her fellow diners in her rush to get to her. Afreyda blinked and wobbled. "You look pretty," she said, her voice barely a croak.

Megan caught her before she could fall and clutched her. "We thought . . . I thought . . . you were . . ."

"You left me again."

"I didn't want to."

"I told him that."

"Him? Who? Damon?" Afreyda's scarred skin scratched Megan as she nodded. "Where is he?"

"He's . . ."

Megan broke the embrace so she could look Afreyda in the eye. "Where is Damon?"

Afreyda managed a brief shake of her head before collapsing.

Nineteen

Damon looked across to Afreyda, who stood hands on hips, taking in the leafy suburb in the exclusive west end of Kewley. Villas were set back from the street, the occasional flash of stucco and terracotta visible behind the shields of walls and railings. This was not the kind of area that concerned itself with war and its consequences—wasn't that what poor people were for? Even the distant boom of guns sounded almost apologetic, as if aware it was intruding where it didn't belong.

"We are lost," she said.

"No, we're not," said Damon. "We're merely at an indeterminate point between our point of departure and our destination."

"We should have followed the others."

"I wasn't stopping you."

"Eleanor told me to get you to the marina," said Afreyda. "And to keep an eye on you."

"I don't need a bodyguard."

"It was not as a bodyguard."

It had only been a few months since he had last been here, but Damon was having a hard time remembering where to go. The villas all looked the same, and none bore a nameplate. It was old money around here—landowners, mine owners, former aristocrats who had accepted the priests' seizure of power in return for keeping some of their cash—and it had learned not to draw attention to itself. The directions he had received mutated in his mind: was it three houses down after the second left past the temple, or two houses down after the third left?

It was the gap in the spikes that alerted him. They were embedded in the seven-foot wall, rusting sentries spaced every few inches or so, except for a space a slender person could just squeeze through. He remembered thinking at the time what a security flaw it was, but even the most paranoid got lax on occasion.

Damon shouted a hello and rattled the gates. They were wrought iron, another foot higher than the walls, and edged with a razor frill. No getting through or over them. The house beyond was silent, devoid of activity. Its occupants must have fled at the first word of the witches' advance. He should have made his way straight here after the Sandstriders' attack instead of trotting around after Eleanor. He should have known she . . . No, he wouldn't dwell on it.

The house might be empty of people, but might not be empty of valuables. It was worth taking a few minutes to find out. Damon checked the street for observers, then slunk over to the gap. He reached up, grabbed the top of the wall and gave an experimental heave. His arms protested at the strain.

"Give us a leg up," he said to Afreyda.

"A what?"

"Help me over."

"That is not the way to the marina."

"No, but . . . I have to retrieve something of mine." A small part of him told him this was not strictly true, but it was a part of him long used to its weary protestations being ignored. "Wait there. I won't be long."

Afreyda made a stirrup with her hands and boosted him up. Damon sat between two spikes atop the wall for a moment, massaging his scraped hands and getting his bearings. He prepared to drop to the ground, then noticed the glittering in the soft mud directly below him: broken glass. Sneaky bastards. This way to the laceration.

He changed plan and launched himself, arcing over the booby-trapped earth and rolling on to the lawn beyond. The impact jarred his knees as if someone had taken a hammer to them. He lay on the neat grass waiting for the throbbing to subside. From the other side of the wall, Afreyda called a warning. Someone was coming. The throbbing was supplanted by an eager need to find cover.

Damon scurried to the porch. Planks creaked under his boots. There was a flash of movement through the window and the front doors were flung open. Before he could run, two burly men burst out and grabbed him.

"Hey!" protested Damon, jerking one way then the other. The men wrenched his arms until they almost popped out of their sockets. "All right, all right, I'm not going to hurt you."

A shriveled old man hobbled on to the porch, supporting himself with a walking stick. His skin was as loose and ill-fitting as a lizard's. Hair like steel wool threatened to drop off his spotted scalp. The eyes though were bright and alert to everything.

He took in Damon and sighed. "I was hoping you were dead."

"Don't think that's an original comment, Kendrick."

"I suppose you've come for . . . ?"

"Uh-huh."

"We were just leaving," said Kendrick. "Maybe you could come back another time? When it's more appropriate?"

"I can't think of a more appropriate time than now," said Damon. His arms were still being forced into positions for which they weren't designed. "Want it known you renege on your deals? Not all your . . . associates are as easygoing as me."

Kendrick considered for a moment. "Very well."

He hobbled back inside. His two men hoisted Damon over the threshold in a manner that didn't completely respect Damon's arm sockets.

"Can't you call your henchmen off?"

Without turning around, Kendrick motioned with a flick of his hand. The two men released Damon from their grip but kept within looming range. He cracked and massaged his shoulders back to life.

"Quality henching, boys."

The hallway was immaculate, a tasteful combination of marble and mahogany. Sunlight coruscated off the crystals of a chandelier high above their heads. Twin staircases curved around to meet on a landing dominated by a painting of the Saviors instructing the Unifier at Statham, the figures a little larger than life sized.

Kendrick pointed to a grubby sack propped up by the banister. "Bill, if you would?"

One of the men de-loomed and picked up the sack. He opened it and held it up in front of Kendrick, who rummaged around inside and extracted a small pouch.

"Could you show Damon the merchandise, please, Ben?" said Kendrick, handing over the pouch.

"You two are Bill and Ben?" said Damon. "That's what I called my . . ." He regarded the pair, who had enough raw material between them to form three normal-sized men. "Never mind."

Ben unfolded the pouch on an occasional table. Diamonds glittered against the black velvet, like a patch of night sky. A small fortune in precious stones.

"Satisfactory?" asked Kendrick.

"Where's the rest?"

"Rest?"

"The Endalay diamond weighed at least five times these scrapings combined. Ten even. This isn't what we agreed."

The skipper who had got them out of Eastport when the witches had first invaded had been ignorant enough to accept a single sovereign for his services, leaving Damon the diamond with which Megan had entrusted him and which he had somehow forgotten to return. However, a jewel that could buy a good-sized city wasn't very practical on a day-to-day basis. During a scouting mission to New Statham, made just before Megan gave birth, Damon had made a detour to Kewley. Kendrick, a trader in items whose provenance wasn't necessarily verifiable, had agreed to convert it into something more liquid.

"You don't want them?" said Kendrick.

Ben's hand hovered over the displayed diamonds, ready to reclaim them. Damn fences, crooked every last one of them, no matter how high class. Kendrick would have raked off at least three-quarters of the sum he'd gained by selling the Endalay diamond. Still, better a small fortune than no fortune.

Damon waved Ben away. "It was a pleasure to be ripped off by you," he said to Kendrick. He wrapped the diamonds back up and slipped the pouch into his boot. "Any chance of someone opening your front gate? I don't think I could make it over that wall again."

Kendrick flicked a finger at Bill, who led Damon outside. They halted. Soldiers of the Realm were trying to pry the gates open with the flat of an ax. Damon and Bill did a U-turn back into the villa.

"What is it?" demanded Kendrick.

"Gatecrashers," said Damon.

They dashed though the villa, skidding and squeaking across the marble, ending up in the prosaic environs of the kitchen, with its sawdust-strewn floorboards and weathered oak table. Ben started working free the bolts on the back door, which was secured tighter than the average bank vault. The final bolt came free. Ben flung the door open. A fist swung in, sending him reeling. The owner of the fist strutted in, hand on his sword. Aldred.

Bill grabbed a cleaver from a block and made to attack, but three soldiers piled in from the front, weapons drawn. He backed off. His colleague looked on sullenly, dabbing his bleeding nose with the back of his hand.

Aldred stared at Damon, confusion on his face. "What the hell are you doing here?"

"Me?" said Damon. "What about you?"

There was something else in Aldred's expression. Guilt mixed with the confusion. He knew about this place, about Kendrick's profession. He was looking to get in a bit of quick looting before the witches got here. Put a man in uniform and he thought it gave him license to thieve.

"You know this man?" Kendrick asked Damon.

"I wouldn't get your hopes up," said Damon. "He's a bit of a jerk."

"We have nothing to rob," Kendrick said to Aldred. "You might as well leave while you can."

Aldred took in the contents of the kitchen. The porcelain arranged on the shelves was worth a few years' of the lieutenant's wages by itself. "I'll be the judge of that, parasite."

"Parasite?"

"You didn't get all this wealth doing a hard day's work, did you?"

Aldred banged through a few cupboards. Kendrick smiled sourly at his back and fiddled with the gold knob of his walking stick. Damon eyed the door and wondered if anyone would notice if he snuck away.

The lieutenant noticed the grubby sack Bill had over his shoulder—the sack that had contained Damon's diamonds—conspicuously not drawing attention to itself. He snatched it and rummaged through it. He swallowed hard and looked over to one of his men.

"Told you so, sir."

"If anything, Norvel," said Aldred, "you underestimated."

Damon affected a sigh. "What's Eleanor going to say when she finds out how naughty you've been?"

"It's her I'm doing this for."

"How d'you work that one out?"

"If she's going to be queen she deserves to be treated like one. They stole her fortune. I'm stealing it back."

"Do you know who Kendrick is?" said Damon. "He'll have half the criminals in the Realm after your head for this."

The kitchen went silent until all that could be heard was ragged breathing and the patter of blood dripping from Ben's nose. Everyone was taking in the implications of Damon's words. Aldred couldn't afford to leave Kendrick alive, but neither was Kendrick going to accept his fate meekly.

There was a clang as the knob of Kendrick's walking stick hit the floor. Before anyone could react, Kendrick twirled the stick and buried the now-exposed spike in Norvel's eye. He twisted. Norvel's scream almost deafened Damon. Blood and puréed eyeball streamed down the soldier's face.

Damon dived under the table as Bill lunged at Aldred with the cleaver. Aldred spun out of the way. In one motion, he drew his sword and took off half of Bill's face. Ben meanwhile charged the other two soldiers, but even his bulk was no match for blades. He was hacked down as if nothing more than a straw man set up for practice.

Kendrick thrust at Aldred's groin, but it was a half-hearted strike that seemed to have been made to provoke the counterattack Aldred delivered. The floorboards shuddered as the old man's body toppled over. The corpse stared at Damon with glassy eyes. Around it, blood soaked into the sawdust and began to clump.

Aldred crouched down and peered under the table. "Are you going to come out from under there?" he said, poking Damon with the gory point of his sword.

Damon drew himself into a ball. "You want to kill me, you'll have to work for it."

"*They* attacked *us*."

"Civilized of you to restrain your response."

Aldred bounced on his haunches and stood up. "You want to cower there, fine. The witches'll be here soon. Is it true they've already attempted to execute you?"

Damon clambered out from his hiding place. "I find it best not to take these things personally," he said, brushing sawdust from his sleeves. "You just end up obsessing over your resentment."

"Healthy attitude," said Aldred. "You're going to need it."

He grabbed Damon and twisted his arm behind his back. Damon howled a protest that went unheeded as Aldred frog-marched him across the room. He found himself flying through the air into the pantry. He collided with a pile of flour sacks that emitted an apologetic cough of white dust.

There was a slam that condemned the cramped storeroom to near darkness. Out in the kitchen he heard the heavy scrape of the table being shoved across the floor. Damon scrambled for the door and charged. It refused to budge. He was trapped.

Damon hammered on the pantry door until his fist throbbed. "Come on, Aldred, let me out! You have her now. What kind of threat can I be?" No response.

There was no other way out, just cold, dark stone. The already-narrow walls inched inwards. He stepped back and kicked. The door objected to the assault in the strongest terms. Damon ended up on the floor yelling enough curses to raise an army of demons. That they didn't appear told him all he needed to know about that particular superstition.

There was a receding clomp as Aldred and his men left. That was something at least. He was surrounded by plenty of food. That was something else. Nothing to drink though. He wouldn't starve, just die of thirst. His throat constricted at the thought. He licked his dry lips, then worried about wasting liquid.

Damon slapped his hands over the surface of the door. Some of the nails were loose, their heads exposed. If he had a knife he might be able to pry them loose. It was at times like this he missed Megan. Still, it was possible somebody had left one in here. He groped around the shelves. He knocked something over and jumped as it smashed by his feet. The pungent aroma of vinegar made his eyes water.

"Damon!"

He perked up at the sound of his name being called, then perked back down when he compared the odds of somebody showing up who wanted to kill him versus somebody showing up who didn't. He crept along the pantry, listening intently. Glass crunched under his soles. So much for stealth.

"Damon!"

A woman's voice—Afreyda. He breathed a sigh of relief. "In here!"

"Why are there dead bodies everywhere?"

"That wasn't me!"

"And why is there a table in front of the door?"

"I think we can rule me out there too."

"Who did this to you?" asked Afreyda. "They were soldiers, yes? Did I see Aldred?"

"Are you going to interrogate me or let me out?"

"Both. In that order. What happened?"

Damon hesitated, wondering what to tell her. There were so many ways of interpreting the facts, and he didn't want Afreyda jumping to the right conclusion. "There was a little disagreement."

"So he locked you in a cupboard?"

"It's a local tradition."

"You are a very strange people."

From the other side of the door there was much squealing and grunting. Damon bounced in the darkness. How many men had it taken to barricade him in? Was Afreyda strong enough to move the table? Was he going to be stuck in here forever? The space around him contracted even further.

Scraping, foreign muttering that could only be swear words. Damon kept testing the door until the weight against it disappeared. He shoved it open and burst into the kitchen beyond. Afreyda stood before him, panting, sweat glistening on her dark skin. Flies were already starting to buzz around the corpses of Kendrick and the others.

Never before was Damon so relieved to step into a scene of carnage. He flung out his arms. "Marry me! Have my children!"

"No! And definitely no!" Afreyda pulled him toward the exit. "We must hurry. The ships will leave without us."

"Relax," said Damon. "I'm an expert on fleeing."

Twenty

The images were burned into Damon's brain: the last boat leaving, Megan's pleas, Eleanor's impassive gaze. They had left him to the witches; their time together meant nothing. He'd been used up, discarded. Part of him cursed them; part of him suspected they had done the right thing.

He and Afreyda had no other choice but to head back into the city, ducking and weaving through the streets, evading the soldiers pouring in, trying to find an escape from the doomed town. No luck. The witches had thrown up an impenetrable perimeter. They were trapped. It was only a matter of time before they were discovered.

They ended up in a garden on the edge of Kewley. Through gaps in a creeper-covered fence they watched as the witches marched their prisoners back into town, a long column of despair and misery. The soldiers of the Faith came first. The witches forced them to kneel in the road, at intervals a few yards apart. A witch took up position behind each one. They made the sign of the star-broken circle and raised their axes. Damon knew what was coming, but he couldn't look away, couldn't even blink.

The civilian prisoners came next, made to march in two lines either side of their beheaded protectors, some of whose bodies continued to twitch. Some looked away, some wept. One man made the mistake of making the sign of the circle. The butt of an ax shaft in his face dissuaded him from such displays of piety. Or the wrong kind of piety at least.

The prisoners, a couple of hundred or so, were arranged into lines and made to kneel. A few, mindful of what this had led to a few moments ago, tried to resist and were beaten to the ground for their pains. A witch marched to the front and barked orders, the specifics of which Damon couldn't quite make out. The prisoners struggled to make the sign of the star-broken circle and recited what sounded like a vow. Damon could guess what it was: the witches' version of the first Pledge. He rubbed his shoulder and pushed down the memories of his own forced conversion. Back then, he'd thought the witches had worshipped demons and the vow was a grotesque parody. Now he knew they were so very, very sincere.

Damon turned around and slumped against the fence. A tranquil lawn spread out before him. Pleasant, controlled, peaceful. "We should find somewhere to hole up," he whispered. "Wait until they've moved on."

"When will that be?"

"I don't know." It looked as if the witches were settling in, regrouping after the battle. "Few days maybe. It won't be long before they want to go around killing things again."

"We cannot wait that long. We have to catch up with Megan and Eleanor."

"Really? They all but made rude signs at us as they sailed away."

"They could not help it."

"Sure."

Eleanor had what she wanted: Damon out of her life and her conscience salved. *We couldn't possibly stop the boat a few seconds to let you on.* She was happy to spend her life with that treacherous bastard Aldred. In a way it was good, this enforced separation. He needed to be rid of her, of the spell she cast over him. Now she had revealed her true colors, he could go back to thinking of himself. He just wished she hadn't left him in a war zone.

"The temple," he said.

"You think your god will help you?" said Afreyda. "He has not been here so far."

"I don't see your dead Uncle Bob stepping up for us either," said Damon. "There'll be tunnels under the temple."

"Are you sure?"

"Priests are paranoid," said Damon. "They like to have an escape route in case things get mob-y. You can't be in charge of anything without pissing someone off sooner or later. It'll probably lead to a nice quiet spot in the orchard." He was trying to convince himself more than Afreyda.

"You have seen such tunnels?"

"Used to take girls down them. If you're not actually under the temple, it's technically not sacrilege."

The sound of something valuable smashing into a thousand pieces came from inside the house in whose grounds they were hiding. Damon and Afreyda shuffled along the fence until they were better hidden by the tangles of a strawberry bush.

Afreyda peered through the bushes. "What are they doing in there?"

"Cleaning?" said Damon. Afreyda flashed him a look. "Looting?"

"The True do not loot."

Damon parted the bushes and calculated the distance to the wall that divided this property from the next. A little too much on the "there's someone there, get him" side for his liking. "The witches might not loot, but what about the men they recruited in Eastport? Auxiliaries might not share their high moral standards."

"We should—"

A man came out into the garden via the one-time method of being thrown through the window. Judging from his expensive clothes, he was one of the residents. He tried to get up, but a hundred cuts made this impossible. There was a final crunch of glass and he slumped to the grass, blood oozing from his body.

"Maybe we should wait until they've moved on," Damon whispered to Afreyda. "Unless you would like taking a class in advanced defenestration."

By the time they reached the temple the sun was starting to sink below the horizon, casting a fiery glow on the roofs and stuccoed walls. It had been a stop-start-cower journey through Kewley. They ducked and dived through the town, holding their breath in alleyways as soldiers clomped past, enduring the thorns and nettles that clawed and stung them as they hid in bushes, powerless to intervene as the witches dragged the screaming Faithful from their homes.

They snuck around the back. The place was deserted. If anyone else had decided to hide here, they were doing a good job of it.

Afreyda rattled the door. "It is locked."

"What?" said Damon. "It's not allowed to be."

"Maybe you should write a letter of complaint."

"People have to be able to go in and pray and seek sanctuary from the law and possibly catch up on their sleep. It says so in the Book of Faith. Well, not the sleeping, obviously." And seeking sanctuary from the law was a bit hard these days, what with the lawmakers running the temple.

"Do you think there are witches inside?" asked Afreyda.

"They're not really temple people."

Afreyda marched to a pile of rubble and selected a fist-sized rock. "No, don't!" said Damon. Too late. She had already put it through one of the temple windows. Damon cringed. "You can't vandalize a temple!"

Afreyda elbowed aside the remaining fragments of broken glass and reached in to lift the window's latch. She hoisted herself up, checked the interior, then dropped inside.

Damon looked up to the heavens. "Forgive her, for she knows not what she does."

"Are you coming?"

Damon continued to look skywards. "Forgive me," he said. "I do know what I do but I'm a bit desperate. As usual." He followed Afreyda inside.

"Where are these secret tunnels?" she asked.

"You're not really grasping the concept of 'secret,' are you?" said Damon. Afreyda gave him the kind of look that suggested he wasn't grasping the concept of "armed and dangerous." "The cellars, I guess."

They crept through the temple and down into the basement. Damon wondered where the priests were—and somewhere as rich as Kewley was bound to have priests plural, including its own high priest. Had they all fled?

He requisitioned a lantern and held its light close to the floor. He was hoping to spot telltale footsteps in the dust, but the flagstones were so pristine they practically shone. This place was so fancy they even cleaned the parts no one ever saw. He was going to have to do this the hard way.

Methodically he circumnavigated the cellar, scanning for gaps, pressing any obtrusions. Priests weren't noted for their nimbleness or daintiness. If there was an escape route, it'd be large and easy to get to. Nothing presented itself though. There was only one way out, and that led back up above ground.

"What now?" asked Afreyda.

Damon pointed at the wine rack. "Might as well."

"Your answer is to get drunk?"

"You're eager. I was suggesting a quick drink to calm our nerves."

"You do not seem nervous."

"I'm always nervous," said Damon. "I've just learned to hide it."

He selected a bottle on the grounds that its protruding cork meant he was able to extract it with his teeth. Afreyda found some hams hanging in the corner—black with a layer of soft fat surrounding them—and sliced chunks from one of them. Damon was hungrier and thirstier than he had realized. He and Afreyda soon polished off the wine and the meat. Afreyda went to hack more off while he chose another bottle.

A dozy feeling of almost contentment settled upon Damon. Down here in the silence and the near dark, it was easy to believe the war was far away. Unfortunately he also remembered what, or rather who, *was* far away. The ham became salty leather, the wine vinegar.

He passed the bottle to Afreyda, whose taste buds had suffered no such reversal. He hadn't really thought before about what a good-looking girl she was. There was an honesty to Afreyda, a lack of calculation and deviousness. She wasn't concerned with political games history had long since ejected her from.

"Afreyda's a pretty name," he said. "What does it mean?"

"First-born daughter."

"Ah. Quite common then, I'm guessing."

"Only for girls," said Afreyda.

"It's getting hot in here. Why don't you take some of that armor off? Let your skin breathe a little."

"My skin is fine."

Come to think of it, it really was getting hot. It must be the wine, the stuffiness of the cellar. Damon loosened the ties on his jerkin. Afreyda showed no interest.

"Do you smell that?" she asked.

"Sorry," said Damon. "Always happens when I've had a few."

"Burning."

Damon sniffed. Among the various body odors and the tang of wine he smelled smoke. His skin prickled. "You know when I said the witches weren't temple people?"

"Yes."

"It was a slight understatement."

"They are burning the place down?" Afreyda was struggling to keep her voice calm. Damon nodded slowly. "With us in it?"

"I think it's important not to panic at this point."

They raced up the stairs to the exit. Damon barged the door open. Flames blasted at him. He yanked the door shut again and backed off down the stairs.

"It's warm out," he said.

"What do we do now?"

"If we had bread we could make ham toasties."

Afreyda hit him on the arm, a little too hard to be friendly. "This is no time for jokes."

"People always say that, but when you're faced with certain death, why not try to lighten the mood a little?"

"We cannot stay here. The fire will eat all the air."

"I'd be more worried about the flammable door if I was you."

Smoke was beginning to curl through the gaps. Damon backed down a couple more steps.

"Do you think we should . . . ?" said Afreyda. "Before the fire . . . ?"

"Bang? Not a bad way to go, I suppose."

"Kill each other."

"I prefer my suggestion," said Damon.

"You want to be burned alive?"

"You want to die a virgin?"

"I am not a virgin."

"Really?" said Damon. "Who's the lucky boy?"

"Boy?"

The ceiling shook as something crashed into it. Sparks rained on them. Damon cringed. Instinct told him to run, but his brain offered no route. His feet tangled over themselves and he tumbled down the final few steps. He clattered into a stack of decrepit crates, which smashed and crumbled to the ground. No, not to it, into it.

Damon stretched out an arm and found himself groping the lip of a shaft. "The secret tunnel! I've—"

"Found it, yes," said Afreyda, hurrying across the cellar.

"Good idea," said Damon, picking himself up. His shoulders smarted from the fall. "The heat'll spoil the wine. Might as well save what we can." Afreyda came back with the lantern dangling from the crook of her arm. "You're boringly practical on occasion."

A ladder took them further underground. Dank air replaced roasting. They found themselves in a tunnel hacked out of the dirt and supported by crude props. Water seeped through the walls, giving them a living appearance. They hunched and hurried along, squelching in the mud. At least with the temple on fire, there was little chance somebody would follow them.

They reached another ladder and Afreyda started to climb. They had reached the end, and in one piece. He waited for her to clear the ladder. Water pooled around his boots, soaking through the holes in the leather and chilling his skin. Shouldn't it be getting drier if they were going away from the lake?

He was glad when it was his turn to climb, even if the mud on Afreyda's feet had left the rungs slimy. Dirt walls gave way to brick. An old well? That'd explain the water.

Damon reached the top and hauled himself out. He stared around in confusion. This was not what he was expecting.

"It is very pink," said Afreyda.

"Uh-huh."

"No trees."

"I'm seeing that."

"It is a bedchamber."

"Can't argue with that conclusion."

They had emerged from a wardrobe into the bedroom of some mansion or other. The walls were the color you usually only saw after eating certain kinds of mushroom. Jewelry was scattered over a dressing table. The drapes of a four-poster bed billowed in the breeze whistling up from the tunnel. Beyond the gauze, a woman in a silk slip lay prone. The tunnel was for escaping all right, but from angry husbands, not angry mobs.

There was a dark stain by the woman's hand. "Is she . . . ?" asked Afreyda.

"I don't know," said Damon.

He peeked through the curtains. The stain was wine, evidenced by the glass the woman was clutching. She didn't seem to be breathing though. Had she taken something? Tentatively he stretched out and placed a fingertip on the mottled skin of the woman's neck. A pulse fluttered beneath his touch. She was—

"Aaargh!"

"Don't scream!" Damon hissed. "You'll draw everybody's attention."

The woman merely took this as encouragement and hollered her head off. Damon flapped his hands in front of her, as if he could bat the yells back into her mouth. Only Afreyda's strategic application of a vase to the back of her head shut her up.

Damon picked up a fragment of fine china. "Shame," he said. "Bet this was worth a bit."

"You would prefer I let her scream longer so I could find something cheaper to hit her with?"

Damon tossed the fragment aside and crossed to the window to get his bearings. They were by the lake on the west side of town. One of the witches' warships sat out on the water, divesting itself of several smaller boats as if giving birth. Those refugees who had escaped by land had been heading east—maybe the witches' forces were less concentrated over here?

A whinny brought his attention back to the house, or rather to the yard below them. A pair of horses poked their heads over a half-door and called for their no doubt absconded keeper. He grinned and beckoned Afreyda over.

"Our way out."

"We should wait until it is properly dark."

"And have the witches find them first?" They were good horses, rested. From what he had seen, the witches didn't have many mounts—they took up too much space on boats—so they'd be looking to scavenge those they could.

Damon eased through the open window and on to the ledge outside. From there it was a quick shimmy along, then a short hop to the slanted roof of the stables. He slid down, dangled on the guttering, then dropped the few feet to the cobbles.

He patted the neck of one of the horses, a chestnut gelding with a white flash down its nose. They were already saddled; whoever had done it must have escaped by sea with the others. The horse nuzzled his palm, looking for treats. Damon spotted a pail of carrots and gave it one. The horse crunched it eagerly. Damon slipped it another one and offered some to its companion.

Afreyda swished out into the yard using the more conventional route of the house's back door. She gave the horses a cursory check, then led them into the yard and handed Damon the reins of what he assumed was the worse horse. Hoofs clip-clopped on the stones as they approached the gates. Damon wished he could muffle the too-distinctive sound, or at least teach the horses how to walk on tiptoe.

A heavy bar secured the gates. He lifted it and eased them open. The leafy lane outside was deserted.

"We're clear," he said. "We find the west road and ride like hell. Any questions?" One of the horses shook its head. "I wasn't asking you."

They mounted and trotted out. The path wound around the house, lined by tightly packed trees. A branch swiped Damon across the face like a jealous lover angry at his departure. He swatted it out of the way.

They paused at the end of the lane, where the path joined the road that ran along the south shore of Lake Pullar. Witches milled around, checking over the goods abandoned by the fleeing citizens. None had spotted them yet, half hidden as they were by foliage.

Damon and Afreyda exchanged glances, nodded in mutual encouragement. They urged their horses into life, kicking up clouds of dust as they wheeled out. Astonished cries sounded behind them, calling on them to halt. Damon wondered if that had ever worked.

They spurred their horses on. The world sped past: the lake a streak to their right; the town a blur to their left. Damon held on tight as he could, half-fearing he would crush his mount's ribs between his thighs. A crossbow bolt whooshed past his ear. Either close or meant for Afreyda.

She pulled ahead of him as they left town. They were speeding to a waterway that fed into the lake, man-made judging by its straightness. Two soldiers stood guard by its bridge. They moved to block their way, then thought better of obstructing a ton of thundering horseflesh and dived clear.

One spun a wheel by the bridge posts. He barked an order to his compatriot, who scrambled to the wheel's twin at the opposite post. The bridge split and began to rise. The wind snatched Damon's curse.

Afreyda's horse leaped from the drawbridge and landed on the other side in a clatter of hoofs. Damon steeled himself and prepared to jump. The angle wasn't too high, he could clear it, he just had to hold his nerve.

His horse reared, throwing him backward on to the road. The impact slammed through his spine and shattered the world into a thousand competing images. He was dimly aware of his horse galloping away, of men surrounding him, of axes being raised.

Damon struggled to his knees and held out an outstretched palm. "Wait! Wait!" An ax swished. He pulled his hand back just in time.

"Rip your bastard insignias off, we can still recognize your uniform."

"What? I'm not . . . I'm not a soldier."

The witch raised his ax. "Not in ten seconds you won't be."

Damon's stomach cramped, forcing him to bend over. The witch shuffled closer, scuffing up dust, the soles of his boots loose and flapping like gossips. Damon wondered whether he'd live long enough to see the bloody stump of his body or whether his end would be instant, another brutalized victim of the witches left to anonymously rot.

It had come to this. He could live or die. He could follow the path God had laid out for him or explain his rejection in person. He could lose everything or reject those who had rejected him.

Damon pulled off his jerkin. He did the same with his undershirt. The witch paused, curious. Some distance away, on the far side of the canal, Afreyda watched, struggling to control her mount. Damon looked away, not wanting to see her disapproval, even at a distance.

Bare-chested, he bowed to the witch, exposing his shoulder and the tattoo of the star-broken circle etched there. Once it had almost got him killed. This time it might save him.

"*Prana salat suctamo procter ō*," he said. "I pledge obedience to God and His Saviors."

Twenty-One

The witch marched Damon back into Kewley, not exactly at swordpoint but not exactly as brothers in arms either. Damon thought about the vow he had made, the second time he had done so, and wondered whether he meant it. It had saved him, hadn't it? Was God not showing him the way? Why assume the witches were wrong because their teachings came after that of the priests? It wasn't as if the latter had set an example of purity and piety. The witches might be right about everything.

More soldiers were entering the city. They waited in neat ranks while corporals and sergeants billeted them into what had once been the homes of the rich, their patience encouraged by the sight of their former comrades lying dead on the streets, coins spilling from their mouths like copper vomit. No one could accuse the witches of a reluctance to enforce discipline. Or of wasting any gold and silver that had been looted.

"Hanging around for a bit?" said Damon, crossing his arms over his chest. It was getting cold. A dank wind blew in from the lake, raising goosebumps across his exposed skin. "Given up on New Statham?"

"The city is irrelevant."

"What is rel—?" Damon started to ask, then he realized. There was only one thing the witches cared about. This phase of conquering and destruction was a mere prelude to the real conquering and destruction that would result when they had their hands on both Saviors. Was that what God wanted—every single one of His enemies destroyed? Couldn't He wipe them all out of existence with a single thought? Why did He need people? Did they have to demonstrate there was nothing they wouldn't do to prove their devotion? Did Damon have to demonstrate it?

They were heading toward a large pillar of smoke, which Damon assumed was the burning temple. "You want to be careful that doesn't spread," he said. "Lot of dry weather we've been having recently."

"God will protect us."

"But a firebreak makes a good backup." The soldier glared at him. "Just in case. Even the omniscient can get distracted."

An ax shaft to the face left Damon on his knees, spitting blood on to the cobblestones. He wiped his mouth on the back of his hand. Best to keep any further theological musings to himself. The witches might encourage a one-on-one relationship with God, but they did like to direct the conversation.

They marched on through the town. Damon could hear screaming now, smell burned flesh; trust the witches to hold the world's worst barbeque. They rounded a corner. Various parts of Damon's anatomy lurched at what he saw. Bare-shouldered civilians—men, women, children—were lined up, pale-faced and trembling, in front of a fiery brazier from which jutted a number of iron bars. A sweating witch pulled one of the bars out. The star-broken circle glowed red hot at its tip. The witch grabbed the man at the front of the line and jammed the brand against his exposed shoulder. There was a sizzle and a howl of agony. Another witch poured water over the burn. Steam billowed.

The next in line was a boy of maybe ten or eleven. He tried to make a break for it. Witches caught him and smashed an ax shaft across the back of his knees. Damon couldn't watch what happened next.

He kept his head down as they passed the line, though he could do nothing to block the stench of voided bowels. He fingered his tattoo and gave thanks the witches hadn't resorted to this industrial brutality when they had caught him. Of course, this marked him out as one of *them* to the unwilling converts they passed. Did they direct some of their hate at him or was it all reserved for the witches?

They entered the main square. The temple was a smoldering carcass; the rest of the buildings looked untouched. They marched over to the town hall and the troops stationed there. Damon's captor made the sign of the star-broken circle at one of the officers; Damon himself managed a brief wave and a small "hello."

"What's this?" asked the officer.

"He was wearing the uniform of the blasphemers, sir, but he bears our sign and knows the Pledge."

The officer peered at Damon's tattoo. "This isn't fresh."

"No."

"When did you become one of the True?"

"I was with the Mother when she . . . when she . . ." *When she slaughtered her own village, her own friends, her own family.* Damon was sure such actions were necessary in defense of God's Saviors, but how was one meant to refer to them in polite conversation?

"You know the Mother?"

"Intimately," said Damon, failing to specify which Mother.

"What were you doing with the blasphemers?"

"I was in her service."

"Doing what?"

"I can't say."

"Don't play games with me, boy."

"You would have me break an oath to the Mother made in the name of the Saviors?" Damon gave the officer a patronizing pat and made to move away. "Nice try. I'm going to grab a drink and a fresh jerkin. See you around."

He yelped as the officer grabbed him and hauled him toward the town hall. "Let's go see what the Mother has to say about this, shall we?"

"She's here?" said Damon, struggling to keep himself from tripping over his own feet.

"Yes," said the officer. "And she won't like you taking her name in vain."

The witches had set up in the courtyard of the town hall. A soldier stood guard at each of the pillars marking the cloisters around the perimeter. Torches set in gilded sconces combated the dusk. Maps were laid out over trestle tables set up in the exposed interior. Captains gathered around them and argued. Figurines were moved around and knocked down, the fate of thousands reduced to a schoolboys' game.

Gwyneth skulked in the shadows of the cloisters, wrapped in snowy-white furs spotted with drops of wine. There was an absent look in her eyes. Reflecting on what she had done, or simply drunk?

The officer pulled Damon toward her. Immediately four soldiers formed a wall of armor and axes. The officer knelt and yanked Damon down.

"If it pleases you, Mother."

The captains glanced up from their maps. Out of the corner of his eye, Damon recognized Tobrytan. Damon kept his head down. He wasn't keen on a reunion. Tobrytan did have a habit of ordering his death.

The soldiers parted to let Gwyneth through. "What?" she said. There was a slight slur to her voice. Drunk it was then.

"This man claims he's been acting under your orders."

"The whole world is acting under my . . . oh."

The drink practically drained from Gwyneth's face as she recognized him. Tobrytan looked around from the map table. There was an incredulous look on his face.

"Leave us," said Gwyneth.

Tobrytan looked unsure. "Mother, we can't leave you with him."

"You think God has delivered an assassin?" Gwyneth looked to the oldest of the captains, a bent old man supporting himself on a long battle-ax. "General . . ."

The general's voice was a harsh whisper. "You heard the Mother."

The soldiers filed out in organized lines, disappearing into the surrounding building. The snap of burning wood was the only sound in the courtyard. Up in the sky, the first stars began to twinkle.

Damon remained on his knees. Gwyneth was looking away from him, no doubt formulating what she was going to say. He could kill her now, wrap his hands around her throat and squeeze as hard as he could. Even if it wouldn't end the war, Megan would thank him at least. He'd never get away though, and given how the witches dealt with minor criminals, what would lie in store for him? Experts could take years to torture someone to death.

"Where's Meg?"

"I don't know."

"I hear she's heading for the Snow Cities."

"It was mooted."

"Is that where she hid him? With barbarians and unbelievers?"

"Barbarians are unbelievers by definition," said Damon. Gwyneth glared at him. "Maybe not the right time to discuss semantics."

"Where is the Savior?"

"How is your little one, by the way? We would have sent a birthday gift, but you kind of disrupted the postal service south of the Speed."

Gwyneth looked a little taken aback. How long had it been since someone had treated her with less than absolute reverence? "She's safe," she mumbled.

"I don't hear the wail of tiny lungs. You didn't bring her to the party?"

"I said, she's safe."

Damon recognized the pain that flashed in Gwyneth's eyes. He'd seen it often enough in Megan's. "You don't know where she is, do you?"

"What . . . ? How . . . ?" Gwyneth's jaw clenched. "It's for her own safety."

Her. She. Gwyneth had a daughter. So did Megan. The prophecy had specified a boy and a girl. He chuckled. The witches had gone to so much trouble to satisfy Joanne's prediction but nature had screwed with them. Maybe God wasn't on their side.

"What are you laughing at?"

"Private joke with . . ." Damon prodded the sky.

"You think this is easy for me?" demanded Gwyneth. *I think your sister suffered more.* "Why won't you tell me where the baby is?"

Because that would be the final betrayal. Eleanor and Megan would never forgive him. Damon wasn't prepared to go that far. Not yet, anyway.

Gwyneth crouched and tugged off a glove. She stroked Damon's bare chest. Her fingers were warm, hot even. Strange; he had been expecting the chilling touch of an ice queen.

"I know you're scared," she said, her voice soft. "Do you know how terrified I was when I first read the prophecy, when I worked out what it meant? There were all these horrible things I was expected to do and

I didn't know why. I had to learn I couldn't expect to understand why. God had chosen me for a purpose and it wasn't my place to question Him. We have to sacrifice all we love because His is the only love. You have to accept the way of the True with all your heart. Only then will you be free of your burden."

It sounded so easy, so simple. If Cate was one of the Saviors reborn, then she belonged with the True; if not, then it didn't matter. Either way, she would be safer with them than with some unknown northerner in the mountain wilds. They would never hurt her; they would treat her like a princess. She wouldn't fear cold, starvation or disease. But she would never know her mother.

Gwyneth brushed his face, spreading the tear that trickled down his icy cheek. "Where is he?" she whispered. Damon closed his eyes. Gwyneth pressed her thumbnail into his eyelid. "I don't want to have to turn you over to . . . I don't want to see you suffer any more than you already have."

Damon hung his head. What he was about to do was inevitable, had been since his horse threw him, had been since Megan and Eleanor had dug him out of the beach near Trafford's Haven, had been since he'd witnessed the massacre at Thicketford. Would he do it if Eleanor loved him or would he be prepared to suffer Gwyneth's torturers? He hoped to think not, but deep down he knew he wasn't capable of such sacrifice. Eleanor would hate him, but didn't she already? At least she might know the hurt she had caused him, know she could no longer take him for granted.

"The baby's no more than a day's ride from Murray."

Gwyneth kissed him on the forehead. She straightened up and held out her hand. Damon took it and hauled himself to his feet.

"Don't you feel better now?" said Gwyneth.

No, thought Damon. *Worse, a lot worse.*

Gwyneth summoned the general and the captains back into the courtyard. They huddled around the maps. Damon took advantage of their distraction to help himself to some wine. It tasted bitter, but he forced it down anyway.

Gwyneth spun around. Damon froze, goblet halfway to his lips. "Sorry," he said. "Thought it was communal."

"Where is this Murray?"

"It's up north, in Keedy," said Damon, joining them. "Somewhere around—" he pointed at a bare patch of table "—there." The map went no further than the southern shore of Lake Pullar. He spotted the mark of a New Statham cartographer in the bottom right-hand corner. There was metropolitan parochialism for you.

"What?" croaked the general.

"Looks like we're going to need a bigger map," said Damon. The officers exchanged looks. "You did bring one, didn't you?"

Another sequence of looks. Damon wondered how they were winning the war—he'd been on better organized pub crawls—until he remembered who they were fighting against. Priests had become generals and generals priests, and no one knew what they were doing.

"There'll be some maps in the temple," he said. "Should cover the whole of . . . ah. Bet you're regretting that little bout of pyromania now, aren't you?"

"Is there any further reason to keep him alive, Mother?" whispered the general.

"He is one of us."

"He needs to learn some respect."

"I have no objection to you teaching him."

"Wait, wait," said Damon, fearing the True's teaching methods followed the principle of spare the agonizing whipping, spoil the child. "I can take you to Murray."

"Really?"

"It's not that complicated."

"Give us directions then."

"Complicated enough though. Don't want you getting lost in the marshlands. They can be a bit, you know, marshy."

"A small force would be best," said Tobrytan. "We don't want the army getting bogged down."

"We can't sail," said another captain. "Most of the fleet's been dispatched back to New Statham, and what ships we have left are needed for your protection, Mother."

A third captain spoke up. "We're wasting time pursuing Joanne's wishful thinking."

"Don't start this again, Sener," said Tobrytan, a warning rumble in his voice.

"We need to march on Stratton and destroy the blasphemers before they have time to regroup instead of wasting time on this prophecy. We're pursuing some madwoman's ramblings, and for what? Apart from the loss of good men?"

Tobrytan and the other captains shouted Sener down. Damon hung back in the darkness of the cloisters, caressing his goblet. They had so long feared the witches as a monolithic force they had forgotten each one was an individual with their own desires and fears. How much of this war had they planned and how much was a reaction to events, instinctively attacking just as the Faithful instinctively ran?

The general rapped his ax-cum-crutch on the flagstones, the sound continuing to echo around the close walls until the squabbling ceased. "The True cannot achieve victory until the Saviors are under our protection," he wheezed, each word as painfully forced out as those from a dying man. "You agreed to accept the council's decision, Sener."

"Not at the cost of—" started Sener. The ax smashed into the flagstones again. "Of course, general."

"Tobrytan," continued the general, "take a cavalry company west around Lake Pullar and make best speed for this Murray. Secure the Savior at whatever cost."

"Sir."

"I'm going with him," said Gwyneth.

The general held up his hand. "We cannot risk you, Mother." *Plus*, thought Damon, *they haven't denied you your daughter only to let you get your hands on your niece.* "We can protect you better here." Gwyneth jerked her head in what might have been assent and sulked over to the wine.

The general turned back to Tobrytan. "I can trust you with this? You're not going to get sidetracked with any personal vendettas this time, are you?"

"No, sir," said Tobrytan, "but what about my daughter? I'd like to dispatch some men to pull her out of Aedran before she runs into the blasphemers."

"She has her mission," said the general. "God will guide her to safety or call her to Him."

"It is on the way," said Damon. "We could pop in, have a couple of quick ones, see if the Tobrytan-ette is around."

A faint look of triumph crossed Tobrytan's face. The general scowled. "Very well, but do not let it divert you from the Savior. Sener, take two regiments and meet up with the fleet at New Statham. Deal with the garrison there. Any questions?"

"Just one, sir," said Tobrytan, fiddling with his sword belt. "What about *her*? What if she tries to stop us?"

"You're frightened of a little girl?"

Tobrytan's eyes flicked to Gwyneth. "No, but . . ."

"My sister made her choice," said Gwyneth. "She no longer deserves God's protection."

Twenty-Two

Megan and Eleanor half-carried, half-led, Afreyda back to their room. Her wounds were mostly superficial—cuts and bruises suffered during the journey north—coupled with exhaustion. They cleaned and dressed them. Rekka brought some broth, which Afreyda sipped at first, then guzzled.

"Now," said Megan, "what about Damon?"

"The True have him," said Afreyda. "I think he is one of them."

Megan shook her head. "They forced him. A long time ago."

"They forced him now too. The True were doing it to everyone. Or killing them."

"It doesn't matter whether he went voluntarily or not," said Eleanor, pacing. "The witches have him. Sooner or later they'll know what he knows. And, knowing him, it'll be sooner."

The world blurred as Megan took this on. She had
to grip the side of a wardrobe to keep herself upright.
"Cate . . ."

"This Damon knows where the baby is?" said Rekka.
Megan and Eleanor exchanged worried looks. "Please.
Let's drop the pretense. I know who the child is, why the
True want him."

"He's a she," murmured Megan, distracted by the
images buzzing in her head: of the witches snatching
Cate, of them worshipping her in some twisted ceremony, of Gwyneth triumphant.

"I'd heard it was a boy," said Rekka. "My apologies."

"Cate's a girl's name."

"Thought you were being modern."

Blood surged through Megan's veins. She scrambled
for her weapons. "We can't sit here talking," she said.
She tried to slip a knife into her arm sheath, but she'd
unstrapped the sheath earlier and ended up slashing the
sleeve of her gown.

Eleanor took Megan by the arms and sat her down
on the bed beside Afreyda.

"I have to . . . I have to go get her," said Megan.

"Not right this second," said Eleanor.

Rekka called out something in Hilite. A guard
appeared at the door. Rekka issued more orders in
Hilite, among which Megan caught Fordel's name.
The guard saluted and dashed off. Fordel didn't

even bother delaying his appearance to disguise his eavesdropping.

"What exactly does this Damon know?" he asked.

Megan thought back to Cate's birth, when the pain of delivering her was far outweighed by the pain of Eleanor taking her away. "You were only gone a couple of days," she said to the countess. "He knows she's a day's ride from Murray." A handful of villages at most. The witches would have no trouble searching them, finding her.

"I'm not that stupid," said Eleanor. "Do you think I took her all the way myself? I met her foster-mother just outside Murray and sent them on their way. I hung around for a bit before returning. It should've been longer but I was worried about you."

Eleanor's distrust had extended to hiding the length of the journey from Damon, but not only Damon. She had also kept the truth from Megan. Oh, Eleanor could justify it, claim it was for Megan's own good, but Megan couldn't help feeling she wasn't worthy of knowing the location of her own daughter. Gwyneth wasn't the only one who regarded her as nothing more than a brood mare.

"She's far away from Murray then?" Megan asked.

"Not *that* far. A few days' ride."

Fordel stroked his beard. "Still," he said, "that gives the True a larger area to cover, and babies do all look the same. Who's the father? Any distinguishing characteristics?"

"Just some boy I thought I liked," said Megan. "I think the witches made him do it. Maybe. I don't know."

Eleanor looked agitated. "There is something . . ."

"What?" said Megan and Rekka simultaneously.

"When I said I wasn't that stupid . . ."

"What have you done?" said Megan.

"The foster-mother . . ." said Eleanor. "She's kind of a Kalvert."

"What?"

"I needed someone I could trust," said Eleanor. "She's one of Grandfather's bastards. It's not as if she bears the name."

"True," said Rekka, "but as a family we do tend to—" she turned to Fordel and twirled a lock of hair "—what did you call them? Distinguishing characteristics."

"I couldn't leave Cate with just anyone."

"But one of us? I'm surprised the baby hasn't been sold to the highest bidder already."

"We have to get to her before they do," said Megan. "We don't know what kind of a head start they have."

"But we do know exactly where to look." He looked to Eleanor. "Which is . . . ?"

"Staziker. It's a small—"

"—town in the foothills of the Kartiks," finished Fordel. "At least you picked somewhere near the mountains."

"The raiding tunnels west of Tiptun?" said Rekka.

"Speed is of the essence. We should still be able to ride over the Destiny Pass."

"Unless the snows have come early."

"They haven't," said Fordel. "It'll be quickest if we sail to Tiptun. We can get horses there."

"Wait a minute," said Megan, jumping to her feet. "What's all this 'we'? Cate's my responsibility. I'll get her. I'll protect her."

Fordel shook his head. "You think you're the only ones the True threaten? Who do you think their next target will be? The same one to which all conquerors of the Realm have turned their attention. This time the mountains won't save us and we have no desire to become a homogenous mass enslaved to a jealous God and your sister."

"We can't let the True get their hands on this baby," said Rekka.

Why did she and Fordel care what Cate might or might not be? They were rational, calculating, scornful of the Faith whether in its pure form or the witches' corruption of it. Unless . . . unless . . . Megan's stomach tightened, the rich food from the feast churning until she wanted to throw up. They didn't fear Cate, they valued her. They wanted her as a hostage, a guarantee against an attack by the witches. Gwyneth knew Megan wouldn't harm her child, but Rekka and Fordel? They wouldn't hesitate.

But what could Megan do? They knew where Cate was now, and she needed their help to reach her before the witches did. If Megan objected, there was nothing stopping them throwing her in a dungeon while they took Cate for themselves. She would have to play along until the opportunity came to rescue Cate from their clutches.

She picked up her uniform. "What are we waiting for?"

"The tide," said Fordel. "We have a little time to rest, gather our forces."

Megan slumped on the bed. Despite the ache in her body, there was no way she would be able to rest. Her mind was too active, a maelstrom of fears, but within them a gleam of hope. She was going to see Cate again. This time she wouldn't give her up, no matter what the rest of the world had planned.

They started loading the boat—the Lord Defender's official yacht—at dawn. Megan paced the dockside, nervous energy sometimes accelerating her pace to a dash. Freezing air tautened her skin. Rays from the sun speared over the mountains, catching the top of the trees and dappling the still waters, but they brought no heat with them. Gulls settled on ropes and bulwarks, squawking demands.

Afreyda appeared, a little wobbly on her feet, and made to board the vessel. Megan intercepted her on the gangplank. "Where do you think you're going?"

"There is only one way I can be going," said Afreyda. "And you are not leaving me behind again."

"You need to rest."

Afreyda edged up the gangplank until she was on the boat proper. "I am told there are bunks in the cabins."

"Proper rest."

"I have . . . unfinished business with Damon. If he has betrayed you, I must kill him. If he has not, I must rescue him."

Megan shivered, despite the heavy-duty furs and leathers Rekka had supplied them with. "You weren't to know."

"No . . ."

"I'm sorry," said Megan. "I should have told you about Cate. I shouldn't have left you. I should have come back for you."

"You had more important things to consider."

"Yes. No. I don't know. Sometimes I feel everyone wants something from me. My life's not my own."

"*Hi n'kata da mo.*"

"What?"

"No one's life is their own," said Afreyda. "We belong to our ancestors, our descendants, our family, our friends, those we serve and those who serve us."

"Is that wisdom?"

"Possibly. My father used to say it to me when I complained about doing my chores."

"Princesses do chores?" said Megan.

"Princesses who cannot afford servants because their father has spent all their money buying titles do."

"I think I'd have kept the money."

"That is what my mother said. My father—he did not have to wash his own clothes." Afreyda pointed below deck. "I must rest."

She disappeared. Megan trudged up the gangplank and rested her arms on the rail at the boat's stern. Eleanor and Rekka swept out of the Lord Defender's mansion, followed by Fordel and Vegar. What did the Lord Defender think about all this? Did Rekka and Fordel allow him to have thoughts of his own? Megan had the suspicion Vegar's role was to sit at the high table and look big at people.

". . . border guards can take of this," Rekka was saying to Eleanor. "Your men need to recuperate from their . . . exertions." She indicated Aldred and his men, who were stumbling bleary-eyed from the grand hall. They were armed and might have been dangerous had they not borne the look of people who had lost more than one drinking game. Their own footsteps were making them wince.

"They'll recover soon enough," said Eleanor. "If only Hilites enter the Realm, people'll think it's an invasion."

The gangplank bent under their collective weight. "Of course," said Rekka. "If the True spot the party, it's important they see enemies they should be attacking, not opportunistic raiders whom they can leave safely alone."

"You haven't met the witches, have you?"

"They have neglected to introduce themselves, yes."

"If they spot us, we fight or run," said Eleanor. "Hoping they'll go away is the fool's option. The priests tried that, and look what happened to them."

Rekka forced a smile. "Of course, cousin. I was merely trying to save your men further hardship." She gave Vegar a kiss—or rather buried her face briefly in his whiskers—and swished along the deck. "I'll be in my cabin if you need me."

"She's coming with us?" said Megan, keeping her voice low. Vegar and Fordel remained ashore.

"As far as Tiptun," said Eleanor, standing aside to let Aldred and his men come aboard. Megan made a mental note to steer clear of them. She doubted hangovers and sea travel were ideal companions. "Some business to see to."

"Some scheming to catch up on?"

"You're so judgmental."

"I'm not the one who insisted on bringing bodyguards."

"They're not for me," said Eleanor.

So, she shared Megan's suspicions. At least Megan didn't feel so paranoid. Well, not unjustifiably paranoid. "Is that why you tipped Afreyda out of her sickbed?"

"She's handy in a fight. And loyal."

"Not that we deserve it."

"Loyalty's rarely deserved."

The yacht left the calm waters of the inlet for the far choppier ones of the open sea. To a man, Aldred and his fellow soldiers raced to the railings and decreased the boat's payload by a few pounds. Megan turned away and contemplated the churning ocean that stretched out north to God knew where. Some said if you kept on sailing you'd go around the world and crash on the southern shores of the Diannon Empire; some said the sea was as infinite as the sky and the only thing you'd find was the truth hidden within your soul.

Eleanor brought up breakfast from the ship's galley: eggs congealed into a pliable mass that looked like it'd be handy for plugging gaps in the hull; bacon that must have broken uncountable religious laws, considering how charred to death it was; sausages loaded with spices to knock out the taste buds before they started questioning what meat was stuffed into the skins.

"I would have thought Rekka'd have better food," said Megan.

"Vegar's requisitioned all the good chefs," said Eleanor. "He might not get to rule but by God he's going to get a decent dinner."

Megan dabbed up scraps of disintegrated bacon with the tip of her finger. "Do you think Damon's told the witches about Cate?"

"Would we doing this if we thought he hadn't?"

"Do you think he told them voluntarily?"

"Who knows?" said Eleanor, shifting her food around the plate as if motion would increase edibility. "Damon always follows the path of least harm. To himself."

"He saved us when we were stuck in the Speed."

"He waited for a bit. After you'd made sure the witches had no way to follow him."

Why was Megan so keen to excuse Damon? Why did it matter? Everyone betrayed her in the end; everyone turned on her. Not that she could claim any superiority. She could have made sure Damon and Afreyda had got on a boat out of Kewley. She could have gone back to rescue them. She could have stayed safe in Murray, kept Damon out of danger and Afreyda in Gwyneth's service.

"Stop it," said Eleanor.

"Stop what?"

"I know that look. You're obsessing about what we've done wrong."

"We have to learn from our mistakes."

"We have to identify what the mistakes are first," said Eleanor, "and that's not easy." She covered her mouth and belched. "Those sausages, however, were definitely a mistake."

Afreyda emerged from below decks, swaying in time with the undulating deck. "Got your sea legs?" said Megan.

"This is nothing," said Afreyda. "I have sailed the Savage Ocean."

"Are you hungry? I can get you some breakfast."

"I wouldn't recommend it," said Eleanor.

"I have eaten, thank you. Lady Rekka brought me some food."

"Rekka?" said Megan. "That was . . . generous of her."

"I am the funny foreigner. People like to stare. Ask me stupid questions."

"Look, when I . . ."

Afreyda wasn't listening. Her attention had been caught by the soldiers at the other end of the deck. She edged toward them, her steps as deliberate as a panther's.

"What is it?" asked Megan.

Afreyda drew her sword and charged.

Twenty-Three

Megan's scream alerted the soldiers to the swords-woman thundering toward them. They drew their own weapons and pulled into tight formation. Afreyda skidded to a halt, but kept the stump of her sword raised. Her body quivered as she prepared to strike.

Megan caught up with her. "What the hell?"

"It was him!"

Afreyda jabbed at Aldred's head. He jerked out of the way. "You really trying to threaten me with a broken sword, little girl?"

"The last man who dismissed her lost his face," said Megan. To Afreyda, "What do you mean, it was him?"

"He was the one who locked Damon up."

"What do you mean, locked—?"

"In Kewley. He locked Damon up. That is why we missed the boat."

"Is this true?" Megan asked Aldred.

The lieutenant took a deep breath, adjusted his sword grip. "We found him among three dead bodies looting a jeweler's."

"What? Damon wouldn't kill anyone."

Megan didn't know what to think, what to do. She looked to Eleanor. The countess had remained at the stern of the ship. Her bow was raised, an arrow notched in it. It was hard to tell who she was aiming at.

Aldred shrugged. "I only know what I saw. Maybe he came across the bodies and saw an opportunity. The priests authorized all us officers to administer summary execution for thieves and murderers. At least I gave him a chance." He nodded toward Afreyda. "I'm sorry. I didn't know you were there too."

"Why didn't you tell us this?" said Eleanor.

"I didn't want to upset you," said Aldred. "I thought you were fond of the boy."

"I wouldn't go that far . . ." Eleanor sighed. "Do you realize what you've done?"

There was a loud crunch. Rekka was sat cross-legged on a huge coil of rope, calmly eating an apple. Willas stood beside her, hand on the pommel of his sword.

"Maybe you should all put your weapons down," said Rekka. "If we hit a big wave, people might start getting skewered. We'll never get our deposit back on the boat if the deck's stained with blood."

Megan took Afreyda's wrist and slowly lowered it. Afreyda allowed herself to be tugged back a couple of feet. Megan turned to Eleanor and nodded. The countess released the tension in her bow. The soldiers sheathed their swords. They and Afreyda glared at each other before Aldred led his men below decks.

"Deposit?" Eleanor said to Rekka.

"After the state Pálmar left it in, the council thought there should be an incentive to keep things clean. Incidentally, if you find any bits of what looks like goat, step away and give one of the deck hands a shout." Rekka tossed her apple core over the side. "It's not goat."

She followed Aldred below. Willas crossed the deck and plucked Afreyda's sword out of her hand. He examined it, taking in the intricately-carved hilt, the lacquered cross-guard, and the stunted blade, which left rusting flakes of steel on his fingers when he rubbed it.

"Where did you get this lump of pig iron?"

"It is the finest steel in the empire."

"You'd be better off fighting with a stick of shit-covered rhubarb," said Willas. "At least then you'd have a chance of infecting someone." He handed the stump back to Afreyda. "No wonder your people had to invent other ways of fighting."

He crossed to a chest. There was a clatter of metal as he rummaged in it. "This should do," he said, pulling out a short sword.

He threw it to Afreyda, a little too hard to be considered polite. She caught it anyway and turned it over in her hands. "Crude."

"Better crude and whole than fancy and not."

Afreyda tried a few experimental swipes. "It will do."

"I think that's Diannon for 'thank you,'" said Megan.

Afreyda frowned. "There is no Diannon for 'thank you.' Not one word, at least. It depends on the difference in rank." To Willas, she said, "*O'di cat mi doh no dela.* That is how a person high in rank thanks someone low in rank."

"How low?" asked Willas.

"Very."

"If this very lowly solider could make a request, please avoid killing anyone. We're going to need all the people we have."

Afreyda restrained herself and they all made it to Tiptun alive. Megan got no closer to finding out what had happened in Kewley. Why would Damon have strayed from the optimum running-away route to rob a jeweler's house, and what had Aldred been doing there? There was a lot more going on than people were admitting to, but when she asked anyone they either clammed up or told her not to worry. In the end, she conceded she had far greater concerns. She had to get Cate, not fret about the reasons why.

Tiptun was at the end of another inlet and a little smaller than Hil. The buildings were arranged in ever-climbing terraces, making it look as if each house was peering over its neighbor. A sequence of fountains lined the dockside. The low afternoon sun sparkled through the spray they threw up, sprinkling a hundred tiny rainbows alongside the water's edge.

A small delegation met them and, after a brief conversation Megan couldn't understand, swept Rekka and Eleanor off, leaving the rest of them to kick their heels on the quayside. Megan wondered how long it took to ask for horses and supplies to see them over the mountains. Someone brought them out a pot of fish soup that, while welcome, didn't promise Eleanor's immediate return.

"What're they doing in there?" said Megan.

"Forms," said Willas. "Whenever people from one of the Snow Cities go through another city's territory there's lots of paperwork to be completed. Where you're going, how many of you there are, why you're passing through."

"Why?" Megan felt a little alarmed. "They're going to tell her about . . . about . . . ?"

"They'll fill in some bland lie. It's the usual way."

"Then why bother with the forms in the first place?"

"Helps remind you what the lie was."

"Why lie?" asked Megan. "Aren't all the cities one big happy family?"

"A family that cherishes its independence. From one another as well as the Realm." Willas wafted away a gull that had become a little too interested in his soup. "The rules let everyone know where they stand."

"Sounds restrictive."

"We did think of having some guy with a big stick making decisions for everyone, but we couldn't find anyone with the right mix of capriciousness, venality and psychosis."

Eleanor and Rekka rejoined them. "Are we ready?" asked Megan.

The cousins exchanged worried glances. "If you hurry," said Rekka, "you should reach the first outpost up on the Destiny Pass by nightfall."

"We wouldn't need to hurry if it wasn't for your form fetish," said Megan.

Rekka raised her eyebrows. A faint air of amusement played on her lips, as if she had been admonished by a three-year-old.

"We had important business to take care of," said Eleanor.

"What kind of important?" asked Megan.

Eleanor looked to Rekka. "I hope we don't find out."

"What's that meant to mean?" Megan said to the countess.

"Don't worry. Come on."

They bade Rekka farewell and departed on horseback, accompanied by Aldred and his three men, Willas and three of *his* men, and a pair of Tiptunites who were to guide them over the pass. Every group saw Cate differently—hostage, prize, bargaining chip, threat. Megan feared she couldn't trust even her closest friends completely. Eleanor had proved ambivalent at best toward Cate's existence, and who knew what Afreyda was thinking? They only had her word for what had happened with Damon in Kewley, and the witches evidently had some kind of alliance with the Diannons. What if he hadn't betrayed them? What if Afreyda had, trading Cate for her freedom and a ship home? Megan hated herself for thinking such thoughts, but doubt ate away at her. It might be best to snatch Cate and make a break for it on her own.

They cleared the tree line and entered the bleak landscape of the mountains. Dull gray rock surrounded them on both sides, only occasionally broken by a patch of lichen. The temperature was dropping. Each breath chilled Megan's insides. The odd snowflake rode the wind that whipped down the pass. Megan pulled her hood tight and snuggled into her mount.

The sky shaded from indigo to black. The outpost—a large log cabin with stables attached—hove into view. Two guards, swathed in enough furs to double their bodyweight, reluctantly abandoned their brazier and waddled toward them. A brief conversation with the Tiptunites yielded an invitation inside. Those guards lucky enough not to have drawn the outside shift were gathered around a blazing fire.

Megan squeezed in by the fire. The sudden heat made her skin prickle. Beer was broken out—icy on the throat but warming on the stomach—and stew ladled into bowls.

"Me Númi," said the Tiptunite to her left. "Who you?"

"Er, me Megan."

"Hello, Megan."

"Hello, Númi. Anything to do around here?"

Númi looked at Megan blankly. She suspected she'd discovered the limits of his Stathian. She mimed tossing dice, playing the flute, dancing. Númi gave an eager thumbs-up and pointed at the bunks that lined the wall.

"Yeah," said Megan. "I suppose that was open to misinterpretation."

After a few more beers the drinking games started. The Tiptunites' favorite involved propelling chunks of wood into the fire with your crotch. Miss the fire, and your penalty was to down your cup; hit it, and your reward was to down your cup. Even Megan, who hadn't spent much time consuming alcohol as a competitive sport, thought the rules needed to be worked on.

When the players started lighting the chunks before propelling them, Megan slipped away from the circle. It was getting stuffy with all the people and the well-fed fire, and the raucousness seemed to be taunting her. She stepped outside and wandered to the north of the cabin, where she would be shielded from the worst of the wind. The sky was acutely clear—were they above the clouds?—the stars brighter than she'd ever seen them. Peaks loomed above her. She felt as if she was hiding among the skirts of stern but protective giants.

Light footsteps on the rock announced Eleanor's presence. "Everything all right?" asked the countess.

"Needed some air."

"Ah."

"What do we do if the witches already have her?"

Eleanor took a moment to process Megan's blurted question. "Cate? We'll fight. We'll get her back."

"How?"

"Don't ask me. You know I don't go in for long-term planning. I'm a bit of a stranger to *short*-term planning, if truth be told."

"How can we fight them?" said Megan. "The witches devastated the largest army since . . . since . . ."

"No one's invincible," said Eleanor. "No situation is completely without hope." There was a loud bang as the cabin door was flung open. A soldier dashed around, clutching his groin, before finally diving into a water trough outside the stables. Steam enveloped him. "See. Ten seconds ago, he thought his world was going to end, well, beneath the waist anyway. And now . . ."

"Are you comparing my situation to that of a drunk who thought it a good idea to simulate sex with a piece of burning wood?"

"One is very rarely presented with the perfect metaphor." She slipped an arm around Megan's shoulders. "Come on, we should get some rest. Long ride tomorrow."

* * *

Megan ached all over by the time they reached the
fort at the southern end of the Destiny Pass. It felt as if
someone had taken a hammer to the base of her spine
while forcing her legs into positions not suffered since
she had given birth to Cate. And to think people preferred to ride. It was a prestige thing, like contorting
yourself to wear a fancy dress whose chief attraction
was that it cost a sovereign rather than a shilling.

The Tiptunites proved to be lovable oafs—like the
boys from back home, who would attempt no number of
ridiculous feats in order to raise a smile—but then they
probably knew the least of what was going on. Númi,
who joined them on their journey, took Megan as his
personal charge, always ready with food and drink and
the best spot by the fire.

"You remind him of his sister," Willas told her.

"Why did he try to get me to sleep with him then?"

"All right, half-sister."

"That doesn't make it as less creepy as you think it
does."

They reached the fort at the southern end of the pass,
where they recuperated, resupplied and reinebriated.
The next morning, as they prepared the fresh horses, the
Tiptunites saddled up with the rest of them, to Megan's
consternation.

"What's going on?" she whispered to Eleanor.

"They're coming with us apparently."

"Why?"

"For protection," said Eleanor.

"Whose?"

Eleanor shrugged. The Tiptunites didn't seem so lovable anymore.

They crossed into the Realm. There was no formal road, just a memory of travelers long gone, whose footsteps had eroded the grass. They were able to spur the horses on and at least get some speed for their pains.

Megan brought her horse parallel to Eleanor's. "Whereabouts are we?" she asked.

"I'm not sure."

"How long is it going to take us?"

"The answer to that is implied by my first response," said Eleanor.

"You do realize it would have been quicker to say you didn't know, don't you?"

"But that way you wouldn't learn."

One of Aldred's men, who had been sent on ahead to scout, emerged from a smattering of trees that covered the hill ahead of them and galloped back. "Witches," he panted.

Everyone halted. "How many?" said Aldred.

"Er . . . some?"

"Care to expand?"

The scout screwed up his face. "More than three, sir."

"How many more than three?"

"A few more, sir."

"You can count, can't you?" said Eleanor.

"Of course, ma'am. One . . . two . . . three . . ."

"And . . . ?"

"And so on."

Willas rolled his eyes. "And you wonder why your side is losing this war."

"When I enlisted, they said I'd only have to hit witches," protested the scout. "No one said I'd have to do math."

Aldred sighed. "All right, we're going to need a volunteer. If you don't know how many there are of us here, don't bother."

Megan didn't wait. She dug her heels into her mount's ribs. "Not you!" shouted Eleanor as Megan ignored her and headed up the hill, not slowing until she entered the woods. She tied her horse's reins around a branch and crept the rest of the way.

She slid around a tree. Down below, by the side of a brook that trickled down the hill, half a dozen witches had set up camp and were roasting an animal over a fire. A few of them had taken off their armor. One of them was even using his breastplate as a makeshift sink, washing the dust from his head and neck.

"We could go around them," said Eleanor, her unexpected presence making Megan jump.

"We're going to fight them eventually," said Megan. "Might as well do it on our own terms."

"I'm sure Aldred won't mind taking on the witches in a fair fight."

"Since when does ambushing a smaller force count as a fair fight?"

"When you're the ambusher, not the ambushee."

The soldiers tied their horses up well out of earshot and took up positions along the tree line above the witches' camp. Aldred stationed Eleanor and one of Willas's men to provide archery support, with Megan and Afreyda covering them, while the rest prepared to rush the enemy. He was of the minimalist school of military tactics, it would seem.

Aldred raised his sword. The archers took aim. "When I say—"

The Hilite bowman fired. There was a spark as his arrow glanced off one of the witches' breastplates. The witches' heads snapped around. They grabbed axes, slotted bolts into crossbows.

"Charge!"

The soldiers careered down the hill, brandishing their swords and yelling. One of the Tiptunites lurched backward and hit the ground, a crossbow bolt jutting out of his stomach. He swiped at it, trying to grab on to the shaft, but his strength gave out.

Battle commenced with a chime of steel, a whirl of limbs, a spray of blood. Eleanor's bow jerked from side to side as she tried to get a clear shot among the melee. Air swished against Megan's cheek as the countess's arrow whistled past. A witch staggered from the morass, clutching in pain at the arrow sticking out of his thigh. Eleanor reloaded and took careful aim, controlling her breathing. The second shot ended the witch's suffering.

A severed head bouncing away like a stray ball signaled the end of the fight. Megan and the others tramped downhill to join the victors, who were crouching or standing with hands on their knees, panting as they recovered. She did a count of their numbers. One missing, even accounting for the shot Tiptunite.

"Who . . . ?"

Aldred pointed at the heap of twitching bodies. One of his men lay there, staring lifelessly at the sky. Megan closed her eyes and made the sign of the circle.

Willas wiped his sword on the grass. "You should stay here," he said to Aldred, "bury your dead. We can escort Megan the rest of the way."

"I hardly knew the guy," said Aldred.

Willas turned to Númi, who was going through the witches' pockets, and said something to him—probably the same thing he had said to Aldred. Númi shook his head and moved close to Megan, making his feelings clear.

These were unlikely to be the only witches in the area. They should get going, reach Cate before they did. Yet Megan couldn't abandon the bodies so callously. These men had fought for her, died for her, even if they didn't know why. She at least owed them the funeral rites.

She cocked her head at Eleanor. The two of them dragged the dead soldier of the Realm clear of the witches. Megan couldn't help but notice his wound, a neat piercing through his neck, in one side, out the other.

He'd been stabbed with a sword: a weapon none of the witches had been carrying.

They covered the bodies as best they could and went on their way. Megan brooded over her slaughtered countryman. Had it been an accident—a desperate thrust in the confusion that hit the wrong target—or someone eager to adjust the odds in his favor? She glanced over to Willas. He betrayed no emotion as they trotted along, his only action the occasional tug at the reins of the now-spare horses, which seemed to be the only living things around not bothered about finding Cate.

They joined the road, a snaking track of packed mud. Manure steamed in the sun. A little way on, they caught up with a cart drawn by a tired shire horse that looked as if it had been revived by some occult ceremony weeks after its death. A farmer dozed in the driver's seat, drool glistening like a slug's trail on his whiskers.

"You there," said Aldred. "Halt."

The farmer slowly opened his eyes and took in the armed men surrounding him. "I stop," he drawled, "this 'orse never starts again."

"How far to Staziker?"

"D'pends where you're starting from."

"Here."

The farmer looked around. "What d'you want to be here for? There's nought around for miles."

"Is everyone as stupid around here as you?"

"Dunno," said the farmer. "Dunno everyone."

Sunlight flashed on steel as Aldred started to draw his sword. Megan flashed an alarmed look at Eleanor. The countess cleared her throat and moved her mount forward, nudging Aldred's horse aside.

Aldred dropped his weapon back into its scabbard. "I don't think you—"

The farmer straightened up as Eleanor came into his eye line. "My lady."

"How far to Staziker?"

"Four or five miles."

"You seen any witches?"

"No, my lady."

"Thank you," said Eleanor.

They pushed on, leaving the farmer to crawl along at his own pace. Megan envied his lack of worry, his satisfaction that wherever he was going would still be there whenever he happened to arrive. She couldn't rid herself of the nagging fear they'd be too late; that they'd arrive to witness the witches snatching Cate.

Aldred caught up with them. "How did you . . . ?" he asked. "With . . . ?"

"You need the hair," said Eleanor, tossing her head.

Staziker reminded Megan of a larger version of home: a peaceful collection of houses in the middle of acres of farmland. Before they entered the town, she pulled her horse up by the bubbling stream that ran parallel to the road and washed her face in its chilly water. She was going to see her daughter again. Her heart thudded so hard it made her tremble. Nausea made a knotted mess of her stomach. She cupped her hands and dipped them in the river. They shook so much that by the time she raised them to her lips there was nothing to drink but a few drops clinging to her palms.

"Are you all right?" asked Eleanor.

"A bit warm," said Megan.

Eleanor handed her a water skin. "Have some of that." Megan had a sip. The skin didn't contain water. Her throat burned, but her nerves subsided a little.

They remounted and made their way into town. The villagers took one look at them and fled inside. Doors were slammed, windows shuttered. In thirty seconds flat the only sign of life in Staziker was a sleepy cat who wasn't giving up his place in the sun in a hurry.

"I think you need to do the hair thing," Megan said to Eleanor.

"That might have been what caused this," said the countess. "For every person who loves you, there are five who hate you." She slid off her horse. "I suppose we start knocking on doors. Shall we try the inn first?"

"How did I know you were going to suggest that?"

Aldred made to dismount. Eleanor shook her head. "You'll scare the natives. Split the men. Cover both approaches to the village. If the witches are coming, we want as much notice as possible."

The atmosphere inside the inn was the usual smell of sweat, ale and involuntary digestive processes. Megan let her eyes adjust to the low light and resisted the temptation to pull out a knife. It might be considered provocative—unless you were in the seedier parts of Eastport, where you had to demonstrate you had a weapon and thus knew what you were letting yourself in for before the bouncers would admit you.

The only occupant was the barman, who was cleaning a tankard, though half-empty cups and a swinging back door suggested the numbers had been greater a few seconds earlier.

Eleanor strutted up to him. "We're looking for Odelia."

"That right?" The barman spat on to the tankard and polished.

"It's a matter of life and death."

"Whose?" said the barman.

Eleanor slammed a knife into the bar. "Yours." The barman backed off. Bottles rattled on the shelves behind him as he bumped into them.

"I thought you didn't want to scare the natives," said Megan.

"Countesses are allowed a little capriciousness."

"Go out and turn right," said the barman. "Keep walking—"

"You trying to threaten me?"

"—keep walking until you reach the end of town. Odelia's is the last house on your left."

The sun was blinding when they got back outside. They traipsed along the road following the barman's instructions. Hostile gazes followed their progress through darkened gaps. Just for once Megan would like someone to be pleased to see them. She remembered Rekka had been. Maybe not the greatest precedent.

Odelia's was a well-appointed two-story house. A young woman who looked dressed for bed despite the hour led them through dimly lit corridors whose thick carpets muffled their footsteps. Incense hung heavy in the air, making Megan drowsy. A rhythmic squeaking came from above their heads—a weather vane? Whatever, Megan felt a little reassured. At least Eleanor hadn't condemned Cate to some hovel.

A woman reclined on a couch that, like its occupant, had seen its best days a few decades ago. Her once red hair was reduced to a few tawny streaks in a sea of white. Wrinkles creased her brow and her neck. An arthritic hand speckled with liver spots clutched a chipped goblet she rested on her stomach. Odelia, Megan assumed.

"You really did come back."

"I said I would," said Eleanor. "How—?"

"Where's Cate?" snapped Megan, unable to wait any longer.

"Who are you?"

"She's the mother."

"The baby actually *was* a friend's? Two truths from a Kalvert. More than my mother ever got."

"Where's Cate?" repeated Megan.

"She's not here."

Blood surged in Megan's veins. Before she knew what she was doing she had a knife ready to thrust into Odelia's throat. "What? Where is she? Tell me now!"

Eleanor and Afreyda dragged her off. "Calm down."

"What? She's—"

"You think I can nurse a baby at my age? I'd have to hold her down by my ankles. One of my girls has her. Synne."

"Where is she?"

"She had some time off so she took Cate for a walk by the lake," said Odelia. "It's a nice day. Or it was, anyway."

The creaking picked up pace. It must be getting windier. "And where can we find this lake?"

Odelia hauled herself off the couch. "I'd better come with you. Synne's got quite attached to the baby, especially since her own little one passed on."

They gave Odelia one of the spare horses and trotted into the fields. The energy coursing through Megan made her want to jump off her mount and run, but she restrained herself. She had to show control. She told herself to relax, enjoy summer's last gasp. The sun shone high in a sky broken by only the lightest of clouds. The air was still, as if the world was holding its breath at the thought of the impending meeting.

Wait—*still*? That had been no creaking weather vane. Megan realized what the squeaking had been, what the young woman who had greeted them did, what Odelia's house was.

She yanked her horse to a halt and indicated Eleanor should do the same. "You took Cate to a . . . ?" she hissed. "Odelia's a . . . ?"

"Not personally. Not unless there're clients with a serious fetish."

"What were you thinking?"

"I'm trying not to now."

"You know what I mean."

"How better to hide an unexpected baby?" said Eleanor. She shrugged. "It's in the nature of the trade that accidents occur. What do you think happens to bastards normally? Not all of them are the Saviors reincarnated. You take what you can. Odelia's done better than most."

They recommenced their journey. Megan soon spotted the lake shimmering on the horizon. By its shore, underneath the shade of a tree, a girl sat cross-legged. She had a full figure, rosy cheeks and golden hair tied in a braid on the verge of unraveling. She was pointing out the butterflies that fluttered past to the baby in her lap. Synne. And Cate.

Megan gripped the reins so tightly it made her horse toss its head and whinny in complaint. Synne shot to her feet at the sound and clutched Cate to her breast. She relaxed when she recognized Odelia, but only a little.

"Who's this?"

"This is Cate's mother," said Odelia.

Synne shook her head and backed up. The water prevented any further retreat. She looked a little alarmed. "You said she wouldn't . . ."

"Yes, well . . ."

Megan slipped off her horse and moved toward mother and child, feeling as if she was approaching a trapped animal. "I'm not going to hurt you."

"Why would you hurt—?"

Megan raised her hands. "Sorry, that wasn't the best thing to say." She licked her lips, which felt dry and cracked like old paint. "I don't know how to thank you for looking after Cate when I couldn't. I tried my best to make the world a safe place for her. I've been from one end of Werlavia to the other and I failed every step of the way. There's only one thing I can do now to protect her: I have to take her as far away as possible. She's the only family I have, the only thing that matters."

Synne's gaze flicked over Megan's shoulder, in Odelia's direction. Megan didn't dare turn around to see what the response was to the unspoken question. Synne shuffled forward. Hesitantly, she held out Cate. In turn Megan held out her arms, tensing the muscles to stop herself from trembling. Into her embrace Synne placed Cate, a squirming lump of warmth and softness.

For the first time since she had given birth to her, Megan held her daughter.

Twenty-Four

The witches found Damon the horse that had refused to jump him over the canal, which impressed neither the rider nor the ridden. At first light, a few dozen of them set off, split evenly between regulars and auxiliaries. Those of the True who had sailed from the Diannon Empire—who had fought in the first war or were descended from those who had—were clad in the usual black lacquered armor, scratched and dented now after so much action, hints of tattoos snaking out on to sunburnt skin. The auxiliaries, who had been recruited from Eastport and the other lands the True had conquered, were relegated to leather rather than steel armor, their crude axes and maces bearing the unmistakable mark of weapons banged out in a hurry.

The days passed in a monotony of riding and silence. The nights didn't even have the attraction of moving scenery. Damon couldn't sleep. Despite his tiredness and the ache in his bones, he spent them staring at the sky, wondering if there was anything beyond the black void and, if so, whether it cared about him, if he was worth caring about.

He brooded over Eleanor and Megan, what he had done to them, what they had done to him. What did he owe them? They had saved his life, he theirs. They had rejected him, the True had accepted him. They were fighting a hopeless war for a cause neither of them had any reason to believe in.

It didn't have to be like this. They had been happy when it was just the three of them, even if they spent most of the time looking over their shoulder as they flitted from place to place. But Megan wanted revenge, and Eleanor to justify the titles that weighed her down. What Damon wanted was to be rid of this whole mess.

He guided his horse level with Tobrytan's. "Do you ever wonder if you're doing the right thing?" he asked the witch captain.

"No."

"No doubts? No misgivings? No niggling worries all this slaughter might be a little bit naughty?"

"The way of the True is the only way. Once you resolve to follow it, you know no doubt. If *you* do, perhaps your acceptance isn't absolutely sincere."

In Damon's view, only simpletons and dogs were absolutely sincere. "I wasn't sensing things were doubt-free back at witch central."

"Do not use that term."

"Sorry, force of habit."

They trotted on for a while, letting the horses clop out a tired beat. "What about that guy?" said Damon. "Sener?"

"He dou—He has an alternative theory regarding Joanne's prophecy."

"That it's a load of crap?"

Tobrytan's jaw clenched. "If he was anybody else . . ."

"Let me guess," said Damon. "The general's son?" Tobrytan nodded. "So he protects his children, whereas yours . . . What's this about a daughter anyway? I thought your family died at Trafford's Haven?"

"I married again," said Tobrytan. "A Diannon woman."

Damon thought about Afreyda, wondered if she'd got away. She could be following them, watching them from the cover of the dense woods that edged the shore of Lake Pullar, waiting for the best moment to rip his throat out. "And where is she, this wife of yours?"

"She remained behind in the empire."

"Keeping the home fires burning while you're off a-killin'?"

"It was at the Emperor's insistence."

"Ah," said Damon. "He's not a nice guy, from what I hear."

Tobrytan glanced over at him. "I can think of other men I'd prefer to see dead first."

"You're a hard one to squeeze a compliment out of, aren't you?"

"Only God deserves praise."

And He's so insistent on receiving it too, thought Damon.

They found a clearing and made camp. Damon failed to fall asleep, as usual, and spent the night watching his breath condense and dissipate in the moonlight. What was he doing? The True cared for him no more than Eleanor had. Did he really want to see Cate in their hands? It meant nothing: their guns were unstoppable. It meant everything: Megan's sole purpose in fighting was to make the world safe for her daughter. And he, like thousands of others, was caught in the middle.

There was a sequence of hisses followed by a splash from the direction of the lake. Damon rolled upright. Around him, witches slept, producing snores of various intensity. The hisses and splash repeated themselves. A bored guard skimming stones across the lake. Damon warmed his hands against the dying embers of the fire and padded down to the shore.

The guard was about to send out another stone when he caught Damon's footsteps. He grabbed his ax. "Who goes there?"

"Do people really say that?"

"Oh, it's *you.*"

Damon joined the solider. Water lapped the ground a few inches from their feet. "I couldn't sleep," he said. "Want me to take over your watch?"

"You know what the captain'll say about that."

"We know what the captain'll say about *everything*. He's so boringly predictable." Damon checked the soldier's armor. Leather. An auxiliary. Maybe open to persuasion. "What's your name?"

The soldier hesitated. Damon jutted his hand out a little farther. Social conditioning got to the soldier. He took it. "Upton."

"Having a good war, Upton?" asked Damon. The soldier grunted. "Wise to get in early. Get all the good loot."

"There's no looting."

"That's just for show, isn't it? Convince the populace you're—we're—better than the other side. As long as everyone's discreet, who's going to mind? The war won't last forever. No point in coming out of it empty-handed."

"What are you getting at?"

"You don't think of a peaceful retirement? Say, a mill out in the country?"

"Can't say I've considered it," said Upton, kicking halfheartedly at the pebbles underfoot.

"Sounds nice though, right? Better than . . . what did you do before?"

"Tanner's assistant. I was in charge of the piss."

"Don't tell me you want to go back to that," said Damon.

"No, but I'm not going robbing. If I got caught . . ."

"You won't have to rob anyone."

Damon knelt down and slipped a hand inside his boot. He fiddled around a bit until he found what he was looking for, then straightened back up and held out his hand, letting the starlight glitter on the diamond's exquisite facets. You couldn't fault Kendrick's eye when it came to precious stones.

Upton's breath quickened. "Is . . . ? Is that . . . ?"

"Yours, yes."

"Why?"

"I don't like to see your hard soldiering go unrewarded."

"What's the real reason?"

Damon closed Upton's hand around the jewel. "Just look away at the right time."

Aedran was deserted when they reached it. Fresh burns scarred the wall of the town's temple, but it had survived mostly intact. Tobrytan stared at them and stroked his beard. There was something akin to worry on his face.

"Your doing?" Damon asked.

"What?"

"I don't like to prejudge, but your bunch does have a reputation for this sort of thing." *Your bunch? Our bunch now, surely?*

A couple of the town's few remaining inhabitants made the mistake of letting themselves be seen peeking from the windows of their houses. Upton and some other witches dragged out a middle-aged woman, her eyes red from tears and sleeplessness, and a soldier with a bloody bandage covering one eye. Damon took a moment to recognize Norvel. He'd survived Kendrick's spiked walking stick then.

"You're working for them?" spat Norvel.

Damon affected nonchalance. "It's a living."

"You know what happens to traitors, don't you?"

"They live."

Tobrytan swung off his horse and approached the captives. He drew his sword, heavy and sharp. The woman went pale and started to pray. *That's really not going to help.*

"Where is everyone?" said Tobrytan, resting his blade on Norvel's shoulder.

"Gone."

"Where?"

"Everywhere."

"Was there a girl here?" Tobrytan said to the woman. "Young, black hair, about . . ." He swung and decapitated Norvel. ". . . about that height." He prodded at the headless corpse, which spewed blood for a moment then toppled over.

The woman screamed and collapsed in Upton's arms. Damon looked away. Norvel wasn't his favorite person, but he hadn't wanted that to happen. Maybe if it had been Aldred . . .

"Well?" said Tobrytan. "Was she?"

"I'm not sure she's in a fit state to . . ." started Upton.

Tobrytan ignored him and slapped the woman out of her hysterics. She told them everything: of the refugees that had come to Aedran, of the spy they had brought with them, of the panic when they learned the witches were on their way. Damon's heart skipped a beat when he heard of a red-haired woman and her bossy friend.

"And the spy?"

"Father Broose spared her," said the woman. "The Faith is merciful."

"Mercy is God's privilege," said Tobrytan, "not man's. It is his job to follow the laws of the Book, not interpret them as he sees fit."

The woman sniffled. "I don't understand. We *should* have killed your spy?"

"If you valued what you believe in, yes."

"This spy's your daughter," said Damon.

"And?" said Tobrytan.

"I thought God was a harsh father."

* * *

The witches marched out of Aedran. Tobrytan brooded in the saddle, his expression even more sour than usual. Damon supposed he should feel sorry for him but he was expending all his sorrow on himself and had none to spare.

They reached a crossroads. "Which way?" Tobrytan demanded.

"Murray's that way," said Damon, pointing to the track heading off to the northwest. He swung his arm to the north. "Hil, however . . ."

"Hil?"

"The nearest of the Snow Cities." Damon saw the glimmer in Tobrytan's eyes. He leaned in. "It'll be where they're taking your daughter."

A muscle twitched under Tobrytan's ear. "That's irrelevant."

"They do have soldiers with them, I guess," said Damon. "You don't want to get into a fight. Not without your guns."

"You think we're scared of the rabble the priests managed to raise?"

Damon shook his head. "They'll only be a quick hop through the Smallwood marshes. Won't take us too far out of our way."

"We have to find the Savior."

"Of course," said Damon. "The cause of the True is more important than anything, even family. The general was very insistent on that, wasn't he?

Honorable fellow. You'd do well to follow his example. He wouldn't bend the rules for his son's sake, not like Megan. She'd do anything for her child, sacrifice anything." *Even me.*

"What do you mean by that?"

"What do you think I mean?"

Tobrytan's horse took advantage of the lull to make for the field alongside the road and its fresh grass. Tobrytan wrenched it back with a snarl and glared at Damon. "Sometimes I wonder whether you're a demon sent to test our faith."

"Ironically, that's what we used to think of you." Damon caught himself. "What they used to think."

He nudged his horse toward the northwest road. "Let's get to Murray then. I'm sure all our souls could do with Savior-ing. Especially your wife's. She might be a bit bereft after . . ."

Damon glanced behind him. Tobrytan was twisting the reins as if he was trying to garrote his horse. A dilemma? Damon doubted the witch captain had faced many problems that didn't have a ferric solution. Would he disobey the general or disappoint his wife?

Tobrytan summoned one of his lieutenants. "Meccus, take a dozen men and head north after the blasphemers. If they have any of us, secure them."

"And the blasphemers, sir?"

"Do what you have to."

Damon wasn't sure if this was what he wanted. Still, it left him with fewer men from whom to escape. Should he find the nerve to do so.

Upton had been assigned the late watch that night, the one long after midnight and an age before the dawn, when the body wanted nothing more than slumber. Tobrytan, determined to make up in time what they lacked in speed, had pushed them until the last sliver of daylight slipped below the horizon. Most of the witches had fallen asleep as soon as they swallowed the last mouthful of their rations. Damon had no trouble staying awake, not with the way his heart fluttered and his thoughts boiled. He waited for Upton to go on duty, then, light on his feet as he could manage, scurried after him.

"You know when I said I wanted you to look away . . . ?"

"Why didn't you just sneak off behind my back?" whispered Upton.

"Didn't want you getting spooked and raising the alarm."

Upton looked around in the traditional manner of someone signaling they were doing something sketchy, then sidled away from the camp, sending Damon meaningful glances. Damon tiptoed after him. "Are you . . . ?" he asked.

"I want another diamond."

Only one? Upton had sold himself cheap: Damon had readied an extra three. "I don't know . . ." said Damon. Upton made to call out. "All right, all right."

Damon handed over the smallest of the stones. Upton rolled it between his finger and thumb before slipping it in his belt.

"I didn't see you."

"God bless the unobservant."

It felt good to be out on his own at last. Damon took long strides in the gloom, stretching muscles unused after the uncountable days jammed in the saddle. He'd head west, to Percadia perhaps, somewhere untouched by the war. He'd change his name, his appearance, his past. A fresh start.

The dark shimmered in his peripheral vision. A trick of the not-light? He strained his ears. An owl hooted, a fox yapped, something pattered among the leaves the trees were starting to become tired of. Mostly, though, there was just the hiss of the night, the noise of the world at rest.

A spark flared in the black, burning itself on his retina. It grew into a flame and multiplied, its children arcing around him. Damon spun on his heel. Witches gathered around, each lighting a torch from his prede-cessors, surrounding him with a ring of fire.

Damon swallowed down his fear, clenched his fists hard to keep control of himself. "Nine out ten for effect," he said, trying to keep his voice from trembling. "You missed out the evil cackle though."

"You have a duty to God," said Tobrytan, stepping into the circle, his sword drawn, "to the Saviors."

"You want *me* to do the evil cackle? All right, I'll give it a try." Damon attempted a laugh. It degenerated into a strangulated sob.

Tobrytan flicked his naked blade. Flame whirled as a couple of witches discarded their torches and pounced on Damon. He was pinned to the ground, his struggles doing nothing more than grinding up dust from the dry soil.

"How are we going to stop you running again?" said Tobrytan. He scraped a whetstone along the edge of his sword, showering the air with sparks. "Make sure you can't run."

He pointed at Damon's foot. Upton scurried forward and yanked Damon's boot off. "You treacherous—" spat Damon. A soldier cut him off by jamming an ax shaft into his mouth. Not just to cut him off. To prevent him from biting off his tongue.

Damon tried to yank his leg away. Another soldier grabbed it and pushed it into the ground, gripping so hard the blood was squeezed from Damon's calf. No amount of thrashing could wrench Damon free.

"Stop squirming," said Tobrytan, "or I'll take the other one off too."

He rested his sword on Damon's bare ankle, working out his angles. Damon's skin stung as the blade pierced it. Droplets of blood welled up. Tobrytan raised his sword high above his head. Torchlight danced in the polished metal. Damon tried to plead, bargain, threaten. His muffled cries were nothing but the grunts of an animal.

The blade hurtled downward. Every muscle in Damon's body contracted, preparing for the onrush of pain. It didn't come. Tobrytan's sword struck the ground an inch past his foot.

"Will you run again?" said Tobrytan, brushing dirt from the edge of his blade. Damon's relief gushed into his pants. He shook his head. "Clean yourself up. You can find your own way back."

The ax shaft was ripped from Damon's mouth, almost taking his teeth with it. As the witches trooped away, he sat up and dried his face, and tried to convince his heart that beating five times its normal rate was doing neither of them any favors.

He groped for his boot. Upton got there before him. He tipped it up and caught the velvet pouch that slipped out. He checked the diamonds in there, then threw the boot at Damon's head.

Twenty-Five

Cate lay peacefully in Megan's arms. For all of five seconds. Then she started bawling, her face red and screwed up, her tiny lips trembling. Megan tried rocking her. That made things worse. The crying increased in intensity. Megan's own agitation grew. She had come all this way for her daughter and she had no idea how to look after her, why she was distressed, what she could do to make it better. And she really thought this was the best thing for her?

She looked up at the others, whose faces expressed varying balances of pity and contempt. "I don't . . ."

Synne eased Cate out of her arms. "She's due her feed."

She slipped off the strap of her dress and guided Cate to her breast. The baby's cries evaporated. She guzzled contentedly. A little milk trickled down her chin. Synne wiped it away with her thumb.

Megan looked away, embarrassed at her failure. Eleanor and Afreyda led the horses down to the lakeside to drink. They muttered between themselves. Megan thought she caught her name, but failed to make out anything else.

Odelia produced a small bottle of something noxious and sucked on it. "What happens now?" she said.

"We leave," said Eleanor, striding back to them.

"You're taking her from me?" said Synne.

Eleanor shook her head. "You're coming with us." Her gaze flicked down to the suckling Cate. "We need you."

"Is that all I am now? A wet nurse? I was the one who was always there for her." Synne glared at Megan. "When you weren't."

"Believe me, you'll be safer north of the Kartiks."

"I'm not going to the Snow Cities!" said Synne, paling. "They'll . . . they'll . . ."

"You'll be well taken care of," said Eleanor.

"And what about me?" asked Odelia. "That's one of my best earners you're taking."

Eleanor pulled a purse out from her furs and tossed it at Odelia. She pulled a handful of gold coins out of it. They flashed as they caught the sun.

"Snow City gold?"

"It's gold, isn't it?" said Eleanor. "No one's going to refuse it."

"The girl's yours."

"No," said Megan, sharp enough to make everyone jump. "Synne's her own. She belongs to no one but herself. However—" she wrapped her hand around Synne's "—I know I don't have the right to ask you this," she said, "but we need you, *she* needs you. We can't get her to safety without you."

"Either way, I'm keeping the gold," said Odelia. "Unlike emotional blackmail, it pays the bills."

Synne looked around—at the clouds drifting in the pale sky, the trees swaying in the breeze, the woman with expectant eyes, and finally at the baby resting in her arms. "I'll come with you," she said.

"Thank you," said Megan.

"For Cate's sake."

"She's all I care about."

Megan fumbled in her furs and pulled out the statuette of the Saviors and child. "I got her this when I was in Statham. It's not much, I know."

"No . . ."

"You were meant to disagree with me."

"Sorry. It's lovely."

Megan proffered the statuette to Cate, who grabbed it with a tiny fist and shoved it into her mouth.

Synne pulled it away, looking a little shocked. "You can't eat the Saviors!" she said to Cate.

"If anyone can, she can," said Megan.

They set off, back up the gentle slopes that led to Staziker. Synne and Cate rode Megan's horse, which

Megan led in a slow walk so as not to disturb Cate, who was enjoying a postprandial nap while sucking on one of the Savior's heads, coating it with drool. Megan wished she could join her, lie down in the soft grass and enjoy the last of the summer's rays. But no, her journey was only half complete, and even then it was only one journey among many.

"How did you end up . . . ?" she asked Synne. "You know . . . ?"

Synne took a while before answering. "There was this boy. I got into trouble. My parents kicked me out."

"This boy wasn't there for you?"

"He ran away, joined the army."

"Bet he's regretting *that* now," said Eleanor.

"It's only for a short while," said Synne. "I'm saving up to start my own inn. A nice one, not some dive. Somewhere you can take children and get food that won't kill—"

A horse crashed down the fields toward them, its saddle empty. Their own mounts started, kicking and pulling as the runaway bolted past. Megan gripped the reins of hers tight, trying to calm it and in turn calm Cate, who had kicked up a fuss at the latest disturbance to her world. Where was the rogue horse's rider? Had it simply been tied up and broken free? If so, why did it appear so spooked?

"Wait here," Eleanor said to Megan. "And this time I mean it."

She cocked her head at Afreyda. The two women galloped up the hill. Megan bounced on the spot, offering the fakest of reassuring smiles to Synne. She tried to work out how long it would take Eleanor and Afreyda to get up to the road at full pelt. Should she go and help or was it her priority to get Cate to safety? She knew what Eleanor would say, but she hated the idea of running away while her friends were in danger.

Afreyda appeared at the top of the hill and beckoned to them. Megan didn't have the patience to plod up there. She swung herself up on to her mount and slipped an arm around Synne's waist. The horse whinnied in protest.

"I'm not that heavy," muttered Megan. "Hold her tight," she said to Synne.

She kicked the horse into a canter, bouncing up the field as fast as she dared. As she got closer she could see Afreyda had her sword drawn, and as she got closer still that there was blood collecting on its point.

"What the . . . ?"

Afreyda indicated the road. One man—a Tiptunite—had a crossbow bolt through his head, a bloody gash where his face should be. Eleanor and Aldred were trying to staunch the flow from a wound of a soldier of the Realm, pressing down on his chest until their hands and forearms were scarlet.

"We were ambushed," said Aldred. He tipped his head toward two other corpses: men in black leather armor scarred with hoofmarks and sword cuts. "Bastards."

"The man's dead," said Odelia. "Slit his throat and have done with."

The wounded soldier summoned up enough energy to make an obscene gesture. "He's dead when we say he is," said Eleanor. "Afreyda, go warn the others. Megan, take Synne and get Cate ready to travel. You—" she looked to Aldred "—help me get him on a horse. We need to get him to Odelia's."

"What?" said Odelia.

"I'm sure you've got plenty of beds."

Megan urged her horse on to Staziker, heart thumping, fear bitter in her mouth. "I don't understand," said Synne. "Who were those men? Why were they all dead? Are they the ones after Cate?"

They reached Odelia's before Megan had to answer Synne's questions. "Pack," she said, bundling Synne toward the stairs. "Dress warm."

Eleanor and Aldred burst through with the bleeding soldier, followed by Odelia. "We need bandages," said Eleanor. "Clean water. Needle and thread to stitch the wound."

"He's dead," said Odelia.

"Don't start—"

"Really dead."

Eleanor halted and indicated for Aldred to do the same. They laid the soldier on the carpet. Eleanor pressed her fingers against his throat, feeling for a pulse. She shook her head. Aldred made the sign of the circle and swore in a decidedly nonpious manner.

"You're going to leave him there?" said Odelia.

"You were the one who was keen to abandon him," said Eleanor, closing the lids on the soldier's glassy eyes. "Besides, he seems comfortable."

"Do you know how much I paid for that carpet?"

"More than a man's life?" said Megan. Odelia scowled and swished off, bunching her skirts so they wouldn't brush against the dead soldier.

There was a thump from above. Synne, Cate slung across her breast, struggled out of one of the first-floor rooms, dragging a heavy trunk behind her. "Any chance of a hand?" she called down the stairs.

"What the hell have you got in there?" asked Eleanor. "Contrary to what it might look like, this is not a bring-your-own-corpse party."

"A few essentials," said Synne. "Tools of the trade."

"Bring what you need for a couple of days' ride. No more."

Hoofs clattered outside. It was Afreyda and the rest of the soldiers: Captain Willas and his men; Corporal Eddy, who had been in charge of the yacht at Kewley; and Númi, the sole remaining Tiptunite. The numbers were tilting in Willas's favor; it had to be a coincidence, right?

"That was quick," Megan said, hurrying out to them.

"They were already on their way," said Afreyda.

"We have company," said Willas. "Witches on the western road. A few miles off."

"How many?" asked Megan.

"About eight or so." Willas pointed at the trail of blood that splattered the streets and led the way into Odelia's house. "Where did that come from?"

"Witches on the eastern road," said Eleanor. "We lost three men. Scouting party, we think."

"More of them on the way?"

"Maybe."

They were coming. Of course they were coming. The universe had conspired to give her one final glimpse of her daughter before snatching her away for good.

"We'll have to fight our way through," said Willas.

"If it comes to it, captain," said Eleanor. "You have your orders from Lady Rekka?"

"We are to do anything to stop the witches getting their hands on the baby."

"And she meant *anything*."

The stony look on Eleanor's face sent a chill through Megan. "What do you mean by that?" she demanded.

Eleanor looked away.

Twenty-Six

Tobrytan cradled the baby as if presented with his first grandchild. The father sprawled on the floor, blood trickling from his forehead. The mother screamed for her child, trying to pull away from the soldiers who restrained her. Damon skulked in a corner, wishing she'd shut up, that she'd accept the inevitable, that he could get the hell away.

"Please," the woman cried, tears streaming down her face, "take what you want. Take everything. Do what you want to me. But don't take my son."

"He does not belong to you," said Tobrytan. "He has a much higher purpose than—" he looked around the dingy cottage, contempt on his face "—this."

"I won't let you get away with this. I'll hunt you down. I'll get him back."

Tobrytan motioned to the soldier guarding the exit, who drew a knife and advanced. Damon swallowed and turned his eyes to the ceiling. Old cobwebs wafted in the breeze.

The woman screamed a series of increasingly pathetic pleas that shredded Damon's nerves. The baby answered with its own wailing, its face all red and scrunched up. *Get it over with, save me from this screeching,* pleaded Damon. What was one more death among thousands? One he could prevent.

"Stop!" he yelled.

Tobrytan turned to Damon. "Why exactly?"

"Because that's not the right baby."

"And you know this how?"

"Because . . ." Damon's stomach cramped in advance of another betrayal. "Because Megan had a girl."

Tobrytan lifted the baby's diaper and peered down it. He frowned. "The prophecy said she'd have a boy."

Damon shrugged. "I don't know anything about that. I was told Megan was the Mother. No one told me there was a specific sex required."

"This is the only child we've come across of the right age."

"He's not her, if you see what I mean. He's too pale anyway. Megan's a southerner. So was the father."

"Where is this *girl* then?"

"They must have moved on after Eleanor handed her over," said Damon.

"They could be anywhere in Werlavia." Tobrytan handed the baby to one of his men and snatched a crossbow off another. "If I have to search the continent, I will, but I'll be damned if I'll do it with you."

Damon was dropping for the floor even as Tobrytan's finger squeezed the trigger. The bolt ripped through the air, skimming over his head and thudding into the wall above him, chewing up the wood. The baby started to cry, heartfelt protests at the state of the world.

Damon tried to retreat, but he was already in the corner. He buried his head in his arms, a child convinced if the danger wasn't visible it didn't exist. "No, no, no," he jabbered. "She'll be around here. Eleanor will have left her with someone she can trust. Some old family servant."

"We're a long way from Ainsworth."

"Not the Endalays," said Damon, "the Kalverts. Her mother's family." Metal scraped across leather with the malevolence of a snake's hiss. "They had land up here. Might even be some of her family left. You can't have bumped them all off in the war."

He risked looking up. Tobrytan had his sword raised over his head, but he was staying his blow for now. Damon licked his dry lips. "Why don't we give the little boy back to his mom and dad—" he glanced at the prostrate man, whose blood continued to soak into the straw scattered over the floor "—well, his mom, at least. We can work out a search plan over a drink?" He tried an ingratiating smile. "There's always the local Vomit Water. It's not as disgusting as it sounds. Well, not unless you have too much, in which case it lives up to its name."

Tobrytan looked at the soldiers holding the woman and cocked his head toward the door. They released her and left. She stood there, unsure what to do, her eyes flicking between Damon, Tobrytan and her son, wailing in the awkward grasp of a soldier.

Tobrytan shoved the baby back in the woman's arms and stormed out of the door. "Thank you," the woman said to Damon through her sobs of relief, "thank you."

Damon slipped a hand into his pocket and fingered one of the two diamonds he'd managed to keep from Upton. He should leave it, provide a little compensation for her ordeal.

"I don't know how to repay you," the woman continued.

Damon left before she could question why he didn't intervene earlier, before the witches had murdered her husband. He kept the diamond.

They split into groups and spiraled out, tramping through the countryside and terrorizing every habitat they passed through. It was a slow, demoralizing journey. Every look of fear made Damon silently beg for the witches to be given what they wanted so they could get away. Every look of anger made him cringe as he waited for the arrow to come shooting his way. Every look of hate scraped another layer off the shell he'd constructed around his soul.

"You could try asking nicely," he said to Tobrytan as they clopped away from a hamlet that had escaped burning only because a recent shower had left everything damp.

"What?"

"The Savior is meant to be a good thing, right? People might be happy he's . . . she's . . . they've returned. They might be willing to help if you explain things to them."

Tobrytan looked blank. Damon might as well have suggested they set up an artistic troupe to tell the story of the Unifier's conquests by means of interpretive dance. "They wouldn't understand."

"Have you tried?"

"Forty years ago," said Tobrytan. "And then they hunted us down. It was a test. Of our strength, our resolve, our faith. We passed it. We kept true to God."

They were circling north. Damon felt it getting colder every day, though that might have been the psychological effect of the nearby mountains that were donning their winter caps. He was beginning to doubt they were ever going to find the baby. Maybe Eleanor had sent it far away; maybe it hadn't survived its first few months; maybe Eleanor had assured it could never be a threat by bashing its head in on some remote rocks.

A faint finger of smoke curled up from the woods to the east. Damon kept its existence to himself, not wanting to face another round of intimidation, but one of the witches spotted it. They diverted right and trudged through the trees. Leaves fluttered down among them, dancing on undetectable currents. One landed on the neck of Damon's horse and stuck to the sweaty coat. He stretched forward and brushed it off.

The source of the smoke was a shack made of timbers and stones piled up in a haphazard manner as if some storm had deposited it there. It was surrounded by pens in which scores of pigs snuffled and oinked and churned the ground into a semiliquid morass. A piglet with the cheery expression of one that had yet to be told about the existence of bacon trotted out to meet them.

Steel glinted at one of the shack's windows: the tip of a crossbow bolt. "What do you want?" a man's voice cried out.

Tobrytan reached for his sword. Bad move. Even plate armor wouldn't save him at this range. Tobrytan realized it as well, and withdrew his hand and held it palm up. "We're looking for a baby."

"I don't care what you heard, we don't sell our kids." Damon heard muffled debate within the house. "I explained that. You got a new couch, didn't you?"

"The baby!" shouted Tobrytan.

"No baby here. We can make you one, but you'll have to wait nine months."

"This is getting us nowhere." Tobrytan waved to his men, indicating they should spread out. More steel flashed at the windows of the shack: this was a multi-crossbow family. Damon's skin prickled as if the points were already piercing his skin.

They backed off. Tobrytan summoned one of his men. "Burn the place."

"You'll never get close enough," said Damon.

The soldier unhooked a gourd shell from his saddle. Tobrytan handed him a pouch. The soldier filled the gourd with coarse black grains and fed a cord into it. Gunpowder. If that exploded in the shack . . .

Steel struck flint with a screech that set Damon's nerves on edge. "There are kids in there. Innocent kids."

Sparks showered the cord but failed to ignite it. "Are they True?" asked Tobrytan.

"No . . ."

"Then they're not innocent."

"I'll talk to them," said Damon.

"You?" said Tobrytan.

"I have the type of face people trust."

"You have the type of face people want to cut off."

More sparks flew. The cord began to smolder. Tobrytan motioned to the soldier holding the gourd, who threw it to Damon. Damon instinctively caught it, realized what he had done and made to drop it. Tobrytan shook his head. The witches produced their own crossbows. Half a dozen bolts pointed at Damon.

"Talk to them," said Tobrytan. "You have until the cord burns down."

Damon swallowed. The tip of the cord glowed a dull orange. Tiny fragments of ashes detached themselves from the burning fibers and danced in the wind. How long did he have until the thing exploded? Minutes? Seconds? He thought about throwing the thing back at Tobrytan and making a dash for it, but he knew the moment he raised his arm he'd be dead.

He transferred the gourd to his right hand and used his left to grasp the reins of his horse and nudge it back toward the shack.

"Do you know anyone connected to the Kalverts?" *Please say you do. Please.*

"The who?"

"They were the lords in these lands."

"No lords around here."

"Back in the days of the kings."

"That was a long time ago. No kings now. You need to speak to the priests."

To say the funeral prayer, if nothing else. The cord shortened a fraction of an inch. Damon held the gourd rock steady, afraid the slightest motion would accelerate its burning.

"How about redheads?"

"Don't know any red-headed priests."

"Just red-headed people in general," Damon said through gritted teeth.

There was a moment of thought, or whatever passed for thought among the shack's inhabitants. "There's that red-headed woman runs that . . .'stablishment."

It wasn't much of a lead, but at least it was *a* lead. "And where do we find this establishment?" asked Damon.

"Over Staziker way."

"What were you doing in Staziker?" demanded the woman.

"I was flogging some truffles to the priest there."

The cord was down to half its original length. Damon's arm was beginning to cramp. He stretched it out slowly, not that extra distance would save him when the gunpowder exploded. "Where's—?"

"Truffles?" continued the woman. "You never told me about no truffles. What if *I'd* wanted truffles? I *like* truffles."

"I got a couple of pigs for them."

"Well, that's great, because Saviors know we're short of pigs. You'd better not have caught—"

There was almost nothing left of the cord. "Where's Staziker?" Damon yelled.

"About twenty miles east," said the farmer.

Damon flashed an imploring look back at Tobrytan. The witch captain nodded. Damon hurled the gourd into the trees and threw himself off his horse.

No sooner had he hit the ground than there was an almighty bang. Animals screeched in panic and bolted. Screams erupted from the shack. Damon pushed himself into the mud and tried to block it all out.

Even though the crows had started on the bodies, Damon could tell they were fresh. Most of them were witches, but off to one side they found laid out side by side a soldier of the Realm and another man who had the rugged look of one from the Snow Cities. The implication was obvious. The Realm and the Snow Cities had allied and, if they were here of all places, it didn't take a genius to work out what had forced them together.

Judging from the apprehension, the True had come to the same conclusion. Tobrytan had thinned their numbers by dispatching scouts to notify other groups to head to Staziker. Their party was currently only a couple of men stronger than the one that had been slaughtered. Gazes flicked nervously up to the tree line, from which the ambush had been sprung if the trampled grass was anything to go by, as if expecting hordes to descend on them any minute.

"We should wait for the others before we proceed," he said to Tobrytan. "We don't know how many of them there are."

"If we die, it'll be in the service of God," said Tobrytan. "Our bodies will mark the way for our successors."

"I love your cheery outlook on life."

Tobrytan gave him a weary look and called for everyone to move out. They rejoined the road and urged their weary horses on. The countryside—all rolling fields and dense forests and chirping birds fluttering from spot to spot—meandered past, unconcerned with their quest. It had seen innumerable struggles over the millions of years of its existence—what was one more squabble?

They crested the hill they were climbing. A thread of sparkling water led to a town on the horizon. Staziker. There was movement down the road. Men on horseback. Was Eleanor among them? Damon trembled. He wrapped and unwrapped and rewrapped the reins around his hands to distract himself. Undoubtedly the countess was there. She wasn't the type to entrust others with such an important task.

The men spotted them. They wheeled their horses around and headed toward Staziker. The witches remained in place, silent, observing.

"Should we . . . ?" Damon said to Tobrytan, indicating the retreating horsemen.

Tobrytan said nothing. His eyes were closed, unheard words twitching his lips. He made the sign of the star-broken circle and reached for the hunting horn at his belt. He blew. A deep note filled the air. A few seconds later, far off to the east, its call was answered.

They proceeded at walking pace—giving time for the party on the other side of Staziker to catch up—a slow, inexorable squeezing of the trap. What would Eleanor be thinking? Was she preparing to fight? *Don't*, he pleaded internally, *it's only a baby; it's not worth throwing your life away for. Surrender peacefully. Once they have the Savior, they won't care about you. Who cares who rules Werlavia: lords, priests, witches? We could go somewhere far away from here, make things like they were before.* Who was he kidding? She hadn't wanted him then; she certainly wouldn't want him now.

They entered Staziker, riding two abreast down its narrow streets. The witches drew their weapons, brandishing crossbows and axes. The town's inhabitants were nowhere to be seen, no doubt hunkered in dark cellars, praying for the violence to pass them by.

Further down the road, hoofs clattered then receded. "They're making a break for it," said Tobrytan. He spurred his horse on. The other witches did the same. Caught in the middle, Damon had no choice but to follow their lead.

He held on tight as his horse gained energy from the excitement, galloping through the town. They burst into the open country. Ahead of them, half a dozen riders—five soldiers and a woman wrapped in furs—were galloping away for all they were worth. They flashed past a pile of bodies, some of which wore the black armor of the True. The rest of the witches couldn't be far away. There would be no escape for Eleanor and the others. Megan would have to surrender her daughter.

Wait, there was only one woman in the party they were chasing. There was no way Megan or Eleanor would have come without the other. He looked back toward Staziker. A lone horse streaked north away from the town, sprinting for the mountains. He caught—or imagined—the flutter of red hair. Eleanor. Unconsciously he brought his mount to a halt. His heart surged. Part of him urged her on, part of him feared the consequences of her escape.

His dropping out caught the attention of the witches. Hoofs that had been thundering away from him now thundered toward him

"Endalay," said Tobrytan, following Damon's gaze. "The soldiers are a decoy." He turned to his men. "After her."

Eleanor's horse was fresher than the witches' tired mounts and she built up a healthy lead on them, but once they reached the foothills of the Kartiks, with their tight, winding paths, and her initial burst of energy dissipated, her progress slowed. They were catching up, gradually but inevitably. Every so often they caught a glimpse of her through the rocks or felt a rain of dust and gravel as she dislodged loose patches above their heads.

She was heading west, as far as the mountains would allow her. There was a pass around here that led over to the Snow Cities. It wouldn't help her. It was miles away, even if she could go in a straight line. They'd catch her before that.

They were close enough to see the worry on her face, the baby slung across her chest, her cry as she urged her horse on, its whinny of protest. They were close enough for one of the witches to take aim with his crossbow. But they weren't close enough to be sure of hitting her and not the baby. Tobrytan's sword flashed. The crossbow whirled through the air, droplets of blood trailing from the hand that still gripped it. Its former owner swallowed his screams as best he could and plodded on.

The path narrowed so much the horses refused to proceed. The riders had to slide out of the saddle and drag them along, advancing inch by agonizing inch. Damon's head went woozy as he made the mistake of looking down—he hadn't realized how high they had come. The county spread out before him. Was that dirty patch on the horizon Staziker? What had become of Megan and the soldiers? They might have been able to fight their way through the other group of witches, but it was unlikely. He stared at his feet, which barely fitted on the ledge they were traversing. Megan would have got the fight she craved, sacrificing herself for her daughter and the countess. No doubt it had appealed to her sense of self-righteousness.

The way became just wide enough for them to ride again. Tobrytan commanded them on at a pace that was just the right side of stupid. Damon forced himself to look ahead, to ignore the drop to his left and the sheer rock face to his right, which he wanted nothing more than to cling to and wait for everything to be over.

There was a cry of alarm as a rider-less horse charged toward them. Eleanor's, it had to be, but where was she? The witches' lead horse panicked, reared. The rider called out, trying to reassure his mount. Too late. Hoofs clashed in midair. The horses slipped on loose shale. There was panicked whinnying as they made a last, desperate attempt to regain their footing. It was to no avail. Horses and rider tumbled over the edge.

They continued, their pace now more measured. It soon became clear why Eleanor had switched to foot. The path climbed steeply in a treacherous spiral around the mountain. Far too precarious for horses.

They tied their mounts around various outcroppings and proceeded upward. The wind picked up, freezing those parts of Damon's skin that were exposed and threatening to nudge him into the void. The path leveled and widened a little, though it still restricted them to single file. Damon relaxed a little. The lead soldier turned a corner formed by the rocks. There was a hiss above the breeze. He managed a pathetic, almost apologetic, cry and toppled off the mountain. An arrow had punctured his armor.

"I don't suppose anyone brought shields," said Damon.

"What's going on?" Tobrytan called out to the soldier who had unexpectedly found himself at the head of their diminishing line. "Where is she?"

The soldier edged forward and poked his head around the rocks. He pulled it back just as an arrow whizzed past. "She's holed up, sir. I think the path's stopped."

"How far away?"

"About thirty yards, sir."

"How good is she with that thing?" Tobrytan asked Damon.

"The bow? She's been using one since she could stand."

"How fast can she reload?"

"I don't know," said Damon. "Never timed it."

"We'll have to charge her. You two," he pointed to the two witches ahead of Damon, "fast as you can. Disarm her. Do *not* let any harm come to the Savior."

The soldiers nodded, pale but determined. Eleanor would kill one of them, that was for sure, but they had their cause. Life must be so much simpler if belief allowed you to be arrow fodder, if your faith allowed you to accept death without question.

"Now!"

The soldiers rushed around the corner. There was a cry and the thud of a body tumbling to the ground. Tobrytan bundled Damon forward. He tripped and went sprawling beyond the corner. The top of his head jutted into empty space. He scrambled backward, then yelled in pain as Tobrytan stamped on him in his eagerness to get past.

A woman cried out. Eleanor fumbled with an arrow as the second witch bore down on her. She forgot about firing and jabbed forward, thrusting the arrow into the witch's eye. A scream echoed around the mountains. Eleanor whipped the bow upward. It struck the witch's breastplate with a deep chime.

Blood streaming down his face, the witch raised his ax to strike. Eleanor pulled a knife from her belt. Oblivious to all this, the baby slept peacefully, wrapped in its sling and tucked in between some rocks. The witch swung. It was a blind, uncoordinated blow. Eleanor sidestepped. Not enough though. Blood sprayed into the air as the tip of the ax sliced across her chest. Grimacing, she whipped her knife hand around, slashed deep into the soldier's throat. He gargled, staggered. Eleanor gave him a helpful kick over the edge.

She grabbed the baby and held her close. Tobrytan raised his crossbow, aiming for her head. "I'm going to take her," he said.

"Knock yourself out," said Eleanor.

She tossed the baby off the mountainside.

Twenty-Seven

Horns blew, first from the west, then answered from the east. The hunters had sighted their prey. Megan hopped from foot to foot, uncontrollable energy surging through her. "We have to get moving," she said.

"Not you," said Eleanor. "Not yet." She turned to Willas and Aldred. "Take the men. Head east. Run, fight, whatever, just lead them away. Megan, give Odelia your furs."

"What?" said Odelia.

"You're going with them," said Eleanor. "Or would you prefer to be here when the witches arrive?"

That was enough to convince Odelia. She practically ripped off Megan's outer layer. Megan shivered in the street, while Odelia huddled in the furs as if the clothes themselves would be enough to protect her.

"I'm staying with you," Aldred said to Eleanor.

"No, you're not."

"Whatever you're planning, let me do it."

Eleanor placed a hand on Aldred's chest. "No time to argue. Now go."

Aldred nodded, then lifted off a grubby sack he had strapped to his body. "Take care of that."

He moved to his horse. Eleanor looked away. Megan caught her glance and jerked her head in Aldred's direction. Eleanor spun on her heel and threw herself into Aldred's arms. His surprise gave away to desire. They kissed—hard, passionately, as if it was the last kiss in Werlavia.

The cloud of dust the horses kicked up obscured the departure of Odelia and the soldiers. Eleanor dragged the remaining women inside and slammed the door. She pointed at the sling across Synne's chest, in which Cate slept with the ignorance of innocence.

"Have you another one of those?"

"A baby?" said Synne.

"A sling."

Synne pointed upstairs at the trunk. "In there."

"I was afraid you'd say that."

Eleanor pressed the sack Aldred had given her into Megan's arms and scurried upstairs. She wrenched open the trunk. Her eyes widened. "Who pays for *that*?"

"There's this pig farmer comes in specially," said Synne.

Eleanor fished out the sling and slipped it on. She began stuffing it with random items. Megan felt her stomach tighten as if a tumor had gestated there and was devouring her from within.

"No," she whispered.

"The soldiers were the first decoy," said Eleanor. "I'm the second."

"But they'll . . ."

"I'll be fast."

Not fast enough. "I can't let you do this," said Megan.

"Let me," said Afreyda.

Eleanor flicked her head. "You don't have the hair."

Horses thundered down the street outside. Everyone froze, held their breath, as if the slightest movement would attract the attention of the witches. Synne held Cate close. Despite everything, jealousy spiked inside Megan. She should be the one comforting her daughter.

The hoofs died away. Eleanor clattered down the stairs. "I'll head north, lose them in the mountains. Once the way is clear, make for the forest. It'll cover you. I'll meet you at the Destiny Pass."

No you won't, you'll never make it. "You can't leave me."

"It's the only way."

"We can all go together."

"Too much chance of the witches seeing us."

"We'll fight the bastards," said Megan. "We'll fight them all if we have to."

Tears blurred her vision. Eleanor brushed them away with a gentle flick of her thumb. She kissed Megan's forehead. Megan held on to her tight, wishing beyond hope they could stay there forever. The witches had taken everyone else from her—not Eleanor as well. Please, God, not Eleanor as well.

Eleanor headed for the door. "I have to go now if the witches are to spot me," she said. To Afreyda, "Look after her."

"I will."

"I can look after myself," snapped Megan.

"I know," said Eleanor. "That's why you'll defeat the witches. You'll make Werlavia safe for Cate, yourself, everybody."

She was gone before Megan could ask how.

Damon stared at the baby smashed on the rocks a hundred feet below them, hardly able to breathe. She had done it, she had really done it. Eleanor's ruthless nature—which had seen her ride south to assassinate two innocent girls, to try to talk Megan into terminating her pregnancy, and to abandon Damon on the shore of Lake Pullar—had asserted itself. She would do anything to avenge herself on those who had destroyed her family's power.

Something rolled away from the body and bounced down the mountain. Damon retched, then realized the unnaturalness of what had occurred.

"It's a fake," he mumbled.

"What?" said Tobrytan.

"The baby. It's a fake. A dummy." Relief seeped through Damon. Eleanor was better than that. Better than him. "*This* was the diversion. Megan'll have Cate."

The mention of Megan's name alerted Eleanor to his presence. "Damon?" She stared at him scrambling around on the ground, an incredulous look on her face. "You're *helping* them?"

"I . . ."

"You didn't even have the decency to get yourself tortured?"

Eleanor's eyes glittered hard and cold as the mountain. Damon withered under her gaze and looked away. She didn't ask him why. Did she understand or simply expect nothing better of him?

"We don't have time for this," he said to Tobrytan. "We should get back to Staz—"

A deep hum echoed around the rocks. Eleanor gave a sharp cry and crumpled. A crossbow bolt protruded from her stomach, blood dribbling from the wound. She tried to push herself to her feet. Her legs refused to support her. She collapsed back to the ground, her breathing labored and arrhythmic.

Tobrytan tossed aside his now-empty crossbow and pulled a knife from his belt. He threw it to the ground in front of Damon. "Finish her."

"What?" said Damon, alarm rising within him.

"Or we finish you."

"No, you can't . . ."

Tobrytan drew his sword. Behind Damon, the two remaining witches raised their axes. The one who'd lost his hand looked ready to keel over any second; the other was fully fit and didn't look in the slightest bit squeamish.

Damon saw himself in the polished metal of the knife, his face distorted by the imperfections in the metal or in his soul. Eleanor squeezed her stomach where the bolt had hit and grimaced in pain. The blood had drained from her face, leaving it an almost pure white. The complexion of a corpse. She would never survive that wound. It would soon go septic, kill her while she suffered tortured dreams on the exposed rocks. He'd be doing her a favor. End the pain.

Nerves and the cold made him fumble the knife. He knelt to retrieve it, used both hands to get a grip. Tobrytan gave the irritated snort of a teacher supervising the class dunce. Eleanor crawled away, dragging herself across the rocks with her last scraps of strength. There was nowhere to run to, no escape. For either of them.

Damon trudged toward her, the blade in his hand twenty times heavier than its size dictated. Eleanor had reached the edge now. Only empty space lay beyond. She struggled to her feet, a painful sequence that made sweat pour from her despite the cold. The wind whipped her hair every which way as she raised her head. Defiance etched itself on her face.

"I'm sorry," whispered Damon.

"No, you're not," said Eleanor, her voice barely more than a wet gasp.

She gave herself to the void.

Megan couldn't tear herself from the window, even though Eleanor and the witches who hunted her had long since disappeared over the hills. The countess was prepared to sacrifice herself for her, for a baby, for a lie? Megan should have gone. Cate was her daughter. Wasn't it a mother's duty to give her life for her child?

"We need to leave," said Afreyda, tugging her away.

"We can help her," said Megan. "Sneak up on those soldiers chasing her. Attack them before they know what's going on."

"That is—" Afreyda waved her hands, thinking of the word "—stupid."

"We can't just let her . . ."

"Yes, we can. She has given you a chance. Do not dishonor her by rejecting it."

Why should Megan be given the chance? What had she done to deserve it? She felt impotent, standing doing nothing as everyone made decisions around her; unworthy, skulking away while others rode bravely into battle. Afreyda and Synne could get Cate away. Megan should be with Eleanor. Since the witches had come, they had always been there for each other. What would she do if she never came back?

"Megan . . ."

"Yes, yes."

Megan snatched the cloak Afreyda proffered and they took the last of the provisions out to where Synne was waiting with Cate. While they loaded the horses, the townspeople started to venture out, the first few giving others the nerve to come out, until they were blocking the road both ways.

"Who were those soldiers?" asked one of the townsmen.

"I don't know," mumbled Megan as she helped Synne and Cate up on to one of the horses.

"Are they after her?"

Megan's hand had wrapped around the hilt of a knife before she realized the townsman meant Afreyda, not Cate. She took a deep breath, forced herself to calm. "They think she came over here to claim alms."

"'Bout time the priests clamped down on sponging foreigners."

Megan made to mount her horse. The townsman grabbed her arm. "I don't think so," he said. "I think those soldiers might want to—"

Megan spun and jabbed her elbow into the man's face. He staggered back, clutching his nose. Megan kicked out, catching him full in his unprotected stomach. The townsman collapsed into a wheezing heap.

The crowd gasped as Megan leaped on him and jerked his head back. She pressed a knife at his throat. "I don't know how many people have died for me today," she spat into his ear, "but I'm damned if I'm going to let you or anyone else make it for nothing."

The townsman held up hands smeared with blood from his broken nose. Megan took that as acquiescence. She shoved him into the road and backed off. Afreyda drew her sword and nudged her horse forward to cover their retreat. The crowd inched backward. They possessed the numbers to overcome the women but not the will. You had to mean it; you had to want it; you had to need it.

Megan swung herself up on the horse behind Synne. The townspeople made an aisle for them to trot through. Megan tensed, expecting a stone or worse to come flying their way. The crowd's hostility remained passive.

Megan relaxed a little as they left Staziker. They followed the road east, in the wake of Aldred and the others, until they were out of sight of the town, at which point they veered south and dashed over the fields. She didn't know if the diversion would fool the witches or merely confirm where they were really headed.

They reached the forest. Megan looked back, fearing the witches would come charging over the ridge, hoping Eleanor would. Neither occurred.

* * *

Damon looked away before Eleanor hit the ground far below, but his imagination was only too keen to fill in the details. The knife slipped from his grasp. His legs crumpled, but he barely registered the stone jarring his kneecaps. He couldn't breathe, as if the grief pressing on him had squeezed the air from his lungs. What had he done? Oh, he'd done it, all right. No matter how he skewed the past, told himself he had merely been swept up by events that were inevitable, he knew he was responsible for this.

"You have to admire her bravery," muttered Tobrytan.

Damon snatched up the knife. "You bastard."

He charged the witch captain. Tobrytan remained still until the last moment, then swatted Damon away with the back of his hand. The world spun. Jagged rocks bit into his skin.

Tobrytan recovered his knife and slipped it back into his belt. "If the Mother does have the Savior, she must have headed west. Is there somewhere to cross the mountains around here?" He rammed his boot into Damon's side. Damon hardly noticed the pain. "I said . . ."

"There's a pass—" Damon waved vaguely in the direction of the setting sun "—that way."

He stared at the space where a few seconds earlier Eleanor had stood, alive, vibrant. She was, then she wasn't. What could he have done? He couldn't take on Tobrytan and the others. Eleanor had chosen to lure them here. She knew they were likely to catch her. She had sacrificed herself for Megan and her child; Damon had merely attended the ceremony. But if Damon hadn't led the witches to Staziker, would there have needed to be a sacrifice? Then Eleanor would be alive and he dead. Same outcome, reversed roles. Except Eleanor had proven herself worthy of life, and Damon, well, hadn't.

"What are you doing down there, you sniveling fool?" said Tobrytan.

What indeed? If Damon remained curled up on the rocks, the cold would eventually numb the pain. He could slip away, forget everything. And then explain himself to God. He couldn't see *that* going well.

Tobrytan gave him another kick, less brutal than before. Almost affectionate for the witch captain. "You're coming with us."

"Why?"

"You have anyone else?"

Megan felt exposed as they emerged from the protection of the trees into the fields south of the Kartiks. The mountains loomed above them, vast and impenetrable. She tried to get her bearings. Had they come out of the forest too early, too late? The area didn't look *un*familiar, but it'd be easy to overshoot the crossing point and wander on forever until they came to the end of Werlavia.

Maybe that wouldn't be such a bad idea, safer than trusting Rekka anyway.

They found the road. A jumble of hoofprints were visible in the mud, heading east toward Staziker. Their own tracks or the witches'? She looked around, trying to match the scene with that of their arrival, when she and Eleanor had trotted down it, oblivious of what was to happen. Megan hadn't taken too much notice of the scenery, too preoccupied with seeing Cate, too sure there would be someone to lead her back to safety. Had she been here before? If so, then west; if not, east.

Afreyda had already made a decision and was heading west. "Hey!" Megan called out. "That might not be the way."

"It is."

"How can you be sure?"

"I recognize it."

Of course, Afreyda had been here too. Megan could simply have asked. She wasn't entirely by herself. Not everything was on her, not every decision had to be made unilaterally.

Dusk was falling. The wind picked up, freezing Megan's neck and increasing her sense of vulnerability. She tugged up her hood and peered over Synne's shoulder at Cate.

"How is she?"

"She'll need feeding soon," said Synne. "And she'll definitely need changing."

There was a distant rumble of thunder behind them. A storm—just what they needed. No, something wasn't right. The way the trees were blowing, the wind rippling across the fields, the dead leaves skittering down the road. They were riding into the weather, not away from it, and they had certainly been through no storm.

Fear sharpened her weary senses, made her kick her horse on. She drew level with Afreyda. "We've got company," she said. "Riders behind us." Afreyda glanced over her shoulder. They weren't in sight, yet. "It could be Eleanor or Aldred or one of the others."

Afreyda's expression told Megan all she needed to know about her opinion on that mindless optimism. Simultaneously, they dug their heels into their horses' ribs and shot ahead. The jolt woke Cate up. She started crying, demanding the world stop and let her rest. *If only I could make it.*

"There!" shouted Afreyda, pointing.

Trampled grass betrayed the start of a trail that veered off the road and up the hill toward the mountains. Megan and Afreyda banked right and started to climb. Their horses slowed, panting with the strain. There was a straggly copse coming up. If they could reach it before their pursuers caught sight of them . . .

Megan willed herself not to look back. Afreyda did the job for her. Her eyes widened. What could only be a swear word spat from her lips. An outrider had broken free from the chasing pack—and there must be a pack, considering the noise they'd made. He spotted them and banked off the road, galloping in their direction. The light was too dim and the distance too far to make an exact identification, but the bulk of armor was all too apparent.

They entered the copse. Afreyda pulled up and drew her sword. "Go on ahead," she said. "I'll deal with him."

"You won't stand a—"

"Go!"

Megan kicked her horse on. They raced out above the tree line. The vegetation was becoming scrubbier, the ground hardening. The Kartiks stood black and jagged against the pale blue of the disappearing day.

Was that a glow in the distance? The Tiptunite fort at the end of the Destiny Pass. A couple of miles away, maybe. They were almost there.

The distant chime of metal upon metal. Megan glanced over her shoulder. There was no sign of Afreyda. The trees were still, silent, indifferent to the fate of those within their circle.

No, she was not going to lose someone else. "You know how to ride?" she shouted in Synne's ear.

"Of course."

"Good." Megan slowed the horse and handed the girl the reins. "Head for the light."

"What?"

Megan slipped out of the saddle. She stumbled, her legs stiff from riding. "Up there. Tell them you're with me. They'll look after you."

The horse—given fresh energy by the halving of its burden—galloped off.

Megan took a deep breath and sprinted back to the trees, almost tumbling down the hill in her desperation to get there. What if she was too late? What if another death was on her hands?

She crashed into the copse. A horse whinnied, a man shouted. Megan forced herself toward the noise. A witch was slaloming toward her through the trees, chasing after Afreyda. She was unarmed and on foot, neither sword nor mount anywhere to be seen. His ax swiped as he shot by. She threw herself to the ground. The blade whistled over her head.

The witch pulled his horse up, reversed, charged again. Afreyda remained still. Was she injured? The witch was almost upon her. Her hand moved to her boot. The witch hacked at her. She ducked, whipped her arm around. Steel flashed.

The horse reared in pain as Afreyda's knife slashed its fetlock. The witch made a desperate attempt to calm it, dropping his ax as he struggled with the reins. The horse bucked. The witch dived in a controlled fall, rolling as he hit the ground.

The horse limped away. The witch scrambled for his ax. Afreyda dashed to intercept him. They collided. She doubled over as he punched her in the stomach, clutching handfuls out of the air as if to fill her empty lungs. The witch picked up his ax and hefted it to reacquaint himself with its weight.

Megan drew both knives from her sleeves and charged. The witch raised his ax high above his head and prepared to bring it down on the gasping Afreyda. Megan screamed and rammed both knives into his neck, either side of his spine.

The ax slipped from the witch's grasp. There was a squelch as he pulled away from the short blades. He stumbled around in a half circle, blood spurting in twin fountains. The color was rapidly draining from his face. He still managed to draw back an armored fist, like a boxer refusing to go down. Megan slashed at his face in a crossing motion. Warm blood splattered her skin. The witch toppled over.

Megan went over to Afreyda. "Are you all right?" Afreyda wheezed something that was either a "yes" or a "do I freaking look all right?" depending on how much sarcasm you were willing to allow for. "Come on. It won't be long before his friends figure out where we are."

Supporting each other, the two women staggered out of the copse. Afreyda's horse was tugging away at a patchy spot of grass. When it spotted them it sidled away. If horses could whistle casually, it would have.

"Not so fast," said Megan. She caught up with it and grabbed its reins. "Just a bit longer." She patted its nose. "Promise."

She helped Afreyda into the saddle. "Thank you," said Afreyda as Megan squeezed up in front of her.

"I've left too many people behind."

"Usually me." She reached around to grab the reins, but Megan already had them.

"Hang on," she said.

The horse lurched forward. Afreyda grabbed hold of Megan, who yelped. "Sorry," said Afreyda. Her hands retreated from Megan's waist. Megan pulled them back around her.

They cantered up to the mountains. Afreyda rested her head against Megan's shoulder. It felt good, to be close to someone, to be accepted for herself and not a piece in some infernal game.

Thunder rumbled again. "Megan . . ."

"I know."

Half a dozen horsemen burst out of the copse. Megan cracked the reins and kicked the horse forward. Their mount shuddered with the effort. *Don't give up on us now*, pleaded Megan, wishing she could give the horse the last of her strength. But what did it matter if the witches caught her, killed her even? They wouldn't have Cate. That was the important thing.

Vegetation gave way to rock. Steel shoes clanged on stone. The horse slowed. Megan urged a last effort from it. It twitched, making a half-hearted attempt to throw its riders with the last of its strength. Megan steadied herself, tried to coax the horse on. It refused to budge.

Behind them, the witches swept forward, *their* mounts perfectly obedient. "We'll have to . . ."

"Stand and fight?" said Afreyda.

"I was thinking run," said Megan, already swinging out of the saddle.

"That works."

They scrambled up the foothills, their feet skidding on shale and gravel. Legs burned, lungs cried out for air. They alternated between pulling up the other and being pulled. It was no use. The witches were almost upon them. Only a hundred yards—a few seconds— away now.

Then a sequence of sighs. Uphill, arrows shot skyward. Megan grabbed Afreyda and dragged her to the ground, remembering the Sandstriders' volley during the battle by the Speed a lifetime ago. These arrows, however, arced over them, then dived, spearing toward the witches as if dispatched by God himself. More than one witch tumbled from his mount and crashed to the rocks. The horses—some pierced—panicked and bolted in every direction.

A phalanx of Tiptunite archers were lined up on a ridge. They reloaded, aimed, fired. The second volley was unnecessary. The witches, those who remained alive and in control of their horses, were already retreating.

Megan picked herself to her feet and dusted herself down. One of the witches glanced back at her. For a moment she thought it was Damon. No, it was a trick of the light, her mind finding familiar patterns.

She heaved Afreyda up and led her to the fort. Deep down in her heart, Megan knew Eleanor wouldn't be there, would never be there, and she'd have to cope without her. But her daughter was waiting.

Epilogue

By the time the Tiptunite patrol found Eleanor, Megan had already given up hope, but that didn't stop her from crying herself to sleep in Afreyda's arms. They took the body back to Hil, sailing gray choppy waters that had even the experienced seamen hanging over the edge. Megan felt as empty as the sea, obsessing over what she had lost, the despair threatening to crush her. It was only as they entered the calm of the inlet, and Cate let her hold her for more than two minutes without a crying fit, that she remembered what she had gained too.

Aldred and Willas were waiting for them when they docked. They were the only ones who had escaped the witches and, judging by their bandages and stitched-up wounds, only just in one piece. Guilt twinged as Megan realized Eleanor's reasons for sending Odelia with the soldiers might not have been entirely altruistic.

In accordance with local tradition, the funeral took place at dusk. Both refugees and city dwellers braved winter's first flurry to attend, drawn by the last connection to a past that led back to before the Unifier's time. As the sun dipped below the Kartiks, and Father Broose intoned the funeral prayer, they bid farewell to the last of the nobility.

Everyone stared at Megan expectantly. She looked down into the grave and shuffled from foot to foot, holding Cate tight to quell her own shivers. "They're waiting for you to say something," whispered Rekka, leaning in.

"I know, but . . . Can't you do it? You're her family. What if I say something stupid?"

"Don't worry," said Rekka. "The amount of booze we've got lined up for the wake, no one's going to remember anything." She held out her arms for Cate. "Here." Megan was reluctant to hand her daughter over, but as she wanted the ground to swallow her up and there was a large hole placed handily nearby, she thought it best, lest she succumb to temptation.

She rubbed the jagged edge of her cut ear and cleared her throat. "Most of you didn't know Eleanor," she said. "Don't get hung up on all the titles. She didn't think they made her better than everyone else—well, not *too* much better—but they reminded her of the responsibility she had to the Realm, to its people. She was fighting for us before we even realized there was a fight, and she fought to the last." She sniffled. "The world's a poorer place without her and I'm going to miss her like you wouldn't believe."

Hundreds of gazes fell upon Megan. She knotted and unknotted her fingers. Afreyda took her hand and squeezed it. Megan squeezed back. "I think we should go get a drink now. It's what she would have wanted."

The mourners dispersed, a few of them expressing sympathy for Megan's loss. "Nice speech," said Rekka.

"Really?"

Rekka wrinkled her nose. "Maybe we should have got Fordel to prepare you some notes."

Megan went to take Cate back, but Rekka handed her to one of her daughters, a spindly teen whose weight had yet to catch up to her height. "Come with me," she said to Megan. "We need to talk about the will."

"Whose will?"

Rekka made a play of looking around. "Was somebody else having a funeral? I must go pay my respects."

"Eleanor can't have left a will," said Megan. "What would she have to leave?"

Rekka was already striding away. Megan scampered after her and followed her into the Lord Defender's mansion. Fordel was in the study, sorting through papers on a desk Megan suspected Vegar, its nominal owner, had never used.

"My ladies," said Fordel.

He offered Megan a scroll tied with a red ribbon. "What's this?" she asked.

"An adoption order."

"What?" Megan dropped the scroll and fumbled for a knife. "You try and take her from me and I'll kill you here and now."

Fordel frowned, then brightened in realization. "Not your baby's. Yours."

"Huh?"

"Eleanor adopted you in her will," said Rekka. "She named you her daughter and the heir to her titles and lands."

"I believe there's a shack somewhere in the foothills of the Endalayan Mountains," added Fordel.

"I don't understand. She can't."

"Your parents are dead, right?" said Fordel.

Megan nodded.

"And you're not married?"

"No, of course not."

"Eleanor did say that was unlikely," muttered Rekka, pouring wine from the pitcher Fordel had next to him.

"Then it's all perfectly legal." Fordel accepted a goblet from Rekka. "The Royal Council legitimized inheritance via adoption after Aldwyn the Second failed to produce a son. It was either that or let him keep executing his queens."

"We're not in the Realm," said Megan.

"But you and Eleanor are still subject to its laws. We recognize your independence, even if you don't recognize ours."

"She left you a letter to explain," said Rekka. "Or apologize, depending on your point of view. Fordel?"

Fordel handed Megan another scroll. Megan twirled it in her hand, fingering the thick paper tube between finger and thumb. She was desperate to read what it said, but all too aware these would be the last words Eleanor would offer her.

Eventually she slit the ribbon off with the point of her knife. "My dear Megan," she read, "I'm so sorry to leave. I wanted to be there for you until this was all over, until you and Cate were safe, but if you're reading this you know I can't, or you're Rekka and being a nosy cow."

Rekka shrugged. "It was a long journey back from Tiptun and I forgot to pack a book."

Megan continued reading.

'I've adopted you not to replace your parents but to become one of them. I can think of no better way to express my love and admiration and pride than to consider you my daughter. Don't dismiss the titles I bequeath you: they can rally people to your cause, help you in your fight. And it is a fight you will win. Don't give up. There will be danger, but you will overcome it. There will be terrible decisions, but you will find the right path. There will be good times—remember to enjoy them. May the Saviors protect you.

Your mother, Eleanor.'

Rekka slid a goblet across the desk. "You probably need—" Megan downed half the wine "—that."

"This is ridiculous," said Megan. "I'm not a countess."

"You are," said Rekka. "You are Megan of the houses of Endalay and Kalvert, Countess of Ainsworth, Baroness of Laxton and Herth, First Lady of Kirkland, Overlord of the Spice Isles and Defender of the Southern Lands." She clinked Megan's glass with her own. "Welcome to the family."

"There's something else," said Fordel. "Another title . . ."

The maelstrom of Megan's thoughts coalesced into dread. "No. Don't say it."

"You're now the only known claimant to the Unifier's throne. You could be queen. We could lead the Realm and Snow Cities against the witches. We could defeat them. If you want it."

Oh God, Eleanor. What have you got me into?

Acknowledgments

Here I go again, as the sage Mr. Coverdale once said. Time to thank some people: my agent, the wonderful Claire Wilson, and Lexie Hamblin and Sam Copeland who acted *in locum parentis* when Claire was playing hookey (or "on maternity leave" as she insisted on calling it); my editor, Sarah Lambert, copy editor, Talya Baker, and all the staff at Quercus, both foreign and domestic; all the members of the Coven for their continued support, in particular Mel Salisbury, Alexia Casale, Lauren James, Cat Doyle, Alice Oseman, Jon Robinson, Tom Easton, Ross Montgomery and Sally Green; Sarah Sky who, along with Lindsay Moakes and Rachael Craw, did her best to keep me sane; and, most importantly, my family—Tom, Mom, Dad, Lyndsay, Peter, t'other Gary, Natalie, Abigail and Cody—for their love and support during what's been a difficult time.

And you, the reader. Give yourself a pat on the back. If you got this far, you probably deserve it.